STORIES BY IRANIAN WOMEN

SINCE THE REVOLUTION

MODERN MIDDLE EAST LITERATURES

IN TRANSLATION

SERIES

Stories by Iranian Women

Since the Revolution

Translation from the Persian
by Soraya Paknazar Sullivan

Introduction
by Farzaneh Milani

Foreword
by Elizabeth Warnock Fernea

Center for Middle Eastern Studies
The University of Texas at Austin
Austin, Texas 78712

Copyright © 1991 by the Center for Middle Eastern Studies
at The University of Texas at Austin.
All rights reserved.

Library of Congress Catalog Card Number 90-086116

ISBN 0-292-77649-7

Printed in the United States of America

Cover: Diane Watts

Editor: Annes McCann-Baker

To Ali Akbar and Soheila

Table of Contents

Foreword

The work that follows is an historical as well as a literary document. We are indebted to Soraya Sullivan for seeing the importance of the outburst of Iranian women's writing in the last decade and for overseeing that fragile and delicate process of translating samples of those works from one culture to another; from one language to another. We also owe a vote of thanks to Farzaneh Milani who has set these stories in the historical, literary and social context of Iran.

Until recently, Western images of Iranian women have been blurred, imprecise, stereotyped: images of Sheherazade, of harems, of shrouded, elusive, veiled figures. These images have been abruptly replaced in the last decade. During the Iranian revolution of 1979, Iranian women suddenly burst upon Western television screens, hooded, yes, and sometimes veiled. But they were scarcely elusive. They were marching in protest down the broad modern boulevards of Tehran; they were shouting at the television cameras and raising threatening arms and hands. These pictures, compelling and troubling, challenged the earlier images of elusive, hidden creatures. Yet the words of these women were lost in the shouting, reduced to slogans, to a few cryptic subtitles. We could not hear or understand much of what they were saying, either in those turbulent early years of the revolution or in the years following the first great changes.

The stories in this collection consist of their words, the words of Iranian women of different ages and socio-economic backgrounds. Their words come to us in different stylistic forms, as a unique record of women's ideas and feelings about themselves and their place in their society.

But what do these words by Iranian women mean for us in the West, who are concerned generally about women's place in history, in economic life, in politics and in literature? Too often we have presumed that the West offers women the greatest opportunity for equality and that Western feminist ideology is the only acceptable ideology. Recent events have suggested that women in the West have been a bit smug, a bit ethnocentric in deciding that *we* know what is best for *others*, even though they might have different histories, traditions and

ix

expectations. Clearly, we can learn from others as we have expected others to learn from us.

The range of human possibilities and adaptability is scarcely limited to western Europe and the United States. This is becoming clearer as the accomplishments of other societies past and present become better known in the West. One of the most important ways these accomplishments have become known is through translation, particularly of literature. The literature of Iran is only now becoming available to us in English. This volume, which offers the literature of Iran as written by its women, then is important in two ways. Not only does it take its place within Iran's long historical literary tradition, but it gives us an example of new creativity within that tradition—the creativity of women, many published here for the first time. Iran is changing, as we can see and read in these stories. Just so are its women emerging as literary forces in their own country, long known for its strong literary contributions to world literature. What do they have to say to us in the West? These "other" people's voices, "other" women's voices, are eloquent and strong. We can learn from those voices—about Iran, about women's lives in other societies. A close look at the words of another culture, another literature, gives us a new perspective from which to examine our own. It allows us to compare, marvel, learn.

We are fortunate to have this collection to add to the growing numbers of books chronicling women and by women in the different parts of our shrinking global village.

Elizabeth Warnock Fernea

PREFACE

In the decade of the 1980s, a growing number of Iranian women took up the writing of fiction as a means to express their self-worth and the modalities of their existence. Presented here are thirteen of their most vivid expressions, reflecting various experiences of today's Iran as examined by women of diverse and often unconventional viewpoints.

Ranging from the mundane to the extraordinary, these stories are attempts to depict the floating world of phenomena that Iranians perceive as their reality. The stories are rich with the ambiguities of human relations, caught up in the dramatic and traumatic upheavals of the period in which they were composed. Each captures, in a distinctive way, some essential characteristic of their time. The result is a series of moving portraits of women and the lives they lead.

Many of the authors have not been widely anthologized; and in some cases, the short story is a first attempt by a writer who is eagerly experimenting with her newly-discovered medium. Each selection is introduced by a sketch of the author's background. Most are translations of what the author herself has provided; but in some cases, the translator has had to compose the sketch from more uncertain sources.

All the stories were written either shortly before the 1978 uprising or since then. The choice of stories has not been made according to any fixed ideological viewpoint. Nor is the selection intended to illustrate or contest any of the currently popular theories about women. The primary criteria of selection have been vision and sincerity, as expressed by women authors during this cataclysmic decade in the history of Iran.

Given the criteria of time frame and short-story format, it was not possible to include the work of several influential writers. Works by Mahshid Amirshahi, Sahrnush Parsipur, Ghazaleh Alizadeh, for example, do not appear here. Furthermore, where two or more stories treated the same theme (marriage, religion, war, etc.), the translator had to make the difficult choice of which one displayed the greater skill or would have the stronger impact on the reader. The practical constraints of time and energy also played a role in limiting the scope of this collection. Many stories that were published while this book was being prepared for print could not be included; nor could those published in periodicals unknown to or unlocatable by the translator.

An attempt has been made to present the stories in the collection according to the chronology of their creation. Such an order is in harmony with the translator's desire to facilitate an understanding of the crucial events that led the authors to act as the expressive media of "their times."

In conclusion I must express my gratitude to all those who helped me in one way or another. I am indebted in particular to Professor Elizabeth Fernea who reassured me of the value of this work for publication; to Dr. Mohamad Tavakoli without whose continued support and assistance in locating the stories this work could not exist; to Ann Marie Afra, Dr. Mark Freeman, Dr. William Hartley, and Dr. Susan Parenti who lent me their editorial skills and supreme enthusiasm to bring this work into existence; to Dr. Ahmad Karimi-Hakkak who was a constant source of inspiration and feedback; to Annes McCann-Baker for assisting me with the details of the publishing procedures; and to still others, all of whom, I trust are aware of my appreciation. In spite of all such assistance, errors will no doubt be found in my work, and for these I claim sole responsibility.

Soraya Paknazar Sullivan

Sheherazade Unveiled: Post-Revolutionary Iranian Women Writers

by Farzaneh Milani

In the early 1970s at the height of Iran's drive toward "modernization," the Cultural Council of the Ministry of Arts and Culture prepared a list of the great figures of Iranian history. This concentrated history of greatness tolerated the presence of only four women. Lost in the illustrious company of three hundred kings, generals, statesmen, philosophers, scientists, writers, artists, calligraphers, and musicians, these four lonely women—all poets—revealed, among other things, the strength of the ties between women and poetry in Iran.

But what about women prose fiction writers? They are conspicuously absent from this honorary inventory. Have Sheherazade's daughters, true to their cultural heritage, never written down their oral narratives? After all, Sheherazade, the ultimate storyteller, is a classic case of the closet artist. Her own father, the Vizir, is not aware of her talent, and never does she have an audience of more than two. Night in and night out, she narrates her tales but only to her husband and her sister. No forbidden man ever hears Sheherazade's voice. Her ceremonies of storytelling might go on for one thousand and one nights, and through her art she might transform the vengeful and embittered king, yet her life-saving art is accorded legitimacy only within the four walls of her home. Time and again, Sheherazade proves the triumph of her art but also of her domesticity. She manages to postpone and ultimately waive her death verdict, yet she can never turn her stories into written texts. Her role never exceeds what propriety allows. She must remain a dutiful housewife, and she does. She is resigned to her role as a private storyteller. Her story, like those of her daughters, is the story of the unwritten word, the oral tradition, the blank page. This is the uncontested territory of women storytellers: the page that speaks only in its unobtrusive voice of silence, the blank page of unwritten books by unknown women.

The appropriation of fiction writing by women is a recent phenomenon in Iran. For centuries female literary talent was

1

mostly channeled away from public forms of written self-expression. Many women wove the fabric of their lives in the warp and woof of tapestry, stitchery, and embroidery. The pen was in the hands of men. It was not until 1947 that the first collection of short stories, *Fire Quenched* by Simin Daneshvar, was published. Two decades later the first novel, *Savushun*, by the same author, saw publication and became a best seller, selling over 400,000 copies—a record for any novel in Iran whether written by man or woman. The seventies and eighties witnessed an unprecedented flourishing in women's fiction writing. In fact, the short-term effect of the Islamic Revolution of 1979 on women's writing has been both dramatic and surprising. Women have finally found an authentic and familiar voice in the novel and the short story. In fact, they have carved out a space of their own in the traditionally male stronghold. The short stories collected in this anthology, along with many others as yet untranslated, exemplify a shift which has taken place in Persian fiction writing. This shift consists, among other things, in women taking a visibly active part and gaining a voice within the public tradition of mainstream written fiction.

Perhaps it is still too soon to talk about the Revolution's real impact in women's literature. Certainly it would be wrong to assume that changes affecting the legal and political rights of women or their personal freedom bring about immediate changes of the same magnitude in their literature. The attempt to replace the "Pahlavi-produced, westernized"[1] woman with an Islamic ideal of womanhood—in literature or in life—will, if possible at all, need more than just a few years. The effort to supplant the previous "poisoned" and "corrupt"[2] literature with one that promotes the Islamic ideal of femininity also requires more than just the few years that have elapsed. All that is known for sure at this point is the surprising fact that at home or abroad, writing by and about woman has been on an upswing.

---

[1] See *Sima-ye Zan dar Kalame-e Imam Khomeini* [Images of women in the words of Imam Khomeini] (Tehran: Sazeman-e Chap va Entesharat, 1987).
[2] Ibid., p.209.

2

Although the Islamic Republic has not as yet openly expressed an "official" view on the role and portrayal of women in literature, it has taken a clear position on the participation and presentation of women in film and video. According to film and video regulations, observes Hamid Nafici, "Muslim women must be shown to be chaste and to have an important role in society as well as in raising Godfearing and responsible children. In addition, women must not be treated like a commodity or used to arouse sexual desires. These general and ambiguous guidelines have had a profound effect on the use and portrayal of women in cinema. The most significant is the avoidance of stories involving women altogether, thus evading entanglement with censors. If women are portrayed at all, a whole new grammar of film is applied, including these features: women actors are given static parts or are shot in such a way as to avoid showing their bodies. Thus, they are filmed in longshot, with fewer close ups and facial expressions. In addition, eye contact and touching between men and women are discouraged."[3] The unwritten yet prevailing attitude toward women's literature also stresses codes of modesty and emphasizes the need to exercise "Islamic" morality.

The creation of the ideal woman in the Islamic Republic has been mainly assigned to the educational system. Textbooks, especially at the elementary level, have been changed in order to train the future ideal Islamic citizen. In such textbooks women occupy the traditional roles of mother and wife in the home. If they have a profession, it is one of the "appropriate" jobs for a woman, namely teacher, nurse, secretary, or office worker. Meanwhile, the ideal role models presented by the Islamic Republic for Iranian women to emulate are Hazrat Fatemeh, the daughter of the prophet Mohammad, and Hazrat Zeinab, his granddaughter, neither attributed with any literary interest. Hazrat Fatemeh is admired mainly for her female virtues as mother, wife, and daughter. Hazrat Zeinab is remembered for her militancy and active participation in what she thought to be a just struggle undertaken by her brother, Imam Hossein, to challenge the despotism of the

---

[3]Hamid Nafici, "The development of an Islamic cinema in Iran," *Third World Affairs*, 1987, p. 459.

caliph who had usurped power. In the words of the Iranian women's delegate to United Nations Decade for Women Conference, the "Zeinabic" way is "to bear the message, to speak out against oppression and injustice."[4]

These two role models betray a fascinating contradiction in the "ideal" role of women within the Islamic Republic. On the one hand, the stress is on motherhood and singleness of commitment to family. On the other hand, there is the demand that women serve the state. Awakened to the revolutionary potential of women, the Islamic Republic has had to change its stance and reinterpret religion according to those values and standards that are consonant with and serve to fulfill its interests.

Whereas in the early sixties many clerics, including Ayatollah Khomeini, objected to women's enfranchisement as "un-Islamic," in post-revolutionary Iran her right to vote and be voted for are not only encouraged but religiously sanctified. Whereas prior to the revolution many religious figures objected to women's military training, by 1986 the Women's Defense Committee offered six months of intensive military training for interested students at universities and teacher-training institutes. Whereas birth control was banned in the early days of the revolution, it is in favor now because of Iran's amazingly high birth rate. Whereas once discussion about woman's equality with man was considered "un-Islamic," now many praise Islam for "empowering woman" and "putting her next and equal to man." In the words of Ayatollah Khomeini: "What they say, that for instance in Islam women have to go inside the house and lock themselves in, are false accusations. In the early years of Islam women were in the army, they even went to battlefields. Islam is not opposed to universities. It opposes corruption in the universities... Islam empowers women. It puts them next to men. They are equals."[5]

Women fully veiled but carrying guns on their shoulders, or in conventionally male arenas, contrast sharply with any traditional or simple definition of womanhood. A woman bearing

---

[4]As quoted in Azar Tabari, and Nahid Yeganeh, *In the Shadow of Islam* (London: Zed Press, 1982), p.1983.

[5]*Images of Women in the Words of Imam Khomeini*, p. 144.

arms is not quite the secluded and segregated mother/wife. Herein lies the paradoxical nature of this neo-traditionalism regarding women: veiled but not excluded from a traditionally male domain; silent and obedient yet outspoken and articulate like Hazrat Zeinab in Kuffeh where, upon the martyrdom of her brother in 680 A.D., she showed amazing courage, resiliency, and eloquence in defending and pursuing his cause.

Thus, the popular prediction that the Islamic Republic would strive to eliminate women from social and productive life and limit them to the four walls of the patriarchal household, has not quite materialized. Intentions and causes aside, women are assigned or have demanded an active, militant role in post-revolutionary Iran. If compulsory veiling was meant to segregate and silence women, then it has not been successful. Women's unprecedented visibility in literature is only one eloquent testimony to this failure.

Considering "the pen to be mightier than the sword," or than "all of Reza Khan's [Reza Shah Pahlavi] bayonets"[6] put together, the Islamic Republic has consistently refused to view literature as a mere source of aesthetic enjoyment. On the contrary, it has regarded literature as an effective means of politicizing, educating, and inspiring. In meeting with representatives of the Writers Association of Iran two weeks after the revolution, Ayatollah Khomeini addressed his audience as "gentlemen" (though it included the prominent woman writer Simin Daneshvar) and demanded that they educate their constituencies like the clerics. "What I request from the writers is that they be committed as we clerics are. You gentlemen writers must be committed. Now, you should use your pen for the welfare of this people and write for the welfare of this society."[7] In the words of President Khamenei at the Congress of Poetry, Literature, and Art in 1982: "If a revolution and a culture does

---

[6]Ayatollah Khomeini's talk to counter-revolutionary writers, as quoted in Ebrahim Hassan Beyghi, *Kine-ye Azali* [Eternal grudge] (Tehran: Bargh, 1988).

[7]Ayattollah Khomeini's talk to the representative of the Writer's Association of Iran, as quoted in *Eternal Grudge*, p. 18.

5

not utilize art to establish and express itself, that revolution will fail to take root and mature."[8]

Paradoxically, today in the Islamic Republic, despite mandatory veiling, control of the mass media, and other restrictive measures taken against women or perhaps partly as a reaction to them, women's literature flourishes in a proliferation of books by and about women inside and outside the country. Despite an acute paper shortage and various forms and modes of censorship in Iran, the number of titles published and of copies sold far exceeds prerevolutionary levels. Between the winters of 1983 and 1985, 126 books by or about women were published. In the course of twelve months more than 500 such articles were written.[9]

At home, Simin Daneshvar published in rapid succession after the revolution the collection of short stories *Be Ki Salam Konam?* [Whom should I salute?] and the memoir *Qorub-e Jalal* [Jalal's sunset]. She is now finishing her second novel, *Jazireh-ye Sargardani* [Wander-Island]. Simin Behbahani revolutionized the ghazal form in two poetry collections published in the early eighties. Shahrnoush Parsipour published in 1989 *Tuba va Ma'na-ye Shab* [Tuba and the sense of night], a long and moving novel which deals with the contemporary history of Iran through different stages in the life of its main character, a woman named Tuba.

In exile, prominent women writers have continued to write even more prolifically than before. After years of silence, Mahshid Amirshahi has published *Dar Hazar* [At home], and she is in the process of finishing another autobiographical novel, *Dar Safar* [Away from home]. Goli Taraghi wrote the short story "Bozorg Banu-ye Ruh-e Man" [The grand lady of my soul] and is putting the final touches on the long novel *Khaterat-e Aghay-e Alef* [The memoirs of Mr. Alef]. Partow Nuri-Ala has published the poetry collection *Az Cheshm-e Bad* [Wind's-eye view] and *Dow Naghd* [Two criticisms].

---

[8]As quoted in Nafici, "The development of an Islamic cinema in Iran," p. 322.

[9]*Vezarat-e Ershad-e Eslami, Fehrest-e Mozui-ye Kotob va Magalat dar Bare-ye Zan* [A bibliography of books and articles about women] (Tehran: Vezarat-e Ershad-e Eslami, 1986).

Younger women in exile have found a more readily available platform for expression and publication in such post-revolutionary women's journals as *Nimeye Dighar, Zan, Peyke Ashena, Forugh, Zan-e Irani,* and *Panjareh.*

At home or in exile, writing by and about women is flourishing. But this is nothing new. Concern over women's issues was one of the focal themes of the constitutional revolutionary literature too, at the turn of the century. What differentiates the two periods is women's active participation in the current debate. Perhaps the novelist Shahrnoush-e Parsipour does not exaggerate when she claims that writing has become a "historic imperative" for women:

> If twenty years ago, you would have asked me why I write, I would have probably answered, I write because I want to be famous; I have something to say; I want to be someone; or I protest without even knowing why.

> Today, however, at the age of forty-one, forty two, I can say I write because the course of events has suddenly pushed my generation in the crosscurrent of events. It seems as if writing now is a historic imperative.[10]

While giving new impetus to established literary figures, the Revolution has created a rush of new writers with widely divergent social and economic backgrounds. Nine women have written their autobiographies and political memoirs since 1979 which is more than throughout the prior thousand years of Persian literature. Although writing life narratives has never been a favorite with Iranians, male or female, women have never before shown such a desire to go public with their personal tales. However limited in number, these nine autobiographies/political memoirs bring together a heterogeneous body of writers. From Princess Ashraf Pahlavi to the singer/journalist Shusha Guppi, from the jewelry designer Sousan Azadi to the widowed Parvin Nawbakht, they include varying political,

---

[10]"Why do you write?" *Doniya-ye Sokhan*, March 1988, No.17, p.9.

religious, and ideological alliances: royalists, revolutionaries, rightists, and leftists.

Most post-revolutionary narratives are acts of definition and self-definition, both personal and social, both autobiographical and political. It is true that from its inception in the late forties women's fiction has been political in the sense that portrayal of the personal and of hitherto omitted themes, voices, and visions is political. But women's fiction in the last ten years is more politicized than ever. One of the most exciting developments is how these writers are extending their range, handling different themes, creating a distinctive atmosphere in which women resist and rebel against repression of any sort. Women are seeking independence and autonomy, raising their voices, telling their tales. Even those who portray themselves as victims of society—conforming, enduring, and suffering—are ultimately victorious, since they succeed in pleading their case and making their stories heard. They are survivors, the ultimate rebels, irrepressible, vocal, and articulate. A sense of sisterhood and identification between the writer and other women dominates this literature.

A more intense sense of political consciousness and more ardent involvement with the issues of the day thematically differentiate these narratives from earlier stories. Women's limitations and suffering are not seen as natural or inevitable. Rather, they are portrayed as endemic to social structures that can and ought to be altered. In fact, anger and revolt emerge as major themes. The expression of private rage is integrated with a more public perspective. In the introduction to her novel *Dar Hazar*, the prominent novelist Mahshid Amirshahi writes:

> Is everyone puzzled like me? Lost like me? Sick like me? Is everyone struggling, questioning, searching like me? Or is it only I who spends her nights in wakefulness and her days in nightmare? Is it only I who is in exile in her own homeland and a stranger among friends? Am I the only infidel among the believers? The only captives among the free?... Sometimes I want to forget everything, sometimes I don't

want to leave anything unabsorbed. Sometimes anger overcomes me, sometimes shame.[11]

The reinstitution of Islamic rule is a major controversy among these women writers. Some consider Islam the major force in women's oppression, while others see it as their sole emancipator. Whereas the latter believe Islam to be fully compatible with the emancipation of women, the former see the Islamic ideology and practice as antagonistic to any kind of feminist aspirations. Manny Shirazi, in her novel *Javady Alley*, has only Islam to blame for women's oppression in Iran:

> But in the land of the sun, in the land of Mithra, there is no love, no passion, no nakedness nor smiles, human touch nor contact, nor free human relationships; but only Islam, its laws and legislation, its binding rules and the controls which chain us, which chain us always, to death, punishment, lashes, and stonings, to black coverings for women and men's violence against women; and to the perpetuation of that violence.[12]

The poet Tahereh Saffarzadeh, like many others, turns to Islam as a viable cure for the ills and afflictions of her society. This upsurge in religious interest, according to the poet, is a political rather than merely a spiritual reaction against oppression. Saffarzadeh identifies her revitalized interest in Islam with "the justice-seeking, uncompromising nature of Shi'ism and the oppressiveness of our time which inevitably provokes a righteous person to rebel."[13]

Traditionally, only men have interpreted the sources on which the practice of Islam is based. They have used the

---

[11]Mahshid Amirshahi, *Dar Hazar* [At home] (Encino: Ketab Corporation, 1986).

[12]Manny Shirazi, *Javady Alley* (London: The Women's Press, 1984), p.179.

[13]Tahereh Saffarzadeh, *Harekat va Diruz* [Motion and yesterday] (Tehran: Ravagh, 1979), p.162.

Qur'an, Figh (jurisprudence), and especially the Hadith literature (the words and deeds attributed to the Prophet Mohammad) to define the ontological status of women and to legitimize a male-dominated, male-centered system portrayed as divinely instituted. Unarmed with masculinity, authority, money, legality, and especially the power of the written word, women have rarely been given a chance to challenge publicly the endocentric "Muslim" ideology that pervades Islamic institutions. Neither have they had the space to emphasize the Qur'anic passages that would support their struggle for the equal treatment of men and women.

This state of affairs seems to be changing in significant ways. Women are increasingly exercising control over how reality is defined by redefining their status from the theological to the political. Secularized women protest, challenge, and resist restrictive laws imposed in the name of Islam. Religiously oriented women discuss issues from within the Islamic tradition itself. For instance, even though concern over the veil has been a constant in contemporary Iran, never before has it been so thoroughly debated by women themselves and from such widely varying perspectives. Not only secularized modern women but also conservative religious women now debate the institution of veiling or methods of its implementation. Zahra Rahnavard, a prolific writer, married to Iran's fifth prime minister, Hossein Mussavi, questions the validity of imposing modest dress and behavior on women alone.

> Unfortunately, after the Imam's message about purification of the workplaces and the country in general from the remnants of the imperial regime, a number of administrators—instead of tackling the roots of the problem—have emphasized one aspect out of proportion and have left other aspects in abeyance. The over-emphasized aspect is women's clothing and the imposition of hejab on them. But we should remember that in Islam men are also required to observe modest dress and behavior.[14]

---

[14]*In the Shadow of Islam*, p.194.

The veil has emerged as a favorite theme of women writers in post-revolutionary literature. Inside the country it has become a barometer of Iranian politics and the level of the regime's tolerance. In women's post-revolutionary literature, the veil has turned into a multi-layered metaphor, conveniently accommodating itself to a puzzling diversity of ideologies. In fact, it functions primarily as a code that allows anyone and everyone to communicate their own aspirations, fears, dreams, and nightmares. Proponents of nationalism, westernization, Islamic revivalism, feminism, and other political ideologies have all found in the veil their own messages and meanings. An emblem now of progress, now of backwardness, a badge now of nationalism, now of domination, the veil holds a central place in this literature.

The symbolism attached to the veil has also become more complex than ever before. For some women, the practice of veiling is not viewed as merely a religious ordinance or a dress code affecting women alone. It is a challenge to western domination, class privilege, sexual license, and corruption. This viewpoint is quite different from the traditional definition of veiling as a clear manifestation of gender-segregated, male-dominated society. The veil has developed strong political and ideological connotations of its own.

Paradoxically, while throughout centuries the veil functioned as a means of segregation, it is now worn by some women in order to desegregate. In this new multivalent context the poet Tahereh Saffarzadeh and the writer Zahra Rahnavard, along with many other educated women, "veiled" themselves voluntarily before the revolution. Allegedly, this voluntary veiling was not intended to exclude them from the public arena. It was to facilitate their access to and participation in the public life. It was not a sign of humiliation or disgrace. It was a return to the exalted position that women rightfully deserved. Both Saffarzadeh and Rahnavard have indeed been by far more accessible to Iranian readership since the revolution than before it. Veiling empowered these writers.

If veiling appears to some people as a retrogressive step, a backward turning of the clock, or an alienated reaction against modernization, to these western-educated writers it is a valid reassertion of independence and indigenous values, expressing a desire to create a new social order, just and honorable. To them the revival of Islamic values through veiling means a mutuality, purity, and communal spirit replacing the previous excessive individuality, mistrust, and corruption.

In the writing of veiled writers, those women who oppose the wearing of a veil are portrayed as senseless slaves of commercialism and consumerism, as "nakedly" exploited for capitalistic purposes. The only freedom these "perpetrators of trivialities, confusion, and immorality" have gained, it is argued, is another form of exploitation. The poet Zeinab Borujerdi sums up this view:

And I saw you, my woman compatriot.
I saw you
Your hair tinted, your lips red, your legs naked,
I saw you
With your pocket ravaged by consumerism,
Your body captivated by passion and show,
Your personality trampled by entrepreneurial greed.[15]

These "captives of passion and greed," these "agents of immorality and sinfulness," are seen as willing victims of the West. The aim of "cultural imperialism," it is reasoned time and again, is to deprive Iran of its own character so that it can be better exploited. Veiled women writers constantly warn against the bewitching influence of this "western" affliction that has infested Iranians. The veil thus becomes for them a revolutionary tool for resisting the West. Hence Borujerdi observes:

Isn't it true that Islam is the fortress, the shield, and the castle imperialists wish to conquer? What is better then than to assault the very personification of this stronghold?

---

[15]Zeinab Borujerdi, *Tufanha va Lalehe-ye Shahrivar* [Storms and tulips of shahrivar] (Tehran: Abuzar, 1978), p.26.

Unveiling, in fact, is the most brutal weapon used to attack this fortress. It is the longest step imperialists have ever taken to invade our country and other Islamic nations.[16]

A veil-less woman is vulnerable to imperialist "conspiracy," her veil-lessness attributed to colonial plots of the West which, like termites, eat away at her soul and little by little erode her identity and resistance. Woman the temptress is rapidly metamorphosed into woman the tempted, the easy prey, the docile victim, the obedient casualty open to alien "penetration."

For a large number of women, however, the veil symbolizes social deprivation and oppression, an anachronism antithetical to progress. With anger and revolt, they oppose its imposition and view all previous steps taken toward liberation as being eclipsed by this forced return to a sort of Dark Ages, with which in their mind the veil is associated. Paralyzing inertia, they argue, is the inevitable result of being engulfed by this portable wall. Azadi explains the sensation:

> As I pulled the chador over me, I felt a heaviness descending over me. I was hidden and in hiding. There was nothing visible left of Sousan Azadi. I felt like an animal of the light suddenly trapped in a cave. I was just another faceless Moslem woman carrying a whole inner world hidden inside the chador.[17]

For the overwhelming majority of women writing in exile, the veil is literally a mobile prison, a terrifying form of solitary confinement for life. Anger against it can be so extreme that unveiling is elevated to the level of a panacea to cure all the ills of Iranian women. Defiance of convention, flouting of masculine authority, or any challenge to patriarchal gender re-

---

[16]Zeinab Borujerdi, "Darsha-i dar bare-ye Hejab" [Some teachings regarding the veil], *Etela'at-e Banovan*, No. 3, August 1980, p.18.

[17]Sousan Azadi, with Angela Ferrante, *Out of Iran* (London: Futura, 1987), p.223.

lations starts with opposition to the veil. Modernity and liberation become inseparable from unveiling. "Modern" becomes synonymous with "unveiled" and almost equivalent to "civilized."

If forced veiling is seen as patriarchy's or the religious zealots' response to women's improved status in the public domain, then women's resistance shows their struggle for freedom and emancipation. As A. Rahmani describes the situation:

> You must be a woman to understand how all the efforts of this massive body of turpitude is directed toward the creation of devices to make women believe that they are contemptible. And if you, as the object of these attempts, fall into their trap, then you have accepted their values and will naturally fall apart. You have to interpret each rock and each shout of "Death to Unveiled Women!" as the sign of their desperate reaction to your resistance. As insignificant as it may seem to you, your struggle to hold up your chin and your endeavor to convince yourself that you exist, is an expression of our freedom—despite those vultures' attempt to reduce our existence to those of slaves whose only recognized right is to breathe. They want me to believe that I do not exist, or make me accept the distorted, unidentifiable images of their Islamic holy saints as my role models.[18]

Iranian women, whether veiled or not, at home or in exile, are writing more than ever before. They are telling their stories, describing their reality, articulating the previously unarticulated. They are reappraising traditional space—literary or otherwise—and renegotiating old sanctions and sanctuaries. The years since the revolution have thus witnessed a remarkable shift in women's fiction writing. For the first time women have found a more powerful voice in prose than in poetry. The

---

[18]See A. Rahmani's "A Short Hike."

short stories collected in this anthology are eloquent testimony to this newly claimed voice and vitality.

(Author's Note: This article is part of a book in progress, "Walls, Veils and Words.")

Simin Daneshvar

(1921–)

Simin Daneshvar was born in 1921 in Shiraz into an upper-middle class family. Her father was a physician, and her mother a painter who directed the women's school of art in Shiraz. Simin spent a happy, comfortable childhood and adolescence with her three brothers and two sisters. Her elementary and high school education were completed in the English-speaking Mehr-e-Aeen school in Shiraz. On the day she graduated from high school, she was nominated the best student in the nation. She then moved to Tehran to attend the college of literature at Tehran University, where she was a resident of the American dormitory. In 1941, after her father died and her family faced a financial crisis, Simin left the dorm and found work. For a while she was an assistant in foreign relations at the Ministry of Foreign Affairs; later, she was hired to write articles for the Iranian radio and *Iran Newspaper*. She signed her articles by the pen name, "An Unknown Shirazi," receiving three dollars for each one. It was during this time that her first book, *The Extinguished Fire*, was published (1948). This book marked the emergence of the female writer in Persian prose. Many of the seeds that were to turn into the enormous garden of *Savushun*, her later novel, germinated in this book.

Simin graduated from Tehran University with a Ph.D. in Persian Literature a year after her first book was published. It was then that she met the man she would later marry, Jalal-Al-Ahmad, one of Iran's most influential writers. Simin and Jalal were married in 1950, in spite of the adamant opposition from Jalal's father, a traditional man who chose to visit the holy city of Qom instead of attending his son's wedding and who refused to visit them for ten years.

In 1952, Simin received a Fulbright scholarship, came to the States, and studied aesthetics for two years at Stanford University. During this period, she published two short stories in English in *Pacific Spectator* and *Stanford Short Stories*. It was the first time the fiction of an Iranian writer appeared in literary publications in the United States.

Upon return from the States, Simin took a teaching position in the School of Fine Arts at Tehran University. She also translated and published numerous works. Her second collection of ten short stories, *A City Resembling Paradise*, was published in 1961. Simin's ambition to join the faculty of Tehran University was never realized. Although she was hired there as an adjunct professor in 1959 and remained on the teaching staff for twenty years, she was never promoted to a tenured position. In 1980 she finally resigned.

Her novel, *Savushun*, became a best seller in Iran immediately after it was released in 1970. This novel has been reprinted thirteen times and sold over 400,000 copies. *Savushun* is a mixture of opposites combining both light and darkness, history and fiction, dream and nightmare. In this novel Simin reached a creative peak. *Savushun*, as one of Iran's prominent writers puts it, "...is truly a contemporary novel. It is a novel because it belongs to the world of imagination and creativity. It is contemporary because it rejects the monotony of the narrative style so prevalent in other works of this period. And it is a contemporary novel because it sets out to acknowledge a sincere and genuine character: that of an ordinary woman." Simin's two later works, *Who Will Welcome My Greetings?* and *Jalal's Decline* published in 1981 and 1982 respectively, were also welcomed by Iranian readers. The story in translation here is selected from her *Who Will Welcome My Greetings?* collection, written shortly before the 1979 revolution.

Simin lives in Iran. She has completed the first half of *The Island of Vagrancy*, a long novel to be published in two volumes.

TRAITOR'S DECEIT

by Simin Daneshvar

It was warm and sunny, up until yesterday. Then suddenly this morning the sky turned brown as though made of bronze. It's a gloomy day. Formerly, at this time of year, their servant would have installed the heaters, carried the plants to the greenhouse, and sealed over with boards the blue-tiled pool in the center of the yard. The sapless leaves would have been gathered and piled up on top of the boards and the yard would have been thoroughly cleaned up. This year, the colonel's retirement messed up everything.

Keyvan came into the veranda, carefully protecting a pigeon under his arm. His grandfather, the colonel, said abruptly, "You skipped school again?" "But Grandpa, my pigeon isn't feeling well and the school bus only honked once," Keyvan replied innocently. The colonel took the pigeon from Keyvan. The bird's body was still warm but its head was resting on its chest with closed eyes. Keyvan pleaded, "Grandpa, we must take him to the doctor." He paused for a moment and started again, "Or I'd be very sad. I'd get up in the middle of the night and sneak out of the house. I'd put my clothes on, take my piggy-bank and run away to my mother. I'd get lost and you'd never find me again. And then you'd be sorry."

The colonel would give his life for this child. He pleaded with his daughter, after her divorce, to move in with them and rear Keyvan in his home, but his daughter ignored him. She sold her dowry, collected her alimony and cashed in all the gold coins she had saved for a rainy day, and went off to Germany. She had told them, "I want to become a hairdresser, and I intend to marry a German. You'll see!" Mansureh, the colonel's wife, was also crazy about Keyvan. So, they agreed to let their daughter go. It wouldn't be so difficult. Besides, they always had an orderly in their house to help. Every two years, the colonel would carefully inspect the files of conscripts and choose the one with the most agreeable family background. He always had him examined before he brought him home. He believed that the Yazdis made the most industrious, the Shirazis the most eloquent, and the Turks the most responsible orderlies... Then too, there was the silly Fatimah, who would always show up at the moment they needed her and say, "Do you need me for anything?" When Fatimah was young, the neighborhood kids had given her the nickname Bridget Bardot. Mansureh was convinced that Fatimah had bleached her hair blonde. "You can tell by the way it's turned frizzy." Fatimah was a hard-worker. She did a good job with the wash and a perfect job with the ironing.

But now, in the morning of this first day of Azar, she was probably sitting by her warm heater, weaving the bath brushes she sold for a living... And there was no orderly... And the fancy title of "colonel" was history. Mansureh declared a strike and stayed in bed. She threatened to stay in bed until the heaters were installed and the house warmed up again.

The colonel was disgusted. He thought, "She wasn't a hot shot even in her youth, always praying and fasting or reading nonsense books. I don't know how I put up with her nasty habit of reading in bed; leaving the light on till wee hours and waking me up every time she turned a page." The colonel himself woke up at six, exercised, jogged a few rounds in their yard, ate breakfast and left the house early. He returned home at dusk. "She was the first to make me acknowledge my retirement. She makes me miserable, always nagging that I get in her way, that I never leave the house, that I wander around like a ghost, that I'm always either playing cards, telling someone's fortune, or smoking. She made me quit smoking. Now she's insisting that I take up another job. And as though all this isn't enough, she's bugging me to take her to see the world, arguing that we need to enjoy what's left of our lives. Now she wants me to take her on a pilgrimage to Mecca, as if it were the grand threshold to the next life."

The colonel took Keyvan's ice-cold hand and led him out of the house. Keyvan was holding the pigeon under his arm. The colonel was thinking, "I'll look up Haji Ali, the heating contractor, at the Asadi intersection. By the time we get there the pigeon will be dead. We'll drop it in a garbage bin and somehow, with Haji Ali's help, we'll distract this kid. Haji Ali must be good at handling these things, having two wives and an army of children. But, who am I? Only a retired colonel, no one listens to me anymore. Not even my own wife and grandson, not

19

even that silly Fatimah, or any of the neighbors." Before reaching Haji Ali's shop, the public drinking fountain caught the colonel's eyes. Above the water-tap, there was a stone-bench with an arch resembling those set up over a water storage tank. The wall of the arch was covered with icons, and a green ribbon made curls and coils all around the icons. Half-lit candles were scattered on the stone-bench. A man, clad in a cloak and nightcap, was sitting in front of the entrance of the mosque. He was reading the Holy Koran. A lit brazier sat in front of him. The colonel had an idea. He told Keyvan, "Take your pigeon and place it on top of the stone-bench! God will heal it." He thought he had found the solution. Keyvan ran off and the colonel followed stiffly. Keyvan reached up and put the pigeon on top of the bench. Then he complained, "But Grandpa, we don't have any candles to light." The man reading the Koran raised his head and said, "If that thing is a carrion, remove it! It's impure." The colonel stared at the man. He had a pale face with light brown eyes. His lips were even paler. He had on a worn out cloak and a caftan but he looked neat. The colonel raised his voice, forgetting that he was not in uniform, and said, "What's it to you, meddler?" Then he took a nickle out of his pocket, handed it to Keyvan and said, "Here, son! Give it to this nosy beggar. Charity pleases God." Keyvan took the coin and stretched his tiny hand toward the man, but he didn't take it. The colonel said resentfully, "Keyvan, throw it to him!" Haji Ali emerged from his shop. Then the grocer next door and his clerk came out and gathered around. By this time a few passers-by had also stopped to watch. Haji Ali wiped his lamp-black hands on his pants and buttoned his jacket around his inflated belly. His face was covered with soot. He spoke calmly, "Colonel, I thought you would be above such a behavior. We have only one reverend like this one in Tajrish... I heard you call him a beggar." The cloaked man closed his holy book and said, "I am a beggar. I beg from Imam Ali and religious leaders." The colonel laughed. He was tempted to say, "Keep it to yourself." But there were six of them on the other side. He wouldn't be able to handle them all, although Haji Ali was on friendly terms with them (Mansureh always saved some of her best dishes for him, especially before they had lost their orderly). Haji Ali removed the pigeon from the bench. Its head was now hanging to one side. He turned to Keyvan, "Well, kid. You've plucked this bird's wings, and the poor thing has frozen to death sitting in the cold." Keyvan said, "It wasn't me. My Grandpa did it." Haji Ali said, "Pigeons fly away but they always come back to their nest." Then he took Keyvan's hand and said, "Look, big boy! Let's go to the garden in the municipal court and bury it next to the transplants. Mr. Avakh, the gardener, is my friend." Keyvan's tears streamed down his cheeks. The colonel wished he could snatch the holy man's cloak and nightcap and trample them. Too bad he wasn't wearing his army boots.

In the afternoon, Haji Ali arrived at the colonel's house and the colonel ended up helping him install the heaters. Setting up five heaters wasn't a simple matter and the rooms were ice cold. By dusk, the work was done and Haji Ali turned the heaters on, letting them go full force. Keyvan and Haji Ali were getting along well. Keyvan followed him from one room to another, handed him the rags and the glazed bowls, and fetched him matches when he needed them.

After the work was done, Mansureh brought tea, but Haji Ali was reluctant to stay. "I missed both my afternoon and dinnertime prayers," he explained. Mansureh said kindly, "You should have said your prayers. You know that you can always find a prayer rug in this house."

After Mansureh left the room, the colonel asked Haji Ali, "Who was that unworthy soul who ruined my mood this morning? If I had been driving, I would've run him over."

"Colonel, please don't talk like that! That man has hundreds of devotees as respectable as yourself, to say the least." Haji Ali said.

"That pathetic preacher?" the colonel asked.

Haji Ali was indignant, "I've eaten at your table many times, or else I swear to God I wouldn't have set foot here today." He didn't touch his tea. "The reverend is the chaplain of Asadi Mosque. He preaches too, but they have prohibited him from performing both duties."

"Who has prohibited him?"

"You, of all people, should know."

"Why? What has he done?"

"The day he was arrested, I was there myself. There on the pulpit, he was saying, 'You the Moslem people should know that all the blood that has been shed for the sake of justice has not been wasted and is running through my heart and yours.' I don't remember his exact words. He was saying, 'Don't blame me for using slogans. I am only following the Holy Book's teachings. Our prophet salutes Ibrahim who was a constructive man, and loathes Abu-Lahab who was seditious and dastardly.' He read some verses in Arabic and interpreted them, and you should have been there to see how he excited everyone... He cursed Abu-Lahab and all who behave like him. He openly shouted, 'Death to...', and well, they threw his turban around his neck and..."

The colonel interrupted, asking, "How does he earn his living now?"

"People haven't abandoned him."

"Well, the way I understand it, he is sitting in front of the mosque, begging."

"No, my dear sir. His house is everyone's house of hope. People go to hear him there, but he is sitting there to show his resistance. He says the mosque is his fortress."

"Does he have a family, too?"

"He has a wife and three children."

"Why should someone with a family to support get himself into trouble like that?"

"People are looking after his family too."

"Why should a man force his family to live off the wages of charity?"

"His wife is a courageous woman. The day after the reverend was arrested, I went to visit them. I saw her sitting in front of a mound of dirty clothes, washing. She was washing the neighbors' clothes. I rushed home and sent both of my wives over to help."

"Are the wives united or hostile? One wife is bad enough to make a man wish he were dead."

"Your wife is a jewel, if you excuse me for being frank. How she looks after people, helping the families of prisoners...!"

The colonel ran his hand over his mustache and said, "You were saying..."

"Anyway, the women had finished the wash and before dusk, they cleaned the rooms and windows in the reverend's house. I heard that in the afternoon, people stopped by, each bringing something. Rice, cooking oil, squash, sugar canes, tea, legumes, slices of bread and meat. One of the devotees brought a sack of eggplants, and a woman a bottle of tranquilizers..."

"What did she do with all the eggplants?"

"The reverend's wife is fair too. She kept a few and distributed the rest among the poor."

Keyvan was sitting there quietly. His teacher had assigned three pages of text for him to copy, and Keyvan had not finished them the night before. He sat by the heater and finished his homework, then he started cleaning his toy gun. The colonel had taken him to Tajrish Square before noon to cheer him up. He bought him wool gloves and an umbrella. Then he took him to a toy shop and bought him a shot-gun Keyvan insisted on. The colonel made him promise that he wouldn't aim at his cat, and taught him how to polish his gun, load the small shots, and aim it. Keyvan's cat was lying next to the heater with closed eyes. Keyvan put the gun aside and asked, "Haji Ali, does this reverend have a son my age?"

Haji Ali said, "His eldest son is your age, young man."

"Is he in the first grade? Which school does he go to?"

"He goes to a religious school. All of our children go to religious schools, young man."

"My name is Keyvan. You keep calling me young man."

Mansureh entered the living room. She scolded Haji Ali, "Why, Haji Ali, you haven't touched your tea!"

Haji Ali said, "I swear on the black stone I kissed in Mecca that if we weren't neighbors, I wouldn't accept any more hospitality from you unless the colonel agreed to apologize to the reverend."

Mansureh moved the cat and sat next to the heater herself. She said, "First of all, a cup of tea isn't worth worrying about." She paused for a moment, "What has he done this time? He's been snapping at everyone like a gamecock since he retired."

The colonel responded sharply, "You go do your crossword puzzle or fry your eggplants, and leave the serious matters to us."

Mansureh answered calmly, "They haven't delivered the paper yet. They are so unreliable, one might as well give up."

Haji Ali rose to his feet and buttoned up his jacket. The colonel rose too, and took a stack of bills out of his pocket. Haji Ali said, "Colonel, when can you come to talk to the reverend?"

"Do you want me to lose this trifling retirement allowance they give me, too?"

The colonel could not find Mr. Avakh, the gardener, at the municipal court for three days. He finally saw him at the Soleymani dairy shop. It was eleven in the morning. Assuming a superior air, the colonel gave him some instructions. As they were walking, they passed Asadi street and reached the mosque. The cloaked man was sitting at the same spot. Mr. Avakh greeted him, bent down and kissed his hand. Spontaneously, the colonel greeted him too, but the reverend ignored his greetings and instead, he read an Arabic verse while staring into his face. The colonel could hear and understand only the word "traitor." Haji Ali hurried out of his shop and said, "Reverend, the colonel has come to apologize. Didn't you say yourself on the pulpit that our religion permits us to repent of our sins?" The colonel's blood was boiling. He wished he could wipe out all three of them. But how could he? He wasn't young and strong anymore.

"Take it easy, man. Who said I want to apologize?"

Haji Ali said coaxingly, "Colonel, come kiss the reverend's hand!"

The colonel retorted, "I won't even kiss my great grandfather's hand, let alone this lousy reverend's." He restrained himself from saying more. After all, there were three of them on the opposite side. If they attacked him... The cloaked man was feeble, but the other two looked hefty. In such a situation he should either withdraw or use some tactical ploy. Fortunately, Haji Ali turned back and started for his shop and Mr. Avakh left without saying a word. The cloaked man tossed another Arabic verse into the colonel's face.

The colonel returned home and took refuge on the living room couch, looking vexed. He couldn't believe that a faltering reverend would humiliate him in front of everyone. Yet, what bothered him most was that he didn't know what to make of the reverend's insults. He couldn't believe that the reverend may have meant the word "traitor" for him. If he wasn't a retired officer, he would teach him a lesson. Traitor? "Me, a traitor? For having served my country for thirty years? True, I never flew a plane during my service as an air force officer, but what about the office work I did? Doesn't that count?... Dealing with all kinds of problems all day long... having to be content in the same position for fifteen years without a promotion... awaiting the promotion to the status of a general year after year... taking this course and that course; military tactics, topography, world strategy... and learning English at my age... taking tests constantly... and in the end instead of giving me a promotion, they retired me. Having to enviously watch my inferiors get promoted to the status of general and commander of the army, and having to abide by the requirement of saluting them each time I pass by them. As though all this isn't enough, they call me a traitor, too. I'll teach him... I should send some plain-clothes soldiers with clubs to beat the life out of him. But where can I get soldiers? I'm only a retired colonel... I can call officer Eyvazzadeh and ask him to take care of him... Why is he sitting in front of the mosque obstructing people's entrance? He has said he would not leave his fortress. What fortress? Fortresses are for soldiers at war."

He took his shoes off and threw them at the door. He yelled, "Hey, bring my slippers!" He took the playing cards off the radio top and played different games, but he couldn't relax. He told rosary beads, but that didn't help either. It was three months since he quit smoking. It hadn't been easy. All the candy, chewing gum, and sweets he had eaten! He went to the closet and took out a pack of Winstons. With trembling hands, he opened the packet. But he realized that he didn't have any matches. He yelled, "Where are the matches in this house?" Mansureh didn't respond. The colonel thought, "She must be saying her midday prayers again. Then she'll read the Koran, then it's time to say the afternoon prayers." He went to the kitchen barefoot and brought back the matches. He wasted three matchsticks before he could light a cigarette.

Mansureh entered the living room and asked, "What's the matter with you?" She saw the smoke clouds and said, "Oh my

God! You're smoking again. Didn't you swear on Keyvan's life that you wouldn't touch another cigarette?"

"Don't rub it in, woman! Today, I greeted that lousy reverend who sits across from Asadi mosque and he didn't even acknowledge me. The day Keyvan's pigeon died, he embarrassed me in front of a lot of people. Today, he cursed me in Arabic. Why does he curse me in a language I don't speak?" Then he yelled, "That wretched, sick, lousy creep!"

"I hope you're not talking about Sheikh Abdullah, the preacher. The one who was arrested and imprisoned. Now he is prohibited from entering the mosque and the pulpit..."

"Yes, it's him alright. Do you know him too? I am damned if I don't drive him away."

Mansureh sat next to the colonel and rested her hands on her knees. She said, "Come on, that's enough! Don't be so headstrong! Do I know him? I used to follow him in prayers when he was a chaplain. When he was in jail, I frequently visited his family..."

"I'll be damned! You, too?"

"I told you I help the families of prisoners."

"You did, but you didn't tell me they were so worthless."

"You're the one who's worthless. But I want you to know that I haven't donated a cent of your money. Your money is tainted, my dear."

"Shut up! Ever since my retirement, you've become impertinent. Watch it or I'll break every bone in your body!"

Mansureh observed calmly, "You're venting your frustration on me, but I won't argue with you. I am not your enemy. We have lived with each other's faults for thirty years. If you're troubled because the reverend has ignored you, you should greet him again, and don't give up until he acknowledges you. It's people like you who have caused him his troubles."

"Woman, this man is opposed to the government. I am being paid by the government. How can I go kiss his hands? How can I be partial to him? Never. Not in a hundred years. Not in his wildest dreams."

"You could and you will. You are not a bad person deep inside... This reverend is a fair man. He distributes all the proceeds from the alms among needy families. His own family lives on pileless carpet."

"Why does he degrade himself like that? Why? Why is he sitting outside the mosque in the freezing cold? Can't he go somewhere else? Why doesn't he stay in his house where he belongs?"

"He has endurance. He must be convinced that he is doing the right thing. He is a Believer."

The colonel was suddenly calm. He looked at his wife with pity. Her hair had turned gray and there were innumerable wrinkles around her mouth. Even the skin on her cheeks was wrinkled. The dimple that used to be so pretty when she laughed had turned into a deep line. She had gained a lot of weight and her knee-caps and fingers were swollen. This was the woman who lived with him for thirty years and gave him three sons and a daughter. Now they have all scattered, each living in a different city. They write to their mother and she sits, with her reading glasses on, and reads them...several times over. They send hello to him... This was the woman who shared her bed with him for thirty years, who soothed him, lovingly, affectionately, and compassionately. She cared for him when he took ill; she fed him... Yes, she told him that she was helping the family of some prisoners, but she didn't say who the prisoners were. It was his own fault. He returned home late, exhausted, and left the house early in the morning. What for? For whom? So that people like the reverend could humiliate him, or his own wife could tell him that it was people like himself who were responsible for the reverend's miseries? Thanks a lot! True, he was used to his wife's bitter criticisms, but...

He would eat his dinner and sit in front of the T.V. set. Then he would fall sleep. His wife would gently touch his shoulder and say, "Get up, dear! Go to your bed. You'll catch a cold here." Then she would help him up and after she had put him to bed, she would cover him with a quilt and say, "Do you want me to rub your feet?"

Mansureh always woke up before him. She said her prayers and made her husband's breakfast. Everyday she made him fresh juice. When she looked at him, her eyes laughed. Of course, they argued too, and she had plenty of harsh words for such occasions, but she was also the one who initiated the reconciliations. She would say, "How many lives do we have to live? Come on, let's not waste this one!" And he had not been a bad husband for her. Didn't she reassure him that he was a good person deep inside? He was always concerned about his family's welfare. He took them to summer resorts and to the seaside. At the beginning of each month, he took his wife to the store where only the privileged army officers could shop, and would buy enough food to last for three months. He would carry all the bags to the car himself....

When he was younger, his friends called him a womanizer. When he looked at his own reflection in the mirror, he would curl his mustache and admire the fit of his uniform on his body. His wife would constantly burn incense to protect him from evil eyes. And he would languish his eyes and stare at her. She would say, "Look at that big nose!" Well, his nose was a little long, but he had a nice angular face, big black eyes and a fashionable mustache to compensate for his nose. And he was agile and brisk....

Some days when he got in his jeep, their neighbor's wife, Sudabeh, would wave at him to stop and ask him to give her a lift to the bank or the clinic on his way... She was always freshly made up. At the end of the ride, she would round her lips, brush aside her hair from her forehead and say, "Right here is fine." But Fatimah was something else. She would appear in front of him out of the blue and greet him. She would stop and look him over with curious eyes... They had all aged now. How women used to admire him!... even Mr. Masruri's young, cheerful daughter, Parvaneh, had openly expressed her wish to marry a man like the colonel.

Mansureh, on the other hand, covered her hair and wore no makeup. Lately, she had stopped plucking her eyebrows, too, but she kept her face clean. Naturally, she would wear no nail polish as it was forbidden by her religion. She no longer went to the parties her husband was invited to. In the beginning she would accompany him, but soon she stopped going. She didn't enjoy the parties because people played cards and made fun of her when she started reading *The History of Sufism in Islam*, which she always brought along. They cracked nuts, smoked, and mocked her. They also drank. One time, when she started knitting, the guests protested again. She lost her patience, rose to her feet and said, "I am the one who should protest. But I don't. They won't make me pay for your sins. And thank God, we won't be buried in the same grave. I won't say any more." And she walked out... The colonel picked her up on the way home. They didn't say a word to one another.

The colonel thought smoking a few cigarettes in a row would calm him down, but suddenly he changed his mind and snuffed out the one he had smoked halfway in the ashtray. Mansureh said, "That's my man! Didn't you feel much better after you quit smoking? And if you repent and give up drinking and gambling, you'd live to see your hundredth birthday."

"Do you call this living?" He took his wife's hand. The veins were swollen, and there were black and brown spots on her hand. Her hands were once as fresh as a tuberose.

Mansureh said, "Say your prayers! Read the Koran! You don't know what you're missing. Your soul will be refreshed."

The colonel was silent. Mansureh continued, "The clergy man I look up to..."

The colonel laughed. He remembered his wedding night. Mansureh's father had joined their hands together, read numerous prayers and Koranic verses and then offered some advice to them. He read more prayers and then brought a large envelope and placed it on their pillow. It was the property title of a house he had bought at the corner of Absardar for his daughter. They lived in that house for many years. It brought them good luck, and the colonel saved enough money to buy their present house on Parvin street just off Asadi Avenue. They rented Mansureh's house to a merchant Haji. He felt that without his wife's wisdom and considerations, he wouldn't be where he was. After all, a gambler's pocket is always full of holes.

That night after everyone had left, the dashing colonel of those days had taken his wife's hand and kissed it. It was a soft and delicate hand, like a flower. Then he said, "Well, talk to me, my lady!" Mansureh lowered her head and asked, "Which clergy man do you look up to? Who do you follow as an example?" Her voice was soft but tremulous. The colonel laughed and said, "What on earth? Come, give me a kiss!"

Mansureh had pursed her lips and stared at him. Her eyes looked hurt and feverish.

The colonel's mind returned to the present moment. He put the cigarette pack back in the closet and locked it. Mansureh said, "Do you want me to give you an epistle to read? I have most of Dr. Shariati's books. I have hand-copied some of them myself. Ayatollah Taleghani..."

"Why?" the colonel asked.

"Why, what?" she said.

"Why have you hand-copied them yourself?"

"Because this poor soul's books are banned. Owning one copy will buy you six months in the prison." She sighed and continued, "He is in jail himself. Taleghani is in jail too. I wish I had permission to visit them."

"What do you want to visit them for?"

"I want to be able to tell them..."

The colonel interrupted, "I don't want to bother with what's unclean and what's pure, what's forbidden by religion and what's not, or what I'm allowed to do and what I'm not."

"Those are mere details. The bottom line is justice."

The colonel said, "O.K. I'll say my prayers provided that you allow me to marry three more permanent and ninety-nine temporary wives."

"I told you the bottom line is justice. If you marry other women you'll break my heart. You will do injustice to me."

In the morning the clouds gave way to a pale sun. A few migrating birds were still in sight. Mansureh told her husband, "We aren't too old yet. Let's carry the plants to the greenhouse." They had no choice. Mr. Avakh had gotten on his high horse and sent a message through Fatimah saying, "I don't want to go to the colonel's house. Who is going to force me?" Fatimah herself said, "I have a pain in my shoulder blades, but I'll come anyway so you don't think that I am unappreciative."

Fatimah's eyelids were inflamed. Her eyes constantly winked, involuntarily. There was no trace of her youthful flirtations and smiling eyes left in her. Those happy days were over now. They were history. Her hair had turned part gray and part a dull yellow and it was kinky, making her head resemble an inflated balloon.

The colonel first extracted the dahlia and gladiolus bulbs from the garden and buried them under the sand pile in the corner of the greenhouse to be planted in spring, if they survived the cold. They took the geranium plants from the garden and arranged them in the open area in the middle of the yard. Keyvan handed Mansureh the small ones, and she picked off the yellow and dead leaves, putting fresh soil in the pots. Fatimah took these from Mansureh and gave them to the colonel to place on the steps of the greenhouse. Moving the verbena and the white jasmine plants required the strength of a youth none of them had anymore. They dragged them one by one to the greenhouse entrance and the colonel carried them inside and arranged them on the greenhouse floor. They spread out the irises in the dining room, living room, and in the hallways. Fatimah cleaned and polished their leaves with olive oil. There was no room for the ferns and cactuses in the greenhouse. They planted them on the surface of the bigger pots and inside the smaller greenhouse they had upstairs. All the plants were neatly put away and arranged in their proper places.

That night they could not sleep; Mansureh because of pain in her hands, and the colonel because of pain in his back. Mansureh got up in the middle of the night and took an aspirin her daughter had sent from Germany. She gave one to her husband, made a hot water bottle and placed it under the small of his back. Fatimah came in the morning. Her neck was stiff. Mansureh had wrapped an elastic bandage around her wrist the day before. She rubbed some liniment on her neck and asked her to move her neck slowly. Fatimah cried, "I can't, my dear, it hurts!" The colonel joked, "That neck is no good anymore. You might as well trade it in when the vendor comes by." The plants in both greenhouses needed watering, and no one wanted to do the job. The colonel volunteered and watered them all. Mansureh said affectionately, "Well done! Your health is impeccable. If you could only do something about your nose. Look, it's reaching your chin! You almost look like a parrot!"

Mansureh started a special soup with legumes that Friday night. The soup was ready at eleven the next day. It was exquisite. She filled a large bowl with soup and decorated its surface with fried mint, garlic and onion. She then added some cooked ground beef and saffron. She asked the colonel to drive her to the reverend's house. Keyvan went along too. The alleys were narrow and muddy, and although the fender of their big car hit an electric post, the colonel did not complain. Keyvan and Mansureh walked into the house carrying the bowl of soup, and the colonel stayed in the car. The alley was covered with rough mud. There was an empty field facing it. A gang of children of all different sizes had set up a worn-out net and were playing volleyball. The house was old and had two platforms on each side of the entrance. A green tile with some Arabic words inscribed on it was built into the wall above the entrance. The colonel took his glasses out and left the car. He put his glasses on and read the inscription on the tile. It said, "Help God and victory is imminent." It was freezing. He rushed back to the car. They were taking a long time, and he was worried that the reverend's wife had rejected the soup and his wife had stayed to beg her to accept it. He honked. Nothing happened. He turned the car radio on. The voice of a man, singing a song out of tune, exhausted his patience. He thought, "This man has a lot of nerve singing with a voice like that."

When they returned, the colonel noticed that they hadn't brought back the bowl. He relaxed. Keyvan sat next to him and said, "Grandpa, please send me to a religious school. I played with Mohsen, the reverend's son. He was telling me that at his school they teach them how to please their *valedein*. What does *valedein* mean?"

The colonel said impatiently, "It means parents. Well, your mother has gone off to Germany to become a hairdresser and your father is remarried... You don't have any parents."

Mansureh said, "Don't talk to the child like that!" And she turned to Keyvan, saying, "For the time being, we are your parents."

Keyvan responded, "Well, then, send me to a religious school so I can learn to please you, too."

Snow covered everything, as though God had created everything in white. The trees, the gable roofs, the television antennas, the clotheslines, the greenhouse, the pool, the garden, the cement bricks covering the yard, all were covered by snow of varying thickness. It was as though all sitting, standing, and sleeping creatures had stopped breathing and were only waiting. The world of the colonel's house turned into a cat lying in wait to catch a mouse.

Keyvan had a cold. Mansureh was boiling camomile in a pot sitting on the heater. The aroma of the camomile carried a soothing sensation through the room. The colonel sat at Keyvan's bed and took his feverish hand in his. He said, "Son, you're going to get well soon and I promise to buy you a couple of pigeons, one male and one female, when the weather warms up. And I promise I won't pluck their wings this time."

Keyvan said, "But, I told you not to pluck the pigeon's wings, that it would hurt."

Mansureh joined them in the room and turned to the colonel, "Dear, go start your car! Drive to Tajrish Square and get some turnips, vegetables, and sweet lemons for this poor kid."

"But, where can I park at this time of day?"

"Then put on your boots and walk!"

Keyvan said, "Grandpa, I don't like turnip soup."

The colonel did not find sweet lemon in the market, but he brought back turnips and vegetables.

The tires skidded on the snow, making the car swerve. The colonel was thinking, "This thing has snow tires. I don't know what the hell is wrong with it." As he turned into Asadi Avenue, the car spun a perfect semicircle. Near the public drinking fountain, he saw the reverend's cloak lying on the snow. His brazier had been knocked over, leaving a pile of ashy snow behind. Before he reached the scene of the fight, he saw the reverend's crumpled nightcap on a heap of snow. He stopped the car. The alley's passage was blocked. As he got out, his shoes sank in the slushy snow. Two men were dragging the reverend away. Haji Ali and Mr. Avakh were trying to stop the men. The men were in civilian clothes but looked strong and brisk, and the colonel could tell that they were armed. They were randomly beating the reverend, Haji Ali and Mr. Avakh. A few men and children had gathered around.

The colonel walked over to the scene stiffly and yelled, "Wait! Hold on a moment! I am colonel Aryanifar..." Everyone was still, but the men did not release the reverend. The colonel moved closer and addressed the men, "What is the meaning of this scene? What do you want from the reverend?" And shockingly he heard himself saying, "Aren't you Moslems?"

The man who was firmly holding the reverend's right hand said, "I have warned him a hundred times not to sit in front of the mosque. He doesn't listen." The colonel shot back at him. "Since when is sitting in front of the mosque against the law?"

The same man responded, "It is against the public interest, my supervisor says."

The colonel said, "Give my regards to your supervisor and tell him that streets are for public use. People can sit on the sidewalk if they want to." And suddenly he regretted having spoken those words. He was overcome by fear. He thought, "Where do you think you're going to end up, stupid loud mouth?" He swallowed his saliva and said, "Tell your supervisor that the colonel will call himself..." Haji Ali and Mr. Avakh beamed with kindness and appreciation. In the reverend's eyes, there were signs of astonishment.

The colonel thought he had to take a chance. He didn't care what would happen anymore. How many more years was he going to live anyway? And his wife... His wife would appreciate it more than anyone else. Hadn't she insisted several times that one must take sides. So what, if his retirement allowance were cut off?...

He spoke paternally, "Tell your supervisor that tormenting people will backfire." He was actually taking a stand, but strangely, he didn't mind it.

He took the reverend's hand and said, "Please take a seat in my car, Reverend!" The men released him. The reverend seemed hesitant. Now the colonel was pulling his hand. Gently he said in his ear, "You'll catch pneumonia."

The reverend got in the car. Haji Ali recovered his cloak and nightcap and gave them to him. The colonel started the car and turned the heater on. The armed men were talking. One of them walked over to the car and asked, "What did you say your name was?"

"Colonel Aryanifar."

He pressed on the gas pedal and the car jumped forward. He told the reverend, "We'll go to my house and drink a hot cup of tea. My wife is a devotee of yours." He was cheerful. He laughed and continued, "Pardon me for forgetting to greet you."

"God bless you!" the reverend responded.

(Publisher's Note: Another English translation of this story was published by Mage Publishers in 1989 under the title "Traitor's Intrigue" in *Daneshvar's Playhouse: A Collection of Stories* translated by Maryam Mafi.)

Lyly Riahi

(1948–)

Lyly Riahi was born in Tehran in 1948 into a middle-class, educated family. She lost her mother, a licensed midwife, at the age of fifteen in a shocking suicide (self-immolation) in Kermanshah. "Mother had to raise me, my sister and brother under extremely difficult circumstances, and because of her demanding career, she was under enormous pressure. She suffered from many diseases and found out she had developed cancer as well. Maybe there were other reasons, too...." Her father, a general in the Iranian army, is among the country's well-known nationalists. Because of his support for the prime minister, Mossadegh, he fell out of favor with his superiors. Consequently, Lyly's family had to move from one city to another. As she puts it, "My youth was a period of intense unrest and insecurity. For many years, I had to keep my packed suitcase under my bed."

Lyly considers her aunt, Ms. Simin Daneshvar, one of Iran's most acclaimed contemporary writers, and her aunt's husband, the late Jalal Al-Ahmad, who is one of the most influential authors of Iran, her mentors. "It was because of their encouragement that I started to write at the age of twelve and was lucky to have a number of my poems published in a book entitled *Pioneers of Free-Verse Poetry*. "The Cactus Flower," the story in translation here, was written and published in the summer of 1978 in a periodical called *Arash*. Lyly's other work is *Heroes in Khosrow and Shirin*.

Lyly entered the University of Tehran in 1967 and received her Bachelor of Arts degree in political science. In 1974 she finished her Masters degree in library science and joined the staff of the University of Tehran library. She resigned from her position in 1983 when circumstances became too harsh on career women. Lyly has married twice and has a three-year old son from her second marriage. She lives in Tehran and continues to write short stories.

THE CACTUS FLOWER

by Lyly Riahi

Parizad stood by the doorway scrutinizing her left hand. She stared at the highly visible dry lines along her forefinger, stretching her rough, cracked skin which resembled the outer crust of the earth. Earth must be the wrong name for the desert surrounding her: a drought-stricken, fractured stretch of land that had long buried, deep inside its dead surface, the hope of water. Neither the incisive cut of a chip-axe, nor the palpitation of a sprout's delicate life was capable of breaking the calloused surface of this earth. The desert and the mounds of the cream-colored sand mountains, whose layers resembled the waves of a stormy ocean, comprised the landscape seen through the window on the opposite side of the room. She imagined looking at the ventilators of a caravanserai complex, housing hundreds of solemn caravans and their sleepy passengers. She imagined the fence around a city turned into stone by a sudden cyclone that destroyed it all, leaving behind nothing except the black sandy silt, so that something else might be built upon it again. But she couldn't imagine what. How long had it been since they had had water?

She couldn't remember. This always happened to her: when something unpleasant occurred, she would forget its origin, as though whether water was available divided time into halves.... with water came the glittering of light, of purity; stale sweat and dust-caked film disappeared. The trees, the bushes, and the flowers in the garden could breathe again, as if God had sprinkled a thousand blessings over this afflicted, mournful land. No wonder Her Eminence Fatimah, the prophet's daughter, had chosen water as her marriage settlement! When there was water, people felt the spirit of freshness, as if the verse—"In the beginning was the word"—were wrong. In the beginning was water, and it was water that gave birth to life. When there was no water, the dishes remained undone, the house unclean, the food unprepared. And she would shrink back in a corner, with her unkempt, sticky hair and unwashed face daydreaming, awaiting its return.

Once upon a time, in a land not so far away, when she didn't look so rusty and was a "somebody," and especially that night when all the candles were put away and the cats looked gray, she had consented to wear that man's ring. The wedding ceremony had been perfect: she sat under a white umbrella while her relatives sprinkled sugar over her hair; young unmarried girls watched the ceremony through a curtain opening; and even the stone-baked wheat bread hadn't been forgotten. She had wanted to cry: the crowd of people in the room, the smell of burning resin and wild-rue incense, and the rudeness of a spoiled child putting his sticky fingers inside the lace and ornaments attached to her hair, looking for coins and candy...

And you, you played your role beautifully, treating me to the traditional cliche "I love you and I promise to make you happy." And that night...you turned into the live image of the macho men whose pictures appear in the centerfold of popular magazines. And I became frightened: Is it life that destroys love, or is it prostitution? Your mother asked during the matchmaking proceedings, "Are you educated? What have you studied? What kind of degree do you have? How much education have you got?" How educated? She had spent endless hours in bus lines to get to her classes; the classes that let out at noon and were an hour's walk from the bus station. She would have to get on the first bus and then transfer to a few others. Her hands would get sticky from holding the slimy overhead bars, as though they were made of jam, and her body would feel like a squeezed lemon. And then she would finally get to the alley and have to walk all the way to the end where their house was. On top of it all, she had to climb the stairs to the second floor and face her father sitting like a king on his throne and throwing orders at her as soon as she stepped in. Thinking about those times made her nostalgic.... "Hurry up!"; "Where are my glasses?"; "Get the paper from Yahya!"; "Where's the brazier?"; "Start it!"; "Why isn't the tea ready?"; "Now, sit down and read me a story from the Shahnameh!"

And her grandmother Bibi grumbling, "She is the only thing left to me, yet she leaves early in the morning, returns home at dusk, and even then, all she does is bury her head in her books. It doesn't even occur to her that this old woman is locked up in the house all day long. She is no companion; she is a cause for grief." Mother would laugh and Father would smoke his opium while flowers of smiles blossomed in the corners of his eyes and mouth.

To hell with those stuffy, congested classrooms with their ugly narrow benches overflowing with bodies! The students hid their freezing hands under their desks for fear of the superintendent who inspected their nails as well as their handkerchiefs and drinking glasses.... The faces of the students in front rows would turn red from the heat, and the ones sitting in the back rows would sit with their overcoats on. And those gray uniforms that smelled of wet wool when they got rained on. They were treated as if they were as color-blind as bats, condemned to wear only gray, brown, or navy blue throughout their youthful years. No flower or bud is condemned to a color like that. Those weary teachers with glassy eyes, who were themselves either too miserable, beset by calamity and deprived to have anything to offer the students, or on the contrary, overwhelmed by some inferiority complex so that they took their frustrations out on the students. The acute fear of failing... the fear of the expulsive "F" and other failing grades. The fear of exams...fear that stayed fresh in her mind for years and caused her nightmares. The same recurring dream: the exam room, the superintendent announcing the remaining time, the complete mental block that froze her mind, and the hand snatching the blank answer sheet from her hands....

All those lessons she had merely memorized without ever learning, lessons she had never found any use for: history of the French railroad construction, the capital cities of countries she would never visit and yet had to memorize. "How could they allow themselves the liberty of sacrificing our childhood and adolescent years as if they were the last flowers of autumn trees? How could they lay waste to our youth? How could they confine our bounding spirits to the prison of such futile knowledge? What is this revenge that the old inflict upon the young? Why are the old so anxious to transmit their experiences and pains to the young (even though the blossoms eventually die anyway)?" She had continued going to school in spite of constantly promising herself that today was to be the last day. She constantly told herself that a wheel that rotated around a base could still function as a wheel if it were dismantled and set around another base. So, she followed their imposed pattern: go to school for the sake of her classmates, use the school as an excuse to escape from the oppressive atmosphere of her house, and act as if the whole world were anxious to know what her final grades would be.

All the troubles she had put herself through...so that she could get here—nowhere...and confine herself to one of these dingy houses and this nothing of a garden plot?... So that she could feel fortunate to have a few flowers and bushes planted there, plants that are now withering away?... Just so that she could wake up early every morning before everyone else, and go to bed late after everyone else was asleep?... So that she could constantly cook, wash, cook, wash, and exhaust herself?... So that she could constantly fold and unfold the bedding?... Constantly mend the seams in the trousers, sew the missing buttons, wash, iron, and witness the futility of all her work?... All so she could play a cheerful hostess to guests, most of them men, and observe them when they all gathered around the table, staring at the suits of playing cards?... So that she could watch their nervous body movements, their meaningless laughter and frowns, their anxious looks, their grudges and their cheating?... So that she could entertain guests who don't even notice when the tea cup is put in front of them?... Constantly empty the ashtrays full of wet nutshells and cigarette butts smeared with women's lipstick, and clean the empty cups?... So that she could sit by herself and look after their children and be accused of being insolent if she took a book to read or did her weaving?

And this man who is living with her like a stranger: no affection, no sense of responsibility, no attention... Having no child, no companion, no friend—she has never caressed a child's soft hair. Other women, mothers, some wrapped in long veils and some uncovered, embrace their infants with their round heads. No baby has she. Small girls with neatly braided hair and unravelled language, girls whose skirts stick out below the skirt of their school uniforms, girls with crooked collars and loose belts that are about to break, girls who run after one another outside the school, boisterously trying to be the first to rejoin their parents. No spoiled little girl has she—nor does she have one of these small boys with shaved heads and curious black eyes, playing with fireworks, marbles, and bows and arrows for her own. She is destined to remain barren—to suffer. "I'm getting older by the day, and so are you. Yet you're never home to at least watch this process with me. If I drop dead one night, where will you be at that moment? In a friend's house? You'll come home late even on that night. And when you are home, you're either sleepy or bored. You put one foot on the table or on a chair, and even when you're not sleepy, you're staring at a point in front of you while chewing your finger-nails, or reading a newspaper, or you'll turn the radio up while I'm talking to you."

Parizad rubbed her reflection in the mirror with a piece of cloth. It was a full mirror next to the moss rose plant, dark with red leaves that used to shine but now looked like old pieces of wrinkled velvet. Parizad thought, "I wish we had water. If I could only give it one drop of..." She dusted the mirror. In the mirror she saw an image with long hair showing a few strands of gray, and two eyes sunken in two dark pits, set on a narrow, emaciated face. These eyes were once glowing like stars in the dark night, like the night of the twelfth Imam's birth in the city where he was born.

In that not so-far-away city, where the ice on the windows formed all kinds of shapes; where hail poured down like the sugar-plums they shower on brides' heads, and sometimes got as big as mothballs; where the ice lantern under the gutters broke, making a loud noise; and where old women swore at children, accusing them of making the alley slippery, old women who sat by the windows watching the streets and occasionally scraping the ice with a coin....

How chilly the bluish snow had been in those days when she heated blocks of brick and wrapped them in a felt carpet for Bibi. She had so many relatives, young and old; she had not comprehended the meaning of loneliness back in those days, days which she now missed so much.

Did anyone force you to come here with me? You should've thought about it the day you committed yourself to me with the biggest smile on your face.

The snowfalls, the pale sun at daybreak, the twilight.... "I hate you. I hate your selfishness and I hate your indifference towards our shared life. Bibi is right to say that when you own something you must take good care of it, otherwise why fancy

41

having something you can't care for? If you have a plant you must water it, take care of it, remove its yellow leaves, and give it sun; same with a pet bird or animal: you can't just stow the poor thing in a cage or tie it to a tree-trunk and forget to even check on it."

You can pack and go back to your mom's house whenever you wish, and don't worry about anyone coming after you!

"Alas! Mother, Mother! I wasn't much help to you... And now that they have interred your body in the cold soil, I can't reach out to you." She had wonderful memories: memories of the books her mother read to her and the stories she told her. She remembered regretfully that she would always fall asleep in the middle of her mother's stories. And then it was her grandmother who had to tell her stories. Nanah's stories were different from her mother's.... Nanah's stories were full of wedding parties, dinner parties and dances, and she would always joyfully send her characters away to live happily ever after. In her mother's stories people had such extraordinary names that she couldn't decide whether they were male or female and she couldn't interrupt to ask because her mother would lose her patience easily and abandon the story altogether. Then she would remain alone with the fixed shadows of the trees on the wall, the moonlight, the seven sleepers of Ephesus, the *jinns*, and the ghosts of Nanah's stories that might snap out of the stories and lie in ambush in the dark....

This story was her grandmother's. She still remembered her as she sat in the dark lighting a cigarette with her coarse hands: "The Prophet Elias, for whom I'd sacrifice my eyes, discovered the water of life. His hair, his mantle, and his shirt were all green and he wore a green velvet hat on his head. His beard and his eyes were green, too. When he smiled, sorrow left the heart, but remember my child, whoever is fortunate enough to see him must grab the corner of his gown and say, 'O Prophet Elias, I implore thee for mercy! I won't let go of your gown until you grant me my wish!' And then whatever her wish may have been, God will grant it to her." Nanah had sighed and said, "Alas! Mother! I wish you hadn't given birth to me." She had talked so much about the *jinns* and ghosts that she had made her and her brother frightened of the dark, so gravely that they dared not use the bathroom at night.

42

Someone mentioned or she read somewhere that Prophet Elias had drunk of the water of life.

God, yes God, you and your 124,000 prophets! Why doesn't the stupid water come back? What are all these stupid plumbing gadgets good for? She used the last bit of water she had saved to cook the cumin rice pilaf in the last piece of clean pot left to her, and anxiously watched it boil. A pipe, a faucet, a sink, and a large bathtub without water: this is a modern shack.

Fortunate are the hut dwellers who have packed their belongings and left this hellish desert for more temperate expanses. With them gone, the destitute market is probably turned into a ghost house. That market is slowly phasing out, too. What's left behind are the inhabitants of tiny houses, most of which are plastered with straw and mud, or the tenants of houses that have only one or two rooms and an air trap. These people have planted television antennas instead of trees. All they have is noisy electric fans, and one or two water faucets through which the city's acrid, salty water flows. But, at least they have that. And the poor? You always hear about heavy-handed charities and disgusting political movements. Suppose the hut-dwellers don't add a golden bangle or two to their wrists. Why can't all these numerous groups, centers, and organizations change anything? Why does everything, so stubbornly, remain unchanged? Why don't they do anything about this poverty, these children with swollen bellies and naked bodies running around the huts?

She bitterly remembered the day when a group of society women gathered, beautifully groomed and reeking of expensive perfume, and wearing sunglasses. While holding handkerchiefs in front of their noses, they snobbishly walked through one of these neighborhoods. They rang a doorbell, and to the person who answered the door, they said, "Since you are needy, we've come to help you. We've brought these clothes for you!" (The clothes were the women's hand-me-downs.) The woman rejected the clothes and said, "Who told you we are needy? We are respectable people." And she shut the door in their faces. They then left the bundle of clothes behind the door and nervously escaped, lest the infective air invade them.

"O boastful ladies! What makes you want to wear fancy clothes and perfume, and go to beauty salons in a ghetto like this? How could you go around shopping in this pile of shit looking like that? Don't you ever look around you? Don't you see the contradiction?"

God, what a city! You can hardly call this a city: A city comprised of a long main street from which crooked streets branched; a city full of flies; a city with no water; a city full of careless mistakes; a city full of "We don't have it...I don't know...We'll have it tomorrow..."; a city full of Pakistani workers sitting on the pavement, counting their money; a city with nuclear radiation; a city of supermarkets and neon lights, of tobacco leaves, of hookah, of whiskey, of mayonnaise; a city of smuggled soap, anti-perspirant, tomato ketchup; a city that used to be inhabited only by the banished and now boasts of being developed, being the capital city of this province, being the king of all harbors. And yet no matter what you do to fix it, you can never make anything work. God, this is the very day of resurrection some people fear so much!

"Oh Mother! Tell me a story, tell me a story. I wish to fall asleep in the middle of your story, the story of that hippopotamus you were telling me about; I wish to drown in the sea of your story or die in my sleep and never return to this world."

"I am delirious from this silence, this loneliness...."

She turned the radio knob. The bass, crisp voice of the Tehran radio announcer, who undoubtedly had a glass of water on his desk, was saying, "In 1971, in the African island of Madagascar which was discovered in the year 1500 by the Portuguese Diego Dias, and is considered an agricultural land, a leftist movement by the name of Monima, attempted....According to reliable sources...." Why don't you say we have no water? Why don't you talk about what prime minister Hoveyda has done? They say he has given our water to the American camps. What happened to the Minabtoon Dam? The Afghani government has blocked the Hirmand, and the Baluchi tribes are dying of thirst. The Hamoon Lake has dried up. Its birds have all migrated. You are talking about 1971...so that the women who are designing Baluchi needle work on their dresses can be entertained? She turned the radio off. Then she restlessly turned it back on again..."Hume said in his speech at the House of Commons that as long as the present crisis has not been resolved, the British government will not lift its economic sanctions...."

When someone sneezes in England, we hear about it, but what about what's going on right here, under our own noses? Water is more expensive than oil here, Sir. Do you know how much they're selling a bucket of water for? In the summer, they deliver water in tankers once a week to people's houses. The tanker has been waiting in line to be filled for three days now...." From a corner where she couldn't see it, there was the feeble buzz of a fly. She herself was crouched down along the wall, thinking, thinking, thinking. She was feeling disconcerted from whirling around herself, from jumping back and forth between present and the past, and from not having anyone to talk to. At sundown, she had wished that someone, anyone, would knock on the door and come in. She would do anything for anyone who would say a few words to her....

What was that accident her aunt Goli had? The poor soul lost all her hair and trembled constantly. The corner of the room in which she had collapsed smelled damp now: a sick odor making the room unbearably stuffy. Goli lost all her eyelashes, her beautiful eyelashes and her massive curly black hair. She bitterly complained, "Everyone has abandoned me, and your visits have become fewer and fewer, too. You may regret it some day."

Mother couldn't decide where to put her purse and was looking for a chair, while one stood right next to her. Like other sick people, Aunt Goli didn't think about anything but her disease. She was wearing a wig that also looked sick: flattened and tangled. Why didn't she comb it? Of course she could if she only removed it for a moment. The poor wig! Poor Aunt Goli, poor anyone who is in a situation like that! And herself, standing like a withered tree holding a bunch of flowers... How distant she felt; she felt ashamed of her own good health.

No, no. She won't let pessimism take over. She will block it and if it tries to enter her mind, she will kill it at conception. She will lift its corpse and pitch it to a distant corner in her memories.... But it somehow appears again with the same intensity and stands in front of her eyes, making her miserable. "I wish a kind voice would tell me a story!..."

There was a sheikh called Sheikh San'an. The story goes that Sheikh San'an and one of his followers took a trip to the West.... What happened then? He fell in love with a Christian girl, and ended up working on a farm cleaning up after the swine.... Oh, God, she is thinking about water again. What if water didn't...? Well, if that happened, lice would invade her body, her feet would stink, and if she scratched her hands, her fingernails would get slimy. But so what? She wouldn't die, would she?

There is one bottle of water left. She can drink thimblefuls for taste and if no one comes to visit her, she will survive. Like the hut dwellers, she will take refuge by the sea and rinse her body. The salty water wouldn't hurt her, since the climate is humid, and besides, so what if it assaulted her? She felt lucky that she didn't have to clean up after the swine. If she did, she wouldn't know how to clean their mess.... Oh, God, what's this lump in her throat? Why can't she swallow it?

The other night she sat in the dark and ate an apple. A cool, large apple. She couldn't see it but she concentrated on the sound it made under her teeth. The walls seemed far off and she suddenly felt that she was no longer a human being, that she was undergoing a transformation, turning into a mouse.... No, she should repudiate these bad thoughts and instead plant positive thoughts. But where are the seeds for them? In stories, maybe?

"I am worried about losing my mind. Loneliness and gloominess is all I have left. Hasn't God already handed down my share of bad luck? Is someone putting pressure on Him to increase my share, or is something wrong with this Old Man's scale? Is He constantly losing His account of time? Could His scale be erroneous?"

"Pardon me. God, pardon me for uttering such blasphemy. I am at fault. You are forgiving. Please don't make it any worse. I can't say my prayers anymore. I am so disgusted with myself; I've become like the devil: nowhere to go...."

"Once upon a time... I better repeat everything I know to myself, otherwise I'll go crazy... There was a man who had lost his luck and was desperately looking for it. He finally found it sound asleep under a lotus tree. He said, 'O luck, you slept right through sunrise!....'"

The entrance to the house is closed. The door to her own house makes her apprehensive. The pyramid of hot sun rays makes her apprehensive. Both the indoors and the outdoors make her anxious. Silence, feeling as heavy as a mound of collapsed brick blocks, squeezes her tightly... All the closed doors she has stood behind, trembling! All the times she has bitten her tongue, lest she appear aggressive, squeezing her hands together, feeling the sweat collect on the down of the nape of her neck, but still unable to say what she wants to say!...

Death! Death! Dear rubiginous, azure death! Death without the agony of death, without pain.... God, even the sheep get a drink of water before being slaughtered.... Before Islam.... Before Islam....

In Bandar Abbas, there must have been people who believed in Buddha, or in Hindu religions, or religions of the black people. She remembers the Temple of Khadar, which has been turned into a water reservoir. But that is dried up too, and a pond of stale water is all that is left of it, water that doesn't even attract the thirsty sheep coming to the city from the mountain villages surrounding it, water infested with tiny, red, mean worms that are constantly struggling and wriggling... Now she is longing for a drop of that water.

What should she do? What has she done to deserve a punishment like this? "No. I won't go crazy. I'll walk around and recite all the poems I know out loud. But when one sees one's reflection on the glass of the door, one gives up the idea. Both the reader and the listener? How could that be? Poems need an audience." She wished she could turn into a rock thrown into a lake, breaking the silence. She wished she could turn into an axe and strike a fatal blow to the ankles of this silence.... She wished she could turn into a bright flame....

It was almost sundown, and the sun had bent like a huge sunflower towards the mountains of Keno. Suddenly she heard a knock on the door. Someone was knocking on the door, instead of ringing the doorbell, with the tip of a sharp metal object.

Parizad thought to herself, "Aside from water, the electricity is gone, too." She opened the door and saw an old man at the threshold of the door, clad in soaking wet clothes. Wet clothes in the midst of a dry desert, by her own sizzling garden? He looked as if he had just emerged from a swamp; his fantas-

47

tic, heavy outfit was covered with moss and a wet, green rope hung around his neck. In his left hand, a pickaxe or something resembling one shone under the sun. His white hair and beard, weltered with green salts, had turned a salty blue, if such a thing is possible, as if he had lived in the sea all his life. He held a bunch of ivy in his right hand, looking as if he didn't belong to that scorched land and as if standing in the sun annoyed him. He awaited Parizad's reaction, acting as if it were her turn to say something, but Parizad couldn't remember what she was supposed to say or do.

"Don't leave! For God's sake don't leave me alone! I hope you don't mind that a strange woman is asking you to stay. I beg of you. If you only knew... If you leave, I'll start talking to myself again. I'll keep talking to myself until I lose my mind. There's no one else but me, the mirror and the plant... In this entire desert, in all these neighborhood houses, there isn't a single soul left. All the women and children have left for other cities.... My canary has withered away in its cage, too. I beg of you. I'll do anything you want me to, but please don't leave me!"

"If you don't feel like telling me your name, I'll understand, but at least sit down on this marble stair! Rest! You've come from the sea... But the sea is far away... How come under this hut sun...?"

As hard as she tried, nothing but a vague hissing sound emanated from her mouth. Words were born in her heart but they did not carry sound. The old man was standing there looking splendid. His eyes had a distant but gentle look: a look that was not ethereal. His hands, tightly grasping his pickaxe, the blue morning glory vines, and the rope hanging around his neck, were covered with large purple blotches. The old man was real. His existence was as real as the reality surrounding her, and as undeniable. He waited some more, then he took a few steps forward. Suddenly something dawned in Parizad's mind. Beseechingly, she stretched her arm toward him. Her temples ached from the violent throb of her pulse but her tongue could not be made to produce her wish...a wish that eluded her consciousness, "My wish! My Wish!"

Her hand had landed on the cactus plant. She found herself standing in the middle of the garden under the reckless sun. The thick, thorny arms of the plant had embraced a pink ostentatious flower, and the sound of water running out of the loose taps could be heard from inside.

Mahdokht Kashkuli

(1950–)

Mahdokht Kashkuli was born in Tehran in 1950 and started her elementary education in the same city. She was fourteen years old when she got married. Unlike similar marriages, hers did not prevent her from pursuing her education. She succeeded in obtaining her bachelor of arts degree in performing literature from Tehran University. Mahdokht continued to study and by 1982 she had completed two masters degrees, one in library science and one in linguistics, and a Ph.D. degree in culture, language and religion of ancient Iran at the same university.

Mahdokht started her career first as a researcher for the Iranian educational television from 1975 to 1985 and then as a professor of performing literature at the College of Arts at Tehran University.

Mahdokht's short stories are: "The Fable of Rain in Iran," "The Fable of Creation in Iran," "Our Customs, Our Share," "The Moon and the Pearl," and "Tears and Water." The awards and honorary degrees she was given for these works have won her national recognition. In addition to children's stories, Mahdokht has published several short stories in Persian periodicals and is presently working on a novel. "The Button," the story in translation here, was written and published in the summer of 1978 in a periodical called *Arash*. Her most recent short story, which is also published in *Arash*, is entitled "Congratulations and Condolences."

Mahdokht, whose daughter studies pharmacology in Spain, is believed to be residing in Europe.

The Button

by Mahdokht Kashkuli

My sister was perched in the doorway, sobbing bitterly; her curly, russet hair was stuck to her sweaty forehead. My mother was doing her wash by the pond, paying no attention to my sister's sobs or my father's shouts, "Hurry up Reza! Move it!" I was holding on to the edge of the mantle shelf tightly, wishing that my hand would remain glued there permanently. It was only a few nights ago that I had heard, with my own ears, my father's voice whispering to my mother, "Woman, stop grumbling! God knows that my heart is aching too, but we don't have a choice. I can't even provide them with bread. What else can I do? This way, we'll have one less mouth to feed." I had cocked my ears to hear who that "one less mouth to feed" was. I remained frozen, holding my breath for a few minutes; then I heard my father say, "Reza is the naughtiest of all; the most restless. Akbar and Asghar are more tame, and we can't send the girls away. It's not wise." Suddenly a dry cough erupted from my mouth. My father called out, "Reza! Reza! Are you awake?" I did not answer him. He fell silent, and then my mother's snorts followed the awkward silence. My father went on, "Woman, who said the orphanage is a bad place? They teach the kids, they feed them, they clothe them. At least this one will have a chance to live a good life." My mother's snorts stopped. She groaned, "I don't know. I don't know anything. Just do what you think is best." And then there was silence.

Why are they going to make me the "one less mouth to feed"? What is an orphanage? I wish I hadn't nibbled the bread on my way home from the bakery; I wish I hadn't quarreled with Asghar; I wish I hadn't messed around with my mother's yarn, as if it were a ball; I wish I hadn't pulled the bottle out of Kobra's mouth, and drunk her milk; I wish I could stay still, like the mannequin in the clothing store at the corner. Then they wouldn't make me the "one less mouth to feed." My pillow was soaked with tears.

I ran outside with puffy eyes the next morning. Ahmad was standing at the other end of the alley, keeping watch for Husain so he could pick a fight with him. I yelled, "Ahmad,

Ahmad! What's an orphanage?" Keeping his eyes still on the door to Husain's house, Ahmad said, "It's a place where they put up poor people's children." "Have you been there?" I asked. He shouted indignantly, "Listen to this goddamn wretch! You can't be nice to anyone these days!" I ran back to the house, scared. If Ahmad hadn't been waiting for Husain, he surely would have beaten me up.

My father's screams shot up again, "Are you deaf? Hurry up, it's late!" I released my grip on the shelf and went down the stairs. The saltiness of my tears burned my face. My father said, "What's wrong? Why are you crying? Come, my boy! Come wash your face!" Then he took my hand and led me to the pond and splashed a handful of the murky water on my face. He wiped my face with his coat lining. I became uneasy. My father seldom showed signs of affection; I suspected that he was being affectionate because he had decided to make me the "one less mouth to feed." We walked towards the door. He pulled aside the old cotton rug hanging before the door with his bony hands. Then he said, in a tone as if he were talking to himself, "One thousand... God knows, I had to pull a thousand strings before they agreed to admit you."

I asked, while I kept my head down, "Why?" My father screamed angrily, "He asks why again! Because!" I lowered my head. My eyes met his shoes. They were strangely crooked and worn out; maybe he had them on wrong.... The lower part of his long underwear showed from beneath his pants. He was wearing a belt to hold his loose pants up, and they creased like my mother's skirt. "I'm telling you, Reza, a thousand strings," he repeated. "You must behave when you get there." I didn't look at him but said grudgingly, "I don't want to behave!"

He threw a darting glance at me and raved, his hand rising to cuff me on the back of the neck but he changed his mind and said instead, "They'll teach you how to behave yourself." Indignantly I said, "I don't want to go to an orphanage, and if you take me there, I'll run away." I pulled my hand out of his quickly and ran ahead, knowing that he'd hit me this time. But he didn't. He only said, "You think they admit everyone? I've been running around for a year, resorting to everyone I know." I said, "Dad, I don't want to go to the orphanage. They keep poor children there." "What, do you think you are, rich?" my father said. "Listen to him use words bigger than his mouth!" And he broke out laughing. When he laughed I saw his gold teeth. There were two of them. I thought to myself, "What does it take to be rich? My father has gold teeth, my mother has gold teeth, and my brother has a fountain pen." I looked at his face. He wasn't laughing anymore; his face had turned gray. I said spontaneously, "Dad, is the landlord rich?" He didn't hear me, or it seemed he didn't, and said absentmindedly, "What?" I said, "Nothing."

I thought about the landlord. He sends his oldest son or his young daughter to collect the rent two weeks before the rent is due. His oldest son enters my father's shop and stands in the front of the mirror, scrutinizing himself, resting one hand on his waist. My father rushes to him and says, "Do you want a haircut?" The landlord's son responds, "No. You just gave me one on Thursday." My father asks politely, "What can I do for you, then?" The landlord's son says, "Is the rent ready?" My father answers, "Give me a few more days. Tell Haji Agha I'll pay before the due date." And the next day his young daughter shows up in the shop. She is so small that she can hardly see herself in the mirror. She holds her veil tightly under her chin with those tiny, delicate hands, and says, "Hello!" My father smiles and says, "Hello, cutie pie! What can I do for you?" The girl laughs cheerfully and says, "My father sent me after the rent. If it's ready, give it to me." My father picks a sugar cube out of the sugar bowl, puts it gently in her palm, and says, "Tell Haji Agha, fine!"

We reached the intersection. My father held my hand in his tightly and stopped to look around. We then crossed the street. He was mumbling to himself, "The damn thing is so far away...."

I felt sick. I said, "Wait a minute!" He eyed me curiously and said, "Why, what's wrong?" I said, "I'm tired; I don't want to go to the orphanage." He mimicked me, pursing his lips, and said, "You don't understand! You were always dumb, dense!"

I remembered that my father was always unhappy with me, although I swept the shop everyday and watered the China roses he had planted in front of the shop. I would take my shirt off on hot summer afternoons and jump in the brook with my underpants. The elastic of my pants was always loose and I always tried to tie it into a knot, never succeeding to make it tight enough to stay. In the brook, I held my pants with one hand while I watered the China roses with a small bowl. It felt nice and cool there. Flies would gather around my shoulders and arms. Grandmother used to say, "God made flies out of wax." But I didn't understand why they didn't melt in the hot sun; they flew off my body and landed on the China rose flowers and I shook the branches with my bowl to disperse them. The flowers were my father's and no fly was allowed to sit on them. In spite of all my efforts, my father was always unhappy with me; he was unhappy with my mother, with my sisters and brothers, with the landlord, and with the neighbors. But he was happy with one person: God. He would sigh, tap himself hard on the forehead, and say, "Thank God!"

I said to him one day, "Why are you thanking God, Dad?" Suddenly, he hit me in the mouth with the back of his hand. My upper lip swelled and my mouth tasted bloody. I was used to the taste of blood because whenever I bled in the nose, I tasted blood in my mouth. I covered my mouth, walked to the garden and spat in the dirt. I looked at the bubbles on my spittle, tapped myself on the forehead and said, "Thank God!" Then I picked up a piece of watermelon skin lying on the brook and smacked it on the head of a yellow dog that always used to nap by the electric post. The yellow dog only opened its eyes, looked at me indifferently, and shut its eyes again, thanking God, perhaps.

We passed another street before we got to the bus station. A few people were waiting in line; one of them was sitting at the edge of the brook. My father took my hand and led me to the front of the bus line. Someone said, "This is not the end of the line, old man!" I only looked at my father.

He said to me, "Ignore him. Just stay right here!" The bus came and my father pushed me towards it. I tore my feet off the ground and jumped on the coach-stop, feeling as if I were floating in the air. Someone said, "Old man, the end of the line is on the other side! Look how people give you a headache on a Monday morning!" My father didn't hear him; he pushed me forward. I was stuck between a seat and the handle bar.... So, today is Monday.... Every week on Monday my mother does her wash. The clothesline spread around the entire yard. I liked the smell of damp clothes. In spite of my mother's curses, I liked cupping my hands underneath the dripping clothes so that the water that dripped could tickle my palms. Every Monday we had yogurt soup for lunch. My brother and I would take a bowl to the neighborhood dairy store to buy yogurt. On the way back, we took turns licking the surface of the yogurt. When we handed the bowl to my mother, she would scream at us and beat the first one of us she could get her hands on.... I felt depressed. I wished I could jump out the window.

The bus stopped at a station and we got off. My father walked ahead of me while I dragged my feet along behind him.

He waited for me to catch up, then he said, "Move it! He walks like a corpse. Hurry up, it's late!" I stopped momentarily and said, "Dad, I don't want to go. I don't want to go to the orphanage." My father froze in his spot. He said incredulously, "What did you say? You think you know what's good for you? Don't you want to become a decent human being some day? They have rooms, there. They have food, and they'll teach you everything you need to learn to get a decent job." I sobbed, "To hell with anyone who has a decent job. To hell with decent jobs. I don't want one! I like staying home. I like playing with Asghar and Akbar. I want to sell roasted corn with the kids from the neighborhood in the summer. I want to help you out in the shop. I don't want to go."

My father sprang towards me, but suddenly retreated and became affectionate. He said, "Let's go, good boy! We're almost there." I felt sorry for him because every time he was kind he looked miserable. My father was walking ahead of me and I was following him, dragging my feet on the street like that yellow dog. On the next street, we stopped in front of a big metal door. A chair was placed inside the door to keep it ajar. A man was sitting on the chair, playing with a ring of prayer beads. He had on a navy blue coat with metal buttons. His eyes were half-closed and his mouth was open. His cheeks were puffy, as if he had a toothache. My father greeted him and said, "Mr. Guard!" The man opened his eyes. Strands of blood ran through the white of his eyes. He said with a gloomy voice, "What is it, what do you want?" My father thrust his hand in both his pockets, took out an envelope and extended it toward the guard with both hands. The man looked at my father, then threw a threatening glance at me. He yawned, stared at the envelope for a while (I didn't believe he could read), shook his head, coughed, and said, "They won't leave you alone; one leaves, another comes!" Then he pushed the door with the tip of his shoes. The door opened just enough to let me in.

After my father walked through the doorway behind me, the guard gave him the envelope and said, "The first door!" My father was walking fast, and when he opened the hallway door, my heart started beating violently and I started to cry. He said, "My boy, my sweet Reza, this is a nice place. The people here are nice, the kids are all your own age...."

He didn't finish his sentence. He pushed on the door. The door opened and I saw a woman inside the room. I wished she were my mother, but she was heavier than my mother, with a deep vertical wrinkle between her eyebrows. She wore a blue uniform and her hair was a bleached blonde.

My father pushed me further in and said, "Greet her, Reza! Greet her!" I didn't feel like greeting anyone.

My father handed the woman the envelope. She opened it, pulled the letter out halfway, and started reading it. Then she turned to my father and said, "Go to the office so they can complete his file."

My father leaped and ran out the door. Then, as though he had remembered something, he returned and stood in front of the door, rubbing his hand on the wood frame of the door. He raised one hand to tap on his forehead and say, "Thank God," but stopped, rubbed his forehead gently and sighed. His eyes were as moist and shiny as the eyes of the yellow dog hanging around his shop. Her head still lowered on the letter, the woman said, "Go, old man! What are you waiting for? Go to the office!" Father took a few steps backwards, then tore himself from the door and disappeared into the corridor.

The woman looked at me, then turned her gaze toward the window and fixed it there. While she had her back to me, she said, "Don't cry, boy! Please don't, I'm not in the mood!" Then she turned around and put her hands on my shoulders. Her hands were as heavy as my mother's but not as warm. She took my hand and walked me toward the door. We passed one corridor, and entered another. Then we entered a room, then another corridor and another room. There were a few people in the room. One was sitting in the doorway, whistling; one was leaning against the desk; one was sitting in a chair writing something. Although the room was furnished with chairs and desks, it was not warm. The woman said, "Say hello to these people!" I looked at her but didn't say anything. I didn't feel like talking to them. I didn't hear what they said to each other, either. I only wanted to sit still and look at them. We left that room and went into another. There was another woman there. I wished she were my mother. She was wearing a blue uniform and had a red scarf around her neck. I think she had a cold because she sniffled constantly. As soon as she saw me, she checked me out thoroughly and spoke with a nasal voice, "Is he new here? I don't know where we're going to put him." She then opened a closet, took out a uniform and said to me, "Take your jacket off and wear this!" Then she continued, "Take your shirt off, too. How long has it been since your last shower?" I didn't answer. Her words hit my ears and bounced right off. She went toward the closet again and asked, "Are you done?" I looked around and then looked at myself, my eyes becoming fixed on my jacket. It had only one button. The button had belonged to my mother's jacket before she used it to replace my missing button. The woman's voice went on, "Quit stalling, boy! Hurry up, I have tons of work to do!"

I put my hand on the button and pulled it out, then hid it in my palm. The woman said, "Are you done?" I said, "Yes!"

I thrust the button in my uniform pocket and wiped my tears with the back of my hand.

Goli Taraghi

(1939–)

Goli Taraghi was born in Tehran in 1939. She finished her elementary and high school education in Tehran, then went to the U.S. and obtained a bachelor of arts degree in philosophy from Drake University. After she completed her master's degree at Tehran University, she joined Iran's Plan Organization and simultaneously began her literary career as a writer. Later, she joined the Faculty of Letters of Tehran University and taught philosophy. She remained in that position until the closing of the university in 1980.

Her first collection of short stories, "I Am Che Guevara," was published in 1969. "The Great Lady of My Soul," the story in translation here, was written in the summer of 1979 and was first published in a periodical called *Ketab-e-Jom'eh*. This story has appeared in English and French translations and received the French Contre Ciel literary award in Paris. In 1980 she published a novel called *Hibernation*, consisting of various related narratives. Around the same time, she wrote the script for a commercial feature length film called "Bita."

Goli is presently living with her two children in Paris where she vigorously continues her literary activity. She recently completed a novel called *The Strange Behavior of Mr. A. in a Strange Land*. English and French translations of this novel are due for publication in 1990. Another collection of short stories which she refers to as "bits and pieces of my own life," is her most recent work. From this collection, "Mr. Aziz's Gold Tooth" has already appeared in print in English and Persian. "A Small Friend" and "The English Teacher" are other completed stories of this collection.

The Great Lady of My Soul

by Goli Taraghi

Kashan. I've arrived, and I am tired. I start for the desert. Being new in the area, I stray. It is cool and light, full of invisible wet particles and pleasant smells.

"Mr. Heydari," I asked, "what is your contribution to the revolution?"

He shuddered; the fear of famine and plunder had kept him from sleeping.

My wife said, "I'm suspicious of the landlord. I think he has contacts with the Israelis."

She was sitting next to the window polishing her silverware. She seemed happy, humming a revolutionary song.

The sky above my head is close and reachable. The plain, extending to the foot of the mountain, is green and covered with wild rue bushes and red poppies. The pomegranate trees scatter themselves abundantly throughout the slopes of the valleys, and the purple, azure, and crimson mountains look naked and feminine with lines like that of a woman in the old times. The horizon is stretched to eternity, to nothingness. And way over there, under the shade of the poplar trees, a man is lying on the ground; and here, near me, at the turn of the damp dusty road, a policeman is praying.

The smallest flower on the earth has grown at my feet.

I asked, "Mr. Poet, where's your historical conscience?"

He said, "I still haven't gotten over the beauty of this flower."

How exceptionally clear and gentle the air is! And the wind smells of grass, of wet trees and blossoms, as if it had run through a sky planted with trees or smeared with a fragrant breath. The policeman is still there. He is bowing, and his forehead is touching the ground.

My father is against the execution of policemen and doesn't understand the significance of war against God.

My wife says, "Revenge is sanctioned in Islam," and stares at the picture of the executed with stupefaction.

Comrades say, "We must leave."

Comrades say, "We must stay, talk, write, fight."

Comrades are hastily planning newspapers, parties, and syndicates.

Mr. Heydari has filled his cellar with flour, rice, kerosene, and grains, and has brought his silk carpets over to our house. He has withdrawn his savings from the bank and has put all his gold coins in a small sack which he hangs from his neck.

My wife has suddenly discovered God and is elated. At night she hurriedly reads religious catechisms so that the next day she can rush to the Ladies' Guidance and Religious Instruction classes. She has cut her red finger nails short, and has stopped putting on the light-green eye shadow she used to wear. She has repented and she no longer gambles. She covers her hair and meticulously hides her earlobes from everyone's sight. She sits by my side and looks at me sadly. She tells me about Imam Reza's magnanimity and God's greatness, of the evilness of imperialism and the maliciousness of the Communists.

"Don't you believe in God?"

I am thinking about a man who committed suicide to prove that there was no God, that human beings governed their own destinies with no determination higher than their own.

"Don't you believe in Heaven and Hell?" she asks.

She holds my hand. Her skin is hot and her breath feverish. She doesn't resemble herself anymore. She doesn't resemble anyone I know. At night, she is always awake. Every time I look at her and see that her eyes are wide open, I become terrified.

There is an uproar at the university. Someone is giving a speech and the crowd is constantly uttering religious slogans. On the other side of the iron fence separating the university from the street, stand kiosks offering boiled beets, baked potatoes, and cooked lima beans. Pictures of Imam Khomeini are hanging from the trees. An old woman stops me and shows me the picture of her martyred son. She had come to plead for justice, and is looking for an unknown Ayatollah.

The street is blocked. I turn around. The sidewalks are covered with books, tape recordings of religious hymns, sneakers, bluejean pants, and pictures of the martyred. Further ahead, a guerilla is illustrating the techniques of using an uzi machinegun to a group of people, and under a tree, a man is distributing food among his family members sitting around a spread cloth. A student stops to greet me. I don't know him. He has painted his face black, and fastened a checked cloth around his head and neck. His jacket is way too big for him. His boots are also a few sizes bigger than his feet.

My class is cancelled. At a meeting, the students are putting their professors on trial in their absence. They are banging their fists against the walls in protest. In the school hallways, my students are hastily searching for the meaning of freedom.

They ask, "Sir, what is the unity of Word? Which is more genuine, 'matter' or 'ideas'? Which is true, history or God?"

My students are reading the *Accounts of Roozbeh's Trial*, Marx's *Theses*, and Imam Khomeini's *Clarification of Problems* with stupefaction.

Someone is at the door. It is past midnight. My wife jumps up looking confused. My father hides the bottles containing alcohol. It is Mr. Heydari. He has brought us dry milk, canned cheese, and Indian fish oil. He is breathless. He says, "There's a gas shortage. Flour is scarce. Plague and small pox are spreading. Soon people are going to eat each other. Everyone will freeze to death."

My wife cries and says that Imam Khomeini will bring us food. My son laughs and punches the flour sacks with disgust. My son believes that the true revolution will come later and victory belongs to the oppressed people. He goes to the factories and awkwardly tries to win the workers' friendship. He wears stained clothes and goes to sleep with his shoes on.

The fields stand far from this mess, plain and untouched. I don't know what made me leave. It was early morning. I got up and left. My wife was praying. She has just learned how to pray and can't recite the prayers from memory. She reads them from a piece of paper she has glued to the wall.

The landlord was in the yard. He jumped as soon as he saw me. He looked at my briefcase. He was trembling. He was waiting for someone.

"Are you escaping?"

"No," I said.

"Is your name on their list also?" he asked.

I nodded my head.

"One of these days, they'll come after me," he said. "They'll get you too. They'll arrest everyone."

My father was up too. He was sitting in front of the window tuning his six-stringed *tar*. He rarely sleeps at night. He has got himself a sack of raisins and a pressure cooker, and is busy making homemade *arak*. He used to give private *tar* lessons, but his students don't come anymore. Monsieur Ardavaz visits him in the evenings and they drink together. Monsieur Ardavaz was forced to close his liquor store down. His store was set on fire and burned down. He has turned one of the rooms in his house into a store and sells biscuits and canned fruit. Monsieur Ardavaz fears imperialism and has voted in favor of the Islamic Republic.

Mr. Heydari is looking for a position with the headquarters of the Islamic Republic police, the Komiteh. At night, while his gold-coin purse is safely placed under his armpit, he performs his duty as a revolutionary guard.

I stop. The gravel road ends all of a sudden. In front of me stand the uniform wheat fields, the rows of cucumbers, and the dye flowers around the hedges. And further away, at the foot of the mountain, a solemn village surrounded by cypress trees is sound asleep, and at the slope of the mountain lie the deserted mills, a forceful river and a bubbling stream emerging from under the huge rocks. I feel weightless, like a floating dandelion. I recite to myself:

How the smell of grass comes from Golestaneh!
In this village,
I was looking for something.
For a dream perhaps,
A light, a pebble, a smile.

Further ahead, on the top of the hills, there is a huge pool and a small cottage plastered with cob, with no doors or windows. I am thirsty. The water is stale, full of tiny fish and floating moss. I rinse my face. I listen. A bird is singing some distance away. I pull out a cigarette. The light of my match scares a lizard. I start again. Something rattles under my feet. A snake? An old man is passing by with his donkey. I pass. The rattle sound is right behind me. I move faster. I look like someone running to make it to a date or an appointment.

The landlord said, "They'll definitely arrest me. They'll arrest you too."

My son says, "We must kill them all!" And yet he is incapable of stepping on a crawling insect. At night he lectures in his room and writes slogans on the walls of our yard with a red pen. He has been beaten up and still has a black-and-blue mark under one eye.

An old woman is sitting on the grass holding a bundle in front of her. The sun's warmth seeps under my skin. I think I would enjoy getting even more feverish. The old woman is chewing on something for a long time.

My father is restless. He swears at everyone and is desperately looking for the best raisins to ferment. His bootleg *arak* stinks, and his friend, Monsieur Ardavaz, has been given twenty lashes of the whip.

I think about my daughter who is fifteen, and in love. She walks in the garden barefoot and mumbles to herself. Her mouth is full. She has become fat—very fat. She hides all kinds of food under her bed and eats a second dinner in the middle of the night. She's always hungry. When she was little, she used to eat her paper, erasers, and colored pencils. She ate mud, leaves, and chalk too. Now she's in love, in love with someone we don't know. And she cries.

Thousands of people are standing at the community prayer session. Thousands of people bow down before God simultaneously. The woman standing next to me is shaking. She is praying. Women, clad in long black veils, have filled the streets.

My poet friend is bedridden. I have heard he has gone crazy and flings his body against the doors and the walls. I go and visit him. My heart is heavy with grief. He is lying down. He is half-conscious. His hair is sopping with sweat. His mother is sitting by the door in the hallway and is talking to herself. I go in. There are black-and-blue marks under his eyes and alongside his lips.

His wife doesn't notice me. She is stupefied. The minute she sees me she starts to cry. She says, "I don't know what he wants. He is frightened and repents constantly. He prays ceaselessly and thinks everything is unclean. He goes to the rooftop in the evening and the neighbors pour out of their houses at the sound of his calling, 'God is Great!' At night he cries, and for fear of God's presence, he can't sleep."

I can't believe it! How quiet, calm, and reserved he was. He used to come to our house on Muharram nights. He would sit without saying anything. We would listen, both in silence, to the wailing of "God is Great," coming from unknown rooftops; to the strange tumult coming from distant alleys; to the sound of sporadic shootings in the dark; and to the scream of a woman who called from her window somewhere in the neighborhood for everyone to rise; and we would hear a hundred windows open, and see the women, children, and old men run outside. And my friend was quiet and said nothing.

I pause. The sky is green as though it were made from a leaf. The plain ends suddenly and a desert covered with dry dust catches me off guard. At my foot, the deadly desert crawls away toward the unknown, dark lands. A muffled clamor is heard from the other end and vague shadows are wriggling together. The dust is frightful and tempting, like a greedy, gluttonous woman, a woman whose presence is felt in all poisonous scents and inflamed breaths of the night.

I am lost. There's no one in sight. I am tired. It's getting dark. I move on although I know I should return. I know that the desert is seductive and cruel, but I continue, enchanted and resigned.

My wife says, "I wish we knew where the hidden Imam was."

Over there, way in the distance, reside the devils and the lost spirits.

The policeman of our neighborhood has been executed. His wife is pregnant, and everyday she and her many children come to the street intersection and throw stones at cars.

My wife dreamed that the sky was burning down, and she was frightened.

My hands smell of fresh blood. Fresh warm blood. The blood of a young boy whose name I don't know. He was beside me. He was talking. He was running. He was throwing his small fist in the air threatening the soldiers. I lost him at the turn of the street. A building was on fire. The street was filled with smoke and fire. Women were running and men were hastily closing their stores. The shooting started. I saw him again. He was bent. His arms were grasping a tree trunk. His mouth was open and his eyes looked at me. He wanted to say something. He was my son's age, my young one. I lost my mind. The siren of the ambulances had driven me crazy. I lifted him. He was heavy. He wasn't breathing. I called someone. I stopped a man. I ran after a soldier. His head was resting on my chest. He was only fourteen or fifteen. I searched his pockets. They were empty. My poor unknown child. His mustache of soft hair had just started to grow. His hand was still in mine.

My wife wakes me up. She wets my face with a towel. My whole body is soaked with sweat. My mouth is dry. I cannot breathe. I open the window. I go to the balcony. It is snowing. I am hot. I am burning. I grab a handful of snow and rub it against my neck. My hands smell of blood, fresh innocent blood.

My father believes that the age of darkness has reached its point of explosion and a catastrophe is underway.

The landlord has been detained at the local Komiteh for questioning.

My son believes that the landlord should be executed. My son is an enemy of the capitalist system.

My daughter is still in love. She is collecting colorful butterflies and dried flowers in an album. She collects pictures of foreign actors and actresses. She is happy that the schools are closed and she sleeps till noon. She decorates her hair with velvet ribbons and paints her fingernails green, yellow and purple.

My wife believes in the formation of a "Construction Crusade." On "Clean the City" day, she swept the dusty lane of our neighborhood and emptied the slime from the gutters. My wife is thinking about building shelters for the poor too. She has donated her silver bracelets to our neighborhood mosque.

Someone is calling me from the other end of the desert. Someone, an invisible being, is walking along with me, breathing heavily. I get frightened. I stop. My heart is beating hard. The desert is staring at me. The desert is swallowing me. A strange air has filled the space, and an anxious soul is whirling around me.

I ask, "Mr. Heydari, what's the secret behind your success?"

My wife says, "An atheist's entire body, even the hair, the fingernails, and the perspiration is unclean."

The desert is beating. It is stirring. The moving hills and the running gravel have surrounded me. I murmur to myself. I sing. I

65

laugh. I shout "God is Great!" I repeat it again louder, from the bottom of my heart. I run.

My students say, "Death to philosophy! Death to reaction!" My students are fond of social sciences.

I stop. The tumult has settled down. The desert is kind and friendly. I cannot believe it. I must be dreaming. There is a green garden ahead of me, and a white house is thrusting its head out of a host of thick branches. It is so incredible and remote, so fascinating and wonderful that it seems totally imaginary. It is as though it grew out of the ground or descended from the sky this very moment. Slowly and hesitantly, I move ahead. I am afraid to look away lest it disappear. I am afraid to breathe deeply lest it collapse. There is a small open door at the south end of the house. I enter. There is a green yard. Empty, secluded, and silent with two rows of old green cedars along the walls and gardens full of many shades of green verdure and tiny white flowers. In the middle, there is a huge pool with still, limpid water. Its tiles are covered with a soft layer of dust. There is no trace of life: not a single foot mark, not a single fingerprint on the walls, no movement among the leaves. The garden is so serene, stationary, and absent, so fantastic and unreal that it looks like it's something from the ages of magic. And the house surrounded by tall columns with azure minarets and crystal-clear windows, is sitting with its back to the sky, so light and brittle that one thinks it is suspended in space.

I lean against the wall. The breath of the water cools me and brushes away the thousand-year-old dust I feel on my body. I sit by the pool. I rinse my face. I drink. I am elated. What a pleasure! The face of the house is glittering at the depth of the water and the green trees are flowing on its marble surface. The pool is overflowing with the blue of the sky. I look around. I don't see anybody. I take my clothes off. I slide in and go under the water. The water is so cold and cutting that my skin is about to tear. My bone marrow is melting. I let my head sink. I go down lower. Deeper. My feet are still not touching bottom. I open my eyes. The bottom is bright. I swirl. I lose my breath. I let my body float. Water has penetrated my soul, causing it to tremble. The sun is moving down the length of the pine trees. The trees have grown taller as the dusk has set in. I see the house again and a strong feeling of longing touches me. How plain, casual, and intimate it is. How real! Weightless, free of substance, free of time dust, it resembles a painted breath in the air. It reminds me of someone or some place I know. Who? Where? Someone close, but forgotten. Someone present in the beginning of a pleasant dream, at the threshold of old memories. So pure and holy as if it were just baptized. It reminds me of an ethereal woman. A woman with a body like that of an angel's and eyes made of water. I know. I remember now. It resembles my mother's wedding picture with the white transparent veil covering her face, the abashed, innocent look in her eyes, and the clover flowers she was holding between her fingers. She resembles a woman who came to see us one late snowy night, and my father told us that she was a distant relative. And a woman even before that time: a woman belonging to my ancestors' kin, a woman flowing in time.

I come out. My teeth are chattering. Dusk in the desert is cool and humid. I put my clothes on. I hold my shoes in my hand and start barefoot. Twelve stairs, I count. Someone has been praying on the balcony. The holy stone is left behind. It's a spacious balcony and a white carpet with tiny blue flowers covers its floor. I go in. It is a bright space with plain walls and platforms for seats. The corners of the ceiling are decorated with plaster flowers and the window frames are modestly decorated with mirrors. At both sides of the balcony, there are two open doors, each opening to a room which itself opens on to another. And everywhere I go something new emerges, something like a secret meeting place corridors leading to other corridors, and a dim spiral stairway.

I am breathless when I get to the top. One can see the four corners of the world from here. The sky is within one's reach and the desert connects with the horizon, the border of the eternal lands. I sit down for a long time. Where am I? What is Time? I don't know. I feel sleepy. Sleep has reached my eyes but not my brain. I lie down for hours. The stars have appeared one by one. What am I thinking about? Nothing. My gaze is floating in the space and my thoughts are whirling on the surface of my consciousness like expanding circles on water. Slowly I become unaware of my arms and legs. My body has lost its material substance and its angular lines have lost their significance. I feel as though I were the continuation of the balcony, the trees and the desert, and my eyes were hanging from the stars. My head is suddenly free of the search for causes and the anticipation of future moments. How distant I am from everyone and everything: from the geometric relation of figures and the rational proportion of objects; from the absolute coefficient of numbers; from embellished relationships and pre-arranged thoughts; from the extensive tablet of laws and the bulky book of ethics; from the "Enjoining the good and forbidding the evil"; from the appropriate way of living and being. How distant I am from the sovereignty of the matter and the authenticity of the history and the absolute legitimacy of ideas; from the commandments concerning menses and childbirth; from the manifestation of a superior mind and the world of similitude; from the fight between the East and the West and the oppressor and the oppressed; from the rites of cleanliness and the ceremonies of burying the dead; from the one who said God is dead; from the one who was afraid of death, from the one who awaited the arrival of the promised hidden Imam Mahdi.

It's dawn when I wake up. Confused and muddled, I look around. I get up. I'm hungry, and feel very good. I feel light, and all the traces of exhaustion have left me.

A pleasant breeze is blowing. A rooster is singing at a distance. A small village, at the other end, at the foot of the mountain, is awake. I put my shoes on. I hear footsteps. I head downstairs. An old man is sitting by the pool performing his morning ablutions. His massive beard is gray. I greet him. He shakes his head. He is praying.

I see the traces of my footsteps on the dust of the stairs. When I get to the door I stop and look back. I know this is the last time I'll see this place. It makes me sad. The house is looking at me over the distance now between us, and in the twilight, it looks so genuine and perfect it scares me. It's telling me something. Something good and healthy. Something unspeakable, yet I understand it, and I am happy that I do.

The way to return is no longer unfamiliar to me. The desert is peaceful and void of frightening temptations. I take a shortcut when I get to the plain and the green land again, and I pass through the fields. When I get to the road a truck stops and gives me a lift. The driver is a young boy with a black beard and tanned skin.

He has pasted pictures of a hundred Ayatollahs to the windows. Near the city, when I get off at a tea house, I notice how hungry I am. The sun has risen. It's a bright and warm summer morning.

The tea is hot and aromatic. I eat clotted cream, eggs, and fresh toasted *barbari* bread. My daughter is crazy about this bread and since she's fallen in love she eats more of it.

I am worried about my son. My wife cries and believes that he has been deceived. She prays for him and begs God to eliminate "matter" and "imperialism" so we can all live happily.

The tea-house waiter asks, "Would you like anything else?"

I shake my head. I look at him. How lively, healthy, and real he is! How present!

I return to my room at the town's motel. There have been many phone calls from Tehran, and the friend I was supposed to meet the night before has gone and left a message. I must return immediately. Something important has come up. There is a note on my desk. My students are on strike and the professors are planning a sit in. I collect my belongings. I take my briefcase and leave. The gas stations are closed. I mumble curses. I have a little gas. It'll last till I get to the holy city of Qom. The road is crowded and full of trucks, donkeys and carts. When I get to Qom, I find that the road is closed. People are carrying a coffin. I wait. The crowd is uttering religious slogans. Women, clad in long black veils, are moving close together. The air is saturated with dust and smells of slime and rotten corpses. It's hot. I wait in the shadow of a wall for the road to open again.

They stop me in front of the courtyard of the shrine. They ask for the title to my car. I show it to them. They search the trunk. They search my suitcase, the floor of my car, and the inside of my pockets. They let me go. I press on the gas pedal hard. I feel dizzy. I chew on my cigarette's filter. I spit. I honk. I scream. A woman bangs on my car's fender with her fist and swears. Her baby starts to cry.

When I get to the road, I speed. Trucks are rapidly approaching me from the opposite side. They look merciless. It would be a miracle if I got to Tehran in one piece. I see myself in the car mirror and feel depressed. I roll the window down. Gray, dead dust and coarse, stone mountains are all there is to see.

My wife asks, "Where's the hidden Imam?"

My father has gotten drunk and chased the landlord's wife. He has broken his *tar* and sings revolutionary songs.

I ask, "Mr. Heydari, where have you exported your rugs?"

Early tomorrow morning I have a meeting. The article I had promised is unfinished and not submitted. I have to go to my friend's funeral.

My wife says, "Dear, be careful! The counter-revolutionaries are laying in ambush."

The brick kilns appear at a distance. The driver of the car behind me is honking ceaselessly and wants to pass me. I can't let him pass because the road ahead of me is clogged. He honks. He screams. He threatens. I want to get out and beat him up. Smells of gasoline and soot have filled the air. Desperately in need of a bit of oxygen, I inhale this air. The sky is the color of asphalt and the horizon is smeared with tar. Cement clouds are hanging over my head. The thick and coarse air hits my vision. I'm depressed and full of anxiety about the afflicted days ahead, when suddenly the face of the house appears from the gray bottom of the horizon, that cement, closed space, a divine aperture, and moves towards me slowly: fresh, clean, and fragrant like a miracle, like a gift. I see that it's there, that it's ever present, that its divine breath is present in everything, and I know that from this moment on it will pay me occasional, unexpected visits, and I know that on gloomy, desultory evenings, on dark hopeless nights, in pleasant early morning dreams, in the painful expectation of a miracle, and at the time of my death, it will be at my side and will console my heart— the ever present being, the perfect being. The great lady of my soul.

Fatemeh Abtahi

(1948–)

Fatemeh Abtahi was born in 1948 to an eccentric and artistic mother who was brought up in Europe, and a physician-poet (or vice versa) father. Fatemeh became interested in literature early on and wrote her first poem at the age of seven. She produced a forty-page novel, *Two Lost Smiles*, at the age of ten and a long poem at sixteen. She wrote nothing more until the age of twenty-two when she was expecting her first child. This was a novel about a prehistoric woman, which she tore up in a fit of disgust. She also burned her early poems. "A Young Walnut Tree on The Messiah's Grave" was written shortly after the birth of her son, which she describes as an "ecstatic event," and published in a periodical called *Ketab-e-Jomeh* in the Fall of 1979.

Fatemeh lives in Tehran. She is a graduate of Tehran University and teaches English. Her interest in painting and music has led her to write and produce children's programs for Iranian Television. A puppet show based on "Jack and the Bean Stalk" and her own short stories and poems have brought her much success. Fatemeh married four times, the last being a re-marriage to the father of her children.

A Young Walnut Tree On The Messiah's Grave

by Fatemeh Abtahi

The Messiah is born. I must give my blessing. I must perform a vow and make an offering. I must pray. I will light tall candles for the Messiah. I will light candles in every mosque and church. Now I am like other women. How worried I am! I feel his forehead several times a day. I want to protect his innocent little body from the filthy heat coming from the outside. I look at his skin, check his pulse, watch his breathing. Isn't this a miracle? How can a dull, dejected woman like me become so affectionate and glowing? I have given birth to the Messiah. No one will erect a statue of us. I kept thinking I was going to give birth to a rock. How could I have given birth to something with veins and vitality? How good it smells! Pieta. I've blown life into marble. He must live and I must pray for him. I'll pray for all children, even those who'll grow wicked.

That day in the dim light of the Isfahan Bazaar, how sad I felt behind my eye-glasses. I walked alone, not looking for anything in particular. Dismally, I carried the weight of my body around. I saw a quilt-making shop. In one corner, there was a huge mound of cotton. An old man was sitting between the cotton and the colorful satin quilts; he reminded me of God. I sat on a pink satin quilt. The old man's needle moved incredibly fast. I took my glasses off. The light of his lamp, gliding down satin quilts, made me sadder. I tried to remind myself that outside the sun was shining on the blue tiles of the mosques. "How long does it take you to make each quilt?" "Has the price of cotton gone up?" "Has the satin factory closed down?" He offered me tea. I'll buy a blue satin quilt for the Messiah. I'll always keep it clean and spread it in the sun once a week. I'll clean the windows. The whole house should shine. I'll show the sun and the snowy mountains to the Messiah through a spotless window. I'll show him the pigeons, the ringdoves and the sparrows that conquer the city in the autumn. "Where's the chick?" "It's gone. It flew away." "Where do sparrows come from?" Hopefully this autumn I'll be more cheerful. That day, in the Isfahan Bazaar, I wanted to bury my head under the pink quilt and cry aloud. I wanted to go outside where the sun and the blue of the mosques were, and scream my lungs out.

Cries for no reason, like the onrush of sparrows. Autumn is supposed to be the season of fruition. I always cry more in the autumn. Women's black and deadly long veils. Pale and skinny children who have to live hidden under their mother's long veils, who have to go to religious and wedding ceremonies hidden under their mother's veils, and who always cry their unhappy hearts out. Slimy drinking fountains and crooked white candles. "How many candles do they light each day?" I also lit a candle. For what? I escaped the mass of the women gathering in the shrine. I reached the square and lost myself in the midst of the blue.

If Nanah Masumeh had not left, I would have gone to Saint Abdullah's shrine with her this year. She always used to take her offerings there; offerings in the name of her daughter Pooran, in my name, in the name of her grandson, and in the name of a canary whose name was Masumeh's Nanah, who had died because of my neglect. She used to wear her elegant velvet jacket and cover her hair with a white embroidered scarf. Her shoes used to shine like the ruby gem of her ring, too. I always felt better after she gave her offerings. Through her massive eyeglasses, I could never tell whether she was crying. In spite of her bad eyes, she had made me a doll. A doll with turquoise earrings and a velvet dress. With a cloth cut from her own jacket, she had made this dress for my doll. If Nanah Masumeh hadn't left, I would also make a doll and give it to the girl who was sitting and crying all by herself on the road to Saint Abdullah's shrine. We would go together. I would buy a huge candle for the Messiah. I would carry the candle on my shoulder. When Nanah Masumeh watered her young walnut tree or looked at it in the garden, the sight of sun rays passing through her thin scarf was fascinating. Now the young tree is growing. I know this time it's not because of Pooran. Nanah Masumeh is gone and won't come back. She won't even miss her walnut tree.

She was always dancing and laughing, always dancing and crying. She was always making dolls for all the children. She always watered the flowers and caressed the leaves. She loved the sweetheart flower and became filled with joy when a flower blossomed out of season. She always prayed and gave her blessings, and even before Pooran was born she was her mother. She drank tea and ate very little. She always went to the baker's and the butcher's cheerfully, and cleaned the vegetables with great care. Sweeping, she always looked out the windows at the garden. Her clothes were always spotless and smelled of heaven. Sometimes she wore her ruby ring. She frequently told us, "My father, God bless him, made me a red and blue wooden horse." She laughed and cried, and I could never tell whether she was crying or laughing even when she was dancing. Sometimes she said, "I have promised God a gift of a hundred *tomans* for my grandson. I am crazy about him. He is going to school now. He is becoming a real gentleman. May God preserve him from the evil eye! I'm going to buy him a real car. Have you noticed how lovely the vegetables have become? Such a delight!" She had made a small satin quilt for my canary, Masumeh's Nanah, and every evening she placed its cage in front of the television and sat next to it to keep it company. She would say, "Lady Pooran, sing! Lady Fati, twitter! Look at that cat... I won't let him eat you, don't you worry!"

When she hadn't heard from Pooran, she would get quiet and solemn. She would water the flowers slowly. Her face would look as sad and heavy as the air inside all the shrines. "Nanah Masumeh! I've shown your doll to everyone." — She was quiet and didn't seem to notice me. She didn't notice anyone. She was looking at some distant spot. Maybe it was the point she imagined her walnut tree to reach, years after her death. Her smile resembled the expression of a helpless infant. Her dress and thin scarf seemed giant waves in the ocean, and she herself a mere coral at its bottom. She didn't seem to hear me. Finally Pooran's letter would arrive and Nanah Masumeh would dance, laugh and cry again. On hot summer days she made hand fans, offered us sherbet, and drank tea. "I used to bake walnut and date pastries and make iced desserts. I used to be able to do anything. I made baklava better than anyone, and I used to weave colorful socks for Pooran and all the relatives' children. But now I've gotten old and can't do anything. 'When you're old, Hafez, leave the tavern for good.'—" I hadn't seen her in her velvet jacket for some time now. Ammeh Khanom said Nanah Masumeh had given it to a poor soul who had nothing to wear. Now they've given her one of Khosrow's jackets. One day she showed me her ring and said, "If you look closely, you'll see the picture of that red and blue wooden horse I told you about." — I know she will never return.

This autumn I'll hold the Messiah in my arms, and at dusk we'll watch the sparrows through the stained windows together. I won't take him out. The crowded streets have become a nuisance. The noises depress me. And Nanah Masumeh and the peaceful air she had about her are gone. — I know she will never return again.

Last autumn and winter Nanah Masumeh didn't have the time to make dolls. She stood in line for bread and kerosene for hours. She had never been talkative like that before. She recounted for us all the rumors she had heard: "They say His Eminence Khomeini is returning to Iran. They say the cruel Shah's time is up. Today when I was at the baker's, I heard gunfire. I was shaken with fear. The soldiers arrested a young boy before my very eyes. What a nice looking young boy he was! Tall as a box tree. He started to run and they shot him down. He became a martyr. Martyrs will go to God's Heaven. I hope the soldier who shot him doesn't live to see tomorrow's daylight! And I hope his death will permanently wound his mother's heart!"

"Dear Fati, let me tell you about the dream I had: I dreamed that I was going to visit His Eminence Khomeini. I didn't know how to find his house, and you were with me. The His Eminence wasn't there, but his wife was. She offered us chairs and a thousand other courtesies and brought us tea. I told her that the soldiers bothered me at the line in front of the baker's.... The His Eminence had arrived and was about to receive us, when... I woke up. I wasn't lucky enough to have the honor of meeting him. I wasn't good enough to see the His Eminence's graceful, blessed face! Why should the His Eminence appear in the dream of a disgraceful soul like me? The His Eminence is a very busy man. He has to attend to everyone's problems."

She bought a glass kerosene lamp which was painted red. She set it in the kitchen window. It was always lit. She said, "Until His Eminence Khomeini's return and until this mess is straightened, I'll keep this lamp going." — She guarded it against the wind and naughty children playing in the alley who threw stones at people's windows. She now cared more for the lamp than for the trees. "When the His Eminence comes, everything is going to be all right. There will be an abundance of everything. We'll be rich. No one will freeze. The His Eminence will come. Roses will grow under his feet. The air around him will smell of rose-water. His face will light up the world."—When Nanah Masumeh talked about the His Eminence, everything glittered like gold: her eyes, the lenses of her eye-glasses, all the windows, and my heart.

One day Nanah Masumeh, Ammeh Khanom, and I went to the Behesht-e Zahra ceremony. Mothers were not crying for the loss of their children. Instead, they were singing revolutionary hymns alongside of their graves. We also sang, while sharing the small amount of halvah we had brought. The graves stretched to the horizon. We sat quietly by a stoneless grave covered with flowers and watched the sparrows peck at the wheat and the millet seeds sprinkled for them on the graves. If I died, Nanah Masumeh would plant a young walnut tree, and every Friday she would recite the fatehah from the Koran, and sprinkle wheat seeds on my grave. Mothers sat peacefully by the graves. I stared at the Pieta statue: how beautiful death was! I also wanted to die. Death without mourning was beautiful. Death for the sake of the soil. From the ground I would smell the sky through soil and stone. I would smell the bitter smell of the walnut that reached for the sky. They were bringing a corpse. They had made a banner with his blood-stained shirt and were singing a hymn. We joined them in the singing of the hymn, following the corpse and the blood-stained shirt.

Nanah Masumeh wanted to plant the entire garden with roses. She had posted pictures of His Eminence Khomeini on all the walls. The ruby lamp was lit. I was constantly day-dreaming in anticipation of the birth of the Messiah. When the Messiah is born, I will tell him stories: "Once upon a time, before you were born, in a land very far from here, there was a fiend who had made everyone miserable. He didn't allow children to play and bothered grown-ups. No heart could be happy and no face could smile." I would put on a grim face and the Messiah would purse his lips, but before his little heart could feel the pain, I would move on with the rest of the story and say, "But one day, a glowing man appeared, equipped with a sword to kill the fiend. He went and stood right in front of the fiend, drew his sword from its sheath, called upon God, and hit the fiend on the neck so fiercely that the sky suddenly filled with thunder and lightning, and the fiend went up in smoke. Then the sky blackened and it began to rain. The rain washed the blood from the soil and made it fertile. Smiles replaced tears and the whole world regained its gaiety." The Messiah would laugh with his mouth, his eyes, and his heart.

The day His Eminence Khomeini came, Nanah Masumeh asked Ammeh Khanom to take care of her lamp; and looking neater than ever, with henna-treated hair and hands, and holding a bunch of flowers in her hand, she left to welcome the His Eminence. She wiped her tears with the piece of cotton she had soaked in tea. She was wearing a new velvet jacket.

When my canary died, Nanah Masumeh's grief-filled voice snapped at me. She blamed herself and wouldn't look at me. She wrapped the small satin quilt in a piece of plastic and put it in the cage. She filled the cage with ornate flowers and placed it in a chest. Then she buried my canary next to a geranium seedling in a pot, and with a sad voice she murmured some song from her native village.

I became lonesome again. Sometimes I had nightmares, and sometimes I dreamed of the Messiah kissing my face and trying to console me. The Messiah would be born at dawn; at dusk, a number of grim-faced men clad in mourning clothes would carry his little coffin away on their shoulders. I was scared.

Nanah Masumeh's face wore an unfading gloom like a veil. Her new velvet jacket was soiled with oil stains. Though still lit, the lamp's red paint had been gradually peeling off and disappearing. She had buried her ruby ring at the bottom of her bureau. Her voice had become hoarse again, like when my canary died. She never mentioned the His Eminence anymore. Early in the winter days, before dawn, she would wipe the snow off the young walnut tree. The snow and the Messiah made me pensive. Anxious, I busied myself with sewing and weaving his clothes. At night I woke shaking with fear. Every night they would bang on the door and try to take my Messiah away from me. Men who didn't speak. Men who had covered their faces and wore long black robes. They banged on the doors with the stocks of their rifles.

One day Ammeh Khanom was telling Khosrow: "Nanah Masumeh has become possessed by the devil again. She won't touch her food." No one watered the flowers. Spring had come, but the garden was dry and gloomy. Only the pine tree was green. Nanah Masumeh was lying down covered by a soiled quilt. She didn't have her glasses on and the gaze of her red, inflamed eyes was fixed to the ceiling. I knew that she had recently heard from Pooran, so that wasn't what had caused her present state. She was altogether different. The henna that she always used to stain her hands had faded away. I held her bony, cold hand; she withdrew it. She didn't see or hear me. She didn't hear Pooran either. Her unkempt red and white hair stuck out of her dirty scarf. "Speak, Nanah Masumeh! You'll feel better if you speak. Shall I get you some tea?"

I went to get tea and noticed that the lamp was out. It was soiled with dirt and grease and its chimney was smeared with soot. It was surrounded by dirty dishes. I cleaned and lit the lamp. Looking out the window, I saw the children trying to hide under their mother's long veils. They looked frightened. Nanah Masumeh didn't drink her tea. With her inflamed eyes and chapped lips, she was staring at nothing. She had turned her back to me. I sat quietly next to her and kept caressing her cold hands until she saw me and felt my warmth. She broke into tears. A graceful, quiet cry, very different from my usual shrill cries. She wiped her tears with the corner of her scarf. Her tears dried up all the gardens: the gardens in which the Messiah and I had strolled every evening. — Desert, the burning desert, the salt marsh of the lips that refused to drink tea.

She put her glasses back on. With trembling hands she rearranged her hair and covered it under her scarf. From her bed, she looked at me and said, "Forgive me for troubling you." I took her another cup of tea. This time she drank it.

The next day she got out of bed. She dressed in clean clothes and sat by the parched garden. Then she went to the kitchen and put out the lamp. I knew she was crying and shivering. How depressed she was! How depressed I was! She packed her belongings in a bundle and said good-bye to us. She got into a cab at the street corner and left for her village. How I wish she could be here when my Messiah is born! I wonder if she can still make dolls for children.

How exhausted I feel! Women holding their pale and skinny children in their arms are going to shrines and mosques to make offerings. I'll stay right here in this room. The throng of the streets annoys me. Autumn is upon us. No one will make a statue of me showing the sparrows to the Messiah. Pieta, how dejected I feel.

The Messiah will grow up in this room. Maybe one day, when the city is not so crowded, I will go buy him a wooden horse. The Messiah will grow up, and I will grow old. I'll keep praying. But one day they'll knock on the door: men who have covered their faces will enter and take him away. I'll remain in this room behind soiled windows, alone. I'll pray and utter my blessings. In the evening I'll water the geraniums on the veranda and sprinkle seeds for the autumn sparrows.

Shahrzad

Shahrzad's actual birth date is unknown, and her age can be deduced only approximately. Because contact with Shahrzad herself or someone who could help in this respect was not possible, included on this page is a short introductory passage found in one of Shahrzad's books of poems published in Iran.

"Kobra was the name of my deceased sister whose birth certificate was saved for me. My mother called me Mariam and my father, Zahra. People called me Shahla in the nightclub where I danced. As a movie actress, I was introduced to the public as Shahrzad and now I use the name M. Shahrzad when signing my poems.

"But to you who helped me find my true self and included me in your circle [reference is made to the circle of Iranian writers] I say that our numbers are too few and our paths too long to allow me the trivial concern of what my name should be. You can call me whatever you want. I will respect your choice.

"When I was a student in elementary school in 1945, I was the heaviest but still the hungriest kid in the school. Because of my weight no one knew how hungry I was. No one knew that I gained weight because I was depressed. Depressed because I did not have what I thought I deserved to have. My sister was younger and more fortunate than I, because she was both hungry and skinny. All my classmates hated me.... They thought I ate my sister's share too. But my sister and I only laughed.

"Now, in 1978 we are all depressed. My sister's daughter is now going to the elementary school. I, my sister and her daughter are all hungry... but we all laugh!"

"Me... Want... Candy," the story in translation here, was published in the Winter of 1980 in a periodical called *Ketab-e-Jom'eh*. It is believed that Shahrzad's *Hello, Mister* (a novel), which is the story of a prostitute, is also her autobiography. Her other works include a book of poetry and her first novel *Toba*. It is believed that Shahrzad left Iran in 1986 and like many other refugees went to Turkey to get a visa for another country. It is not known where her present residence is.

Me... Want... Candy

by Shahrzad

Not much was left of my father's life after my mother gave birth to Afsaneh.

That day I was returning home from school, as usual, reading a used *Keyhan For Kids*, a supplement of the daily newspaper I had rented from the "bag-maker" — the man who turned newspapers into shopping bags and sold them to the neighborhood grocer and dairyman. A new *Keyhan* cost half a *toman* and only Nasrin, who wouldn't allow a soul to touch it, could afford to buy one. The bag-maker had agreed to lend it to me for ten *shahis*, provided I didn't tear or dirty it, and that I keep it only from Wednesday evening till Thursday morning....

In the streets and alleys, I had jostled everyone and bumped into everything, from the wooden electricity pole, hurting my forehead and nose, to Mrs. Karbalai who poured forth a hundred insults upon me:

"Abject bastard, look where you're going! This little bastard walks as arrogantly through the alleys as if she's strolling through the heavenly gardens. The little bastard doesn't even look where she's going. Bitch!... I hope you die before the new day's light."

A harsh voice whose origin remained unknown to me said, "She's reading her father's bullshit. You have to stick it up their...."

I was finishing the section with the story of the "Voyages of Sindbad." It was so exciting that I bumped into the blind beggar who supposedly stinks so bad no one can get within ten feet of him. He gave me a hard blow in the groin with his broken stick and said, "Filthy bitch, instead of giving me something she knocks me over. Fucking bitch! If only I could see, I'd teach you...."

"I know Mr. Kalduz, it's my fault. But what should I do? By the time I get home and do my chores, it'll be night time. I have homework to do, too. And I have to give this to everyone to read so I can return it tomorrow morning. That's why I have to finish it before I get home...."

"Shut up, you blabber mouth! Go get something for me if you really care...."

I got to our street corner before finishing the last page of the paper. Bagher's wife, Soraya, who was my classmate till last year and is now married to a street vendor, looked out the window cautiously and said, "I've left a piece of candy on the tile near the entrance for you. Take it and throw the paper to me. I'll finish it before the hour's up. Hurry up now before someone sees us and tells Bagher about it."

I took the candy, rolled the magazine, pitched it towards the window and said, "Finish it before dusk. I have to give it to Nahid."

Soraya caught the paper and said, "Hurry home. Your brother Yousef has been throwing up blood since this morning and your mother is going to have the baby soon. You know Bagher doesn't let me leave the house; otherwise I would've gone to your house to help...."

Yousef... Yousef... Blood...

There was a big crowd of veiled women at the end of the alley. It's always been like this, but normally I saw a bigger crowd in the morning than the evening when I returned from school. In the morning women gathered around the cloth on which Mr. Ahmad, the greengrocer, spread the vegetables he brought to sell in the neighborhood.

I would give my life for Yousef. I ran all the way to my house. Every one of the neighbors was there. All the women and children were gathering in the rooms, in the yard and in the alley....

Maryam was standing in one corner getting hot water from a boiling pot, pouring it into a basin and giving it to Zahra who took it from her and passed it on to Omar who stood by the window. Kobra was busy stirring the porridge over the kerosene stove. Zina, the Assyrian woman who was a waitress in the evening at the restaurant owned by Soraya's mother, who was neither invited nor admitted to anyone's house and cared for by no one but my father, was pouring tea into glasses and setting them on a tray, quietly weeping. My brother Ahmad was breaking sugar lumps into small pieces and placing them with his tiny hands into the bowls. My aunt Sakineh, who had a cataract and couldn't see a thing, was cleaning the rice. Mrs.

Arshym was nervously walking up and down the room. She was holding the holy Koran above her head, and in spite of the hump on her back, was walking back and forth along the corridor leading to the yard, constantly mumbling: "Damn the devil! Just when one child is being born, the other is dying.... But, what for? What's the difference between these two? What the hell is the meaning of this? Only one of them should be, either this one or that one. How the hell is this whelp different from the other? Pray for her! God damn you, pray for her! Hey you, don't step into the room with your dirty shoes. Everyone pray for her!"

My mother's shrieks filled the windows and the hallways like my father's papers did the day those fat, austere men threw them out the windows. Her voice could be heard everywhere: in the yard, in the alley and in the whole neighborhood.

I was confused and dizzy. I wanted to find Yousef right away. I cleared my way through the crowd of women in black and colored veils to the children's corner of the room.They had laid my mother down in the middle of the room where my grandmother was reciting the Koran over my mother's head. Fatimah and Senobar were tearing pieces off the sheets and giving them to Robab who arranged them in a pile. Asghar's mother was holding a pair of scissors over the lamp. I found poor Yousef withering away in the arms of Afagh's mother, who was both crying and mumbling prayers which she blew into the air. All of a sudden my aunt Rezvan saw me and banged the copper tray she was holding on my head and said, "You impudent whore! What are you standing there staring at me for? Go to your damned father's shop and drag him over here. Or tell him to find someone with a car or something, so we can take your mother to a doctor. Or ask him to bring a midwife along... No one can hear me in this damn place."

The hallway was swirling around my head. I had bitten my tongue and the pain was killing me. My eyes were filled with tears. All the people around me turned into *jinns* clad in black and white outfits; long and short arms tossed Yousef to each other like the paper, lifted his shirt, looked at his stomach and said, "It's red. He's had measles and they've treated him with henna. The henna's heat has penetrated inside. The henna's heat has reached his liver and is suffocating him..."

My mother's screams got louder and her long black hair fell on her face: "O holy Masumeh! O holy Fatimah! O God! O Great Zeinab! O holy Khadijah! O holy Hind! Someone help me..."

The sound of people's prayers filled the whole house... Mrs. Arshym stuck her head in the window from outside and shouted, "You child of cursed parents! Don't say holy Hind. Don't you know which is which yet? Say, O Great Zeinab, O holy Fatimah! Keep saying, there's no God but Allah, until the unworthy creature comes out and spares our souls from this pain!"

I wiped the blood running down my tongue with the corner of my school uniform and ran toward Afagh's mother. In spite of the pain I managed to say, "Khanom Bozorg! Khanom Bozorg! Let me have Yousef so I can get him out of here. I'll take him to the rooftop. It's more quiet there and the air is fresh..."

Yousef opened his arms for me as soon as he saw me through his exhausted, sleepy eyes.

"Khanom Bozorg, this child is fainting!"

Yousef, who could hardly talk yet and made only unrecognizable words, said, "Nanny. Nanny."

My mother's voice broke all the others:

"O day of Resurrection! O day of Resurrection! Why doesn't anyone come to help me? Why doesn't anyone come to deliver this unworthy bastard?... If I were stranded in a desert, I could at least find a slab of rock to lie on. If I were stranded in the mountains, at least a lizard would hear me... O day of Resurrection!"

The sound of the women's cries and prayers got louder. My mother's shrieks grew even more powerful. My aunt Rezvan's eye caught sight of me again. I shrank with fear and was about to pull myself into a corner when she yelled, "What are you standing here for? I told you to go to your father's shop, you whelp!"

My mother's shrieks had reached their climax: "O Imam Husain! O Ummo Kulsum!"

My grandmother who was sitting next to her said, "The other ones didn't cause so much pain. The other ones came much easier. Why should this one be so difficult? This one is supposed to be the easiest."

My sister Roghieh grabbed my arm through the space underneath Afagh's mother's legs, fixed her tearful eyes to mine and said, "Shadi, did you bring today's *Keyhan for Kids*?"

Yousef seized my hair with his tiny hand and with his simple tongue which was now as red as a fire ball, said, "Na... Nan... Nanny."

Khanom Bozorg hit me in the chin and said, "What does this child want, you brute? What's he saying? What's nan... nanny? You can make out what he's saying. Why don't you give him what he wants?"

My tongue started to burn again. I said, "Khanom Bozorg, please Khanom Bozorg. Give him to me. He is suffocating. Don't you understand? Why are you taking it out on me? This is not the best place to be standing either, is it?"

I pulled Yousef out of Afagh's mother's arms and made my way to the hallway through the mass of noises and women. I was looking for a corner when my aunt Rezvan saw me again and slapped me hard. "You shameless bitch! I'm telling you for the thousandth time, go drag your goddamn father here. You whelp, how many times does one have to repeat the same thing before you get it?"

She stretched her arms to take Yousef away from me when I somehow lost control and kicked her hard in the shin and gave her a piece of my mind: "You're the bitch! You're the whelp! You don't know anything. Don't you know that they've closed down my father's shop? Don't you know that they've arrested him too? Where can I find him if I go after him? Where can I get him?"

My aunt Rezvan was whirling around in pain. Her face had turned as dark as a blackberry and her open mouth was facing the ceiling. Her voice was trapped in her throat.

My mother's shrieks had now become intolerable. I hauled myself to the rooftop. Both I and Roghieh, who followed me, were crying. Yousef leaned his head against my shoulder tamely and rubbed his face against mine.

The sun was setting. I snatched my father's white underwear off the clothesline and sat in a corner on the roof with Yousef and Roghieh....

Something like a breeze, running through the damp clothes, touched my face.

Roghieh said, "I wanted you to read the story of the 'Voyages of Sindbad' to me..."

I was wiping Yousef's sweaty face and his mouth which was filled with blood when my mother's shrieks stopped. Then Afsaneh's detested cry along with the women's cries of exultation and Mrs. Arshym's prayers were heard all over the neighborhood.

Roghieh said, "Here, Shadi. Here's my ten *shahis*. Will you read the paper to me tonight?"

Yousef thrust his small hands into the collar of my black uniform and with tiny fingers whose nails had turned as pale as the moon and as soft as the wax paper covering *halvah*, reached into my bosom and said, "Shatu... Canny... Me want... candy...."

Yousef coughed up a large clot of blood that landed on my father's white underwear, and his head fell on my shoulder...

I remembered that in the midst of the commotion at the house I had forgotten all about the candy.

The graves of my father and Yousef aren't the same size, but I will love them both for ever.

Ghodsi Ghazinur

(1943–)

Ghodsi Ghazinur was born in Lahijan (a northern city in Iran) in 1943. She studied painting and graduated from Tehran University's College of Visual Arts. She then pursued her education in library science and obtained a master's degree from the same university.

Ghodsi, who knows several foreign languages, is a widely established author of children's stories. Her beautiful stories are illustrated by her own drawings, and many have appeared in translation. She is one of a few authors whose writings have been reviewed in a well-known Iranian journals of literary criticism.

During the 70's, more than thirty books were written and published by Ghodsi. "Aboud's Drawings," the story in translation here, was written and published in the winter of 1981 in a periodical called *Bidaran*. It is believed that Ghodsi is presently living in Iran.

Aboud's Drawings

by Ghodsi Ghazinur

The twelfth person stood next to the others along the wall on the left-hand side of the alley. The rest of the boys were standing along the wall across from them. Mohsen and I were chosen by a drawing to pick our teammates. We were going to play the "war" game.

The trouble started when the two teams were selected: one team was to play the Iraqi, and the other the Iranian soldiers; but neither team wanted to play the enemy.

We decided to pick the teams from scratch.

This did not solve the problem, either, since none of the boys wanted to be an Iraqi soldier. We tried casting lots, but everyone was willfully against it. Then we decided that smart and agile boys play the Iranian soldiers and lumpish, sluggish boys, the Iraqi soldiers.

"Then Javad, who is both a good student and the monitor of his class, should be an Iranian soldier and Mahmoud..." Mohsen began.

Akbar interrupted him, protesting that: "Who said being the class monitor makes you a good guy? Aside from Javad, monitors are all spies. They constantly watch us, and just to get some brownie points, they give our names to the superintendent so we get beat up."

"Let's ask the boys," Mohsen said. "Whoever is chosen by everyone will be an Iranian soldier and whoever we determine unworthy will be an enemy soldier."

But things were not as easy as we had expected. We were all friends; there was no reason to look for weak points in each other. We wouldn't be able to call this a game anymore.

We finally decided to arrange a race: the first twelve boys to reach the electric pole would be the Iranian soldiers and the rest the Iraqi ones.

Now we needed a referee. Akbar suggested one of the boys accept the job and in return for this favor he be allowed to be an Iranian soldier. We consented.

"Look boys," Ali said. "Since Javad's brother is now fighting at the war front, let's make him the referee."

"My brother is due at the front any day now," I said anxiously.
The boys protested simultaneously, "But he hasn't gone yet.
Anyway, everyone's brother is eventually going."

Finally, Javad was elected and we took our places along the
line. Everyone was anxious. We were so nervous that we could
hear our own heartbeats. Some of the boys were stalling: we
were getting ready for a big race. Javad blew the whistle as we
all stood straight. He counted, "One... two... three..."

We shot off like arrows. I don't know how long we ran but
when Javad blew into the whistle again, my hand touched the
post. Some boys were still far behind. The twelve of us who had
made it to the post first were relieved. Our faces beamed as we
moved towards the left wall and stood there like we had just
won a war; the rest of the boys dragged themselves towards the
other wall and stood there with lowered chins. They looked as
if they were about to be hanged. Some of them leaned their
backs against the wall and some shrank back like frightened
geese. They glowered, as if they had been given a harsh
penalty.

The teams were finally organized. Two teams, one elated and
one indignant, stood facing each other.

After a short meeting we decided to play in the alley to the
north of our own, since it had ditches on both sides. Some said
they were fixing the electricity, and some said it was the tele-
phone cables they were working on. Whichever it was, we
didn't care. What was important was that we could use the
ditches for trenches. When we arrived there, it was three in
the afternoon. A few workers wearing bandanas and loose
Kurdish pants were working under the oppressive sun. A group
of women, clad in black clothes, entered the alley and disappeared through an open door. We heard someone reciting verses
from the Koran.

Javad said: "Hey, look kids, there's a canopy!" And he ran
towards the curtained canopy to read the framed obituary of a
recently deceased youth. When he returned, he said, "One of
the boys in the neighborhood has been martyred at the front.
He was nineteen years old. The canopy is for him."

We looked at one another. It would be too embarrassing to
play in the alley. Our mere presence had already annoyed
them. We returned to our alley, concluding that although we

wouldn't have any trenches there, we were sure no one would bother us. All the neighborhood kids, except for the girls and the younger children, were playing this game. Besides, our parents wouldn't object to our noise, knowing that it meant fewer kids in the house.

Our neighborhood is one of the oldest and poorest in Tehran. Its alleys are long and narrow. Each house is inhabited by a dozen people. The houses remind me of a story I once heard about an old woman who lived in a house with a yard as big as a matchbox and a tree as tall as a matchstick. This is why even one person's absence from the house was a godsend, and in this case, there were two or three boys from each house involved in our game.

When we were back in our alley, my younger brother opened our door and suddenly jumped out, screaming, "I want to play, too."

"No way," I retorted. "Our game is only for older kids."

But he stood firm and said, "I'm older, too. I know all your games. I want to be in this one, too."

As hard as I tried I couldn't discourage him. I could have forced him to retreat with a cuff on the back of his neck, but I knew he would get my mother involved, so I gave in.

The boys exchanged pleading glances. There wasn't much they could do, so they consented.

"Go stand in the line of the Iraqi soldiers," I said grudgingly.

"What?" My brother asked unexpectedly.

"You heard what I said! We're playing the 'war' game, and you have to play an Iraqi soldier." I said.

"No, I won't be an Iraqi soldier!"

"Either do what I say, or get lost!"

And I gave him such a mean look that he obeyed me instantly. As he walked towards the line of the enemy soldiers, he looked like a mouse with its tail curled up on its back. But the game wasn't as simple as we had anticipated. It was a "war" game and war requires preparation. First of all, we needed guns and other equipment. Most importantly, we needed to build trenches. To prepare it all would take time. We sat down to do the necessary planning. We had to find gunnysacks for the sandbags. But where could we get all the sacks we needed? All of us had to go after things that would be useful: gunnysacks, plastic bags, tin cans, and buckets. We stuffed the gunnysacks with anything we could get our hands on, from mud to the garbage left outside.

When the sandbags were finally made, it was already dark. We decided to take the sandbags home at night, so the garbage man wouldn't take them. We had to be careful about this; if anyone saw the sacks, they wouldn't last a twinkle of the eye. My mother had made us promise that we wouldn't take any junk or garbage inside the house. How could we convince her that these sacks that were stuffed with trash weren't garbage?

My brother and I tiptoed in, each carrying a sack, both shaking with excitement. We hid the sacks in a corner of the yard and then walked into the house, relieved. But we still needed guns. Each boy was to have his gun ready by the next day. My problem was that I had to make my gun without my brother seeing; after all, he was an enemy. I didn't want him to copy mine. But he was still very young and couldn't understand my logic. He begged me to make one for him, too.

"You want me to make you a gun so you can kill my friends?" I asked. "Make one yourself! It serves you right!"

"You're the one who made me an Iraqi soldier! I didn't have a choice," he said with tears coming to his eyes.

He was right. I had forced him to join the line of the enemy. Since I knew that he wouldn't make a good soldier anyway, I didn't argue with him and he didn't insist because he was afraid I would throw him out of the game altogether. Nevertheless, he looked so dejected that when my mother's eyes fell on him, she said, "What's wrong? You look like it's the end of the world."

My brother didn't respond. He just sniffled and looked at me indignantly, as if he had fought against the idea of being an Iraqi soldier all day long. In the morning my mother told him, "You eat so much junk that you can't sleep at night. You were having this nightmare about a war and having been taken for an Iraqi soldier. I'm not letting you have dinner from now on so you can rest at night."

I couldn't help feeling sorry. I knew he hadn't touched his food the night before.

After my brother fell asleep that night, I got to work. I found a piece of cardboard, drew a picture of a J-3 gun, cut the picture out in the dark with a pair of scissors I took out of my mother's sewing box, then I took the half-ready gun to my room and painted it black with a magic marker. It turned out perfect. My brother cried his eyes out when he saw my gun the next morning. My mother who had lost her patience with him bought him a squirt gun. But my brother kept on crying that that was not a gun and that he wanted a gun and my mother, not knowing what was going on, ignored him. Eventually she got disgusted and started beating him. I felt so sorry for him that I had to rescue him from her, in spite of the fact that he was an enemy, and make him understand that a hand gun was as good as any gun in a war.

When he was calmer, he stuck his gun in his pajama pants. His wet, stained face made him look so pitiful that I decided to make a fake holster for his gun with a piece of cloth. I was trying very hard to see him as a brother and forget that he was an enemy. Having noticed the color of his gun for the first time, he said, "But brother, this gun is yellow!"

And tears filled his eyes again. I said, "So what if it's yellow?"

He balled, "Whoever saw a real gun that's yellow? This is no good, it's made of plastic."

Reluctantly I painted his gun black with my magic marker.

At eight o'clock in the morning, all of us reported to our posts, each carrying a gun on the shoulder and a bag in hand. We got stationed and marked our sandbags so that they wouldn"t get mixed up. Akbar remembered at the last minute that we didn't have flags. We decided to find fabric and make the flags ourselves. Mohsen and Javad were assigned to draw the flags of both countries so that the flags could be made accurately.

At night I asked my mother, "Will you give me some cloth?"

My mother said mechanically, "Did you cut your hand?"

I said, "No, I want it for our game."

She said astonishingly, "Good Lord! You've run out of all other games and now you want to play with dolls? The trouble is you have nothing to do. Get up and bring some oil for the samovar."

To keep her from getting more resistant, I jumped quickly. I ran and filled the oil bottle and hurried back. When I handed the bottle to her, I said, "Now, give me the cloth!"

"Shame on you! Don't you know only girls play with cloth?" She answered.

"Just give it to me, I need it!" I said.

Murmuring, she left and brought back a few pieces of cloth and dumped them in my palm. My brother, having felt left out, demanded, "I want some, too."

My mother said, "For God's sake!... Look how they get on my nerves!"

But my brother kept insisting. My mother said, "Share it with each other!"

I thought to myself, "Sharing with an enemy? No way!" I said to my mother, "I won't share it. If you want him to have some, you give it to him."

My mother was shocked. "What do you mean?" She asked.

"Just do it yourself, will you?" I said.

Irritated, she took a couple of pieces and threw them at my brother.

When we went outside, we saw Akbar's sister, Akhtar, standing with the boys, stubbornly demanding that she be allowed to play, too.

A female soldier, in our game? No way! But Akhtar wasn't going to give in. Her mother, a worker in the local mill, had asked Akbar to help his sister with her math in the morning. Akhtar was threatening that if we didn't include her in the game, she would tell her Mom that Akbar was loose in the streets all morning instead of working with her.

We had to choose between including Akhtar in our game and giving up Akbar if his sister meant what she said. Mohsen, believing himself smarter than Akhtar, tried to dissuade her by saying, "Akhtar, it's not proper for a girl to play in the alley."

Akhtar boldly shot back, "The only thing improper about it is that it will make your clumsiness more apparent."

Mohsen blushed. Akbar glared at his sister but Akhtar dismissed his threats lightly, concluding that, "You don't want to play with me because I'm not a boy, otherwise you all know that I am more clever than you are."

She wasn't exaggerating: she was a spark of fire. She ran faster than a bullet. None of us could beat her. We were left with no choice. She imposed herself on us, and to top it off, she refused to be an enemy soldier. She joined the team I was on.

When we collected the pieces of cloth everyone brought, we found we had a large pile of it. Akhtar agreed to sew our flag. She bragged that her sewing skills were superior to everyone else's in her class. We thought she was bluffing, but when the flags were ready, everyone stared at our flag admiringly. It was truly gorgeous. We were all set.

With the explosion of the firecracker Ali had set up, the war began. We stood at attention. When Akhtar's fireworks flashed into the sky, the shooting began.

Akhtar had saved these fireworks from the last holiday and she volunteered to use them provided that we let her set them off herself. We agreed grudgingly. We all issued gunfire noises from our mouths. Some boys imitated the sound of grenades.

There were no casualties until noon, since no one wanted to leave the scene. The game went on nonstop. At noon we all went home for lunch. We declared a cease-fire as soon as we heard the usual calling of the faithful to prayer at noon. Later that afternoon, the boys showed up one by one in the line in front of the bakery. Only Akhtar, who stayed home to prepare lunch, and my younger brother, who stayed home to help my mother, were missing.

We all forgot that we were in two opposing armies. We joked around and laughed the whole time. But I got into an argument with my brother at lunch when he told my mother, "I want the same amount of food you give Morteza."

I mumbled, "You miserable, enemy, spy! What are you counting my bites for?"

My older brother who had just arrived, broke in angrily, "Aren't you ashamed to talk to your brother like that?"

The news came on the radio, "The Iraqi enemies bombed several houses in Ahvaz today."

"May God strike them dead. They've killed so many of our young boys and made so many of our people homeless," my mother said.

And she turned to me and added, "These are the enemies, stupid ass, not your brother!"

It was almost three o'clock when we resumed our game. Most of the boys came early and the rest showed up one by one. We occupied our posts and sat there alert. I don't know what made Javad raise his head and stand straight all of a sudden. Taghi took advantage of this opportunity and shot at him. But Javad sat down again behind his trench, totally ignoring him, as if nothing had happened. Taghi's screams filled the air.

"You must drop, Javad! I hit you right in the head."

Javad jumped like a gamecock, saying, "Not a chance! It didn't touch me."

"You bet it did and you must drop right now!"

Their argument was getting out of hand. They were at each other's throats, when suddenly the door to Javad's house opened and his mother, who had stuck her head outside, called, "Javad!"

Javad answered her from his hiding place, "Yes!"

"Come here, right away! I need you."

Javad got up and walked towards his house. Taghi shot at him again. Javad started running and ran all the way to his house, while Taghi kept on screaming: "What's he going to say now? I hit him."

Javad returned a few minutes later, walking leisurely. When he reached the middle of the alley, Taghi opened fire at him again. Javad didn't pay him the slightest attention, calmly sitting behind his trench. Taghi exploded, livid with rage. He jumped out of his trench, threw his gun on the ground indignantly, and screamed: "You call this a war? You're all cheating. I'm not playing this stupid game."

"No way! It didn't hit me," Javad responded.

"You're saying that I missed when you were in the middle of the alley, too?" Taghi shouted angrily.

Javad, realizing the situation was getting sticky, said gently, "When someone has to leave his post to go to his house, the game has to stop, even if as you claim he is hit by the enemy."

We had to interfere: it was decided that from that point on if someone was hit he should drop, but instead of leaving the game, he can enter as a new soldier. No more sweat! We also decided that if someone had to leave to attend to something urgent, he should get the group's permission so that a cease-fire can be announced. We were in business again.

Although everything was going smoothly on our war front, the real war was heating up. The neighborhood youth joined the soldiers at the front in shocking numbers. Some of the mothers also went to the front to provide what help was needed. They made clothes, wove, cooked jam, and in short did anything they were good at.

That day my older brother informed us that he was joining the army on Monday. My mother looked at my father. My father's hand, holding a cigarette, started trembling. They acted as if it were the first time they learned it. I sat by my brother and said, "Brother, are you going so you can fight the enemy?"

He caressed my hair and said, "Yes."

"With a real gun?" My younger brother asked enthusiastically.

My brother smiled bitterly. My younger brother went on gleefully, "We're fighting, too. In the alley... But our guns are fake."

I glared at him but it was too late. I expected my older brother to scorn us, to say that instead of engaging in nonsense like that we should be studying. But he gently said, "Sweet Mostafa! No one really wants to be in a war. You are too young to know what war is, otherwise you wouldn't be playing a 'war' game."

"What would I be doing then?" Mostafa asked astonishingly.

"You could be playing a 'school' game, for example."

I was let down. I thought to myself, "To hell with school! We just finished nine months of it. Isn't that enough?"

"Then why are you going to the front?" I asked.

My mother interrupted, "Come! Can't you leave him alone?"

And she went and sat down next to my brother, as if she didn't want to share his attention with anyone else. "Do you really have to leave on Monday, son?" she asked.

"Yes, mother."

She started crying. My brother said. "You know, Mom, that most of the boys in the neighborhood are at the front now! You aren't alone, thank God!"

Mother said sheepishly, "I wasn't complaining, son..."

My brother kissed her hair. She closed her eyes trying to hold back the tears that poured down her cheeks. My father only smoked, nonstop. My brother moved next to him and started whispering something. I couldn't hear what he was saying. I could only see my father shaking his head helplessly.

My brother finally left. Since that day, my mother would leave the house in the morning with the rest of the neighborhood women and return in the afternoon. At home, she would constantly knit sweaters to send to the front. We dared not make noise when the news came on; she wanted to hear every word.

A few days later a new boy appeared in our neighborhood. He was our age, with a dark complexion and curly hair. We soon found out that his name was Aboud. Akbar was the first to meet him. He brought us the news that we would have a new playmate the next day.

When we went to the alley the next day, we found Akbar and Aboud waiting with the rest of the guys. Akbar introduced him to us. When Aboud saw the sacks in our hands and the guns on our backs, he asked, "What are these for?"

"For the 'war' game."

He lowered his head and remained silent.

"Why don't you join us?" Ali asked.

"No, I don't want to play."

"Why?" Ali asked in an exaggerated tone.

"Because war isn't a game."

The boys looked at one another. What did that mean? Hadn't Akbar said Aboud was going to play with us? This kid didn't seem excited at all. Maybe he didn't know how to play. We were all annoyed. We searched Akbar's face for an explanation, but he was surprised, too. Aboud looked down and started walking away.

"Why did he come in the first place?" Taghi asked.

"How do we know? Ask Akbar, who invites everyone he finds on the street to play with us," Jafar said.

"Drop it guys!" Ali said. "It's no big deal! Just forget he's in the neighborhood. Back to the game!"

It wasn't a bad idea, particularly because Akbar himself looked confused, and our teams were intact. We resumed our game, but to tell you the truth, I couldn't stop thinking about Aboud.

The next morning we went to the alley as usual. We hadn't finished setting up our sandbags yet when Aboud appeared. He was holding a big roll of cardboard under one arm. Everyone exchanged curious glances. I decided to act as if I hadn't seen him, but before we had a chance to discuss it among ourselves he came and stood in the middle of our circle and said, "Good morning, brothers!"

His tone was so friendly that everyone's attention went to him.

"Since I left you yesterday, I have been working on this. I worked on it all day so I could finish it in time to bring it today."

And he opened the roll. On the extra-large piece of cardboard, there were several pictures of war, each scene neatly drawn. On the top of the sheet he had written in bold black print, "The Damned War." A scene showing bomb explosions appeared on the right hand side. Aboud had drawn pictures of wounded birds on the edge of the scene, writing underneath the picture, "This is what war is all about." On the left hand side there was a picture showing a few small children staring sadly at a demolished house. The words underneath the picture read, "This used to be Zaer Abbas's house." Another picture showing a classroom was pasted at the lower section of the poster. Aboud had depicted a teacher writing something on the blackboard. The words read, "There will come a day when wars won't exist, a day when all the garrisons will be transformed into schools and children will sing the song of peace."

We gazed at the pictures for a few moments.

"Who was Zaer Abbas, Aboud?" Jafar asked.

"Mahmoud's father," Aboud answered, squinting. "Mahmoud was a friend from school. An explosion destroyed their house. When my friends and I arrived at the scene, they had closed the alley off, preventing us from getting near the bombed house. The only thing we could find out was that none of the inhabitants had survived. They lifted the restriction in the afternoon after they removed the corpses. I walked towards the house. Mahmoud's sneakers were tossed outside and lay on a mound of dust next to his sister's plastic doll with its missing hands and eye sockets filled with dirt. I wanted to scream. I wanted to knock my head against the wall. All my memories of Mahmoud came alive in my mind: the days we used to set fire to car tires during the uprising; the afternoons we used to spend playing soccer; the days we used to go to the river bank and sprinkle bread scraps for the ducks and the fish. Now Mahmoud is dead. The river is contaminated with bodies of ducks and fish killed by bombs, and it stinks. There's not a single bird left. The explosions have scared away not only the people but also the birds.

"Where did they escape to?" Mostafa asked.

"God knows. They've become refugees, too." Aboud said. Then he fell silent.

"Aboud! Is this your school?" Ali asked.

"Yes, but it's now occupied by Iraqi soldiers."

"Then, they must have erased the board," Mostafa said.

Aboud smiled. Then he caressed Mostafa's hair and said, "I wish that was all they had done. They're going to destroy everything. When my younger sister heard on the radio that her school was taken over, she cried in her sleep all night."

We were moved, but unable to say anything. Aboud said, "My father was baking bread for the soldiers on the front when a bomb killed him. My brother's head was smashed by a piece of grenade, while fighting. Now, my mother talks with them in her sleep every night."

In Aboud's eyes, we caught a glimpse of all the suffering of the world. We had completely forgotten our game. The sandbags lay piled up in a corner. The guns were scattered on the ground. No one said a word.

Mostafa took his beloved gun out of its holster, pitched it to the ground and said, "I don't want to play the 'war' game anymore."

Once again I stared at Aboud's drawings. All of the sketches showed a small boy with curly hair, resembling Aboud himself.

"Your drawings are beautiful, Aboud," I said. "Have you done all of them yourself?"

"Yes. Now we can color them together, and when it's done we can paste the whole thing up in the alley so everyone can see what War really means."

Mojdeh Shahriari

(1961–)

Mojdeh Shahriari was born to a Zoroastrian family in 1961 in Tehran. Her father was a well-known mathematician, translator, and teacher, and her mother was both a teacher and a librarian. While in high school, Mojdeh was a troublemaker and refused to take any subject but literature seriously. Nevertheless, because of her keen interest and knowledge in the field of literature, she managed to direct several plays, start a newsletter, and set up occasional book exhibitions in school. "Charghad Goli," the story in translation here, which was published in a periodical called *Chista* in the summer of 1981, is the first short story she wrote. Her parents encouraged her to publish it. She comments, "Although 'Charghad Goli' is not a true story, it has been inspired by several true stories one of which is my own, which occurred less than a year after the publication of the story."

In addition to literature, Mojdeh was fascinated by dancing and acting. She took up ballet while very young and joined the National Pars Ballet Group. During the five years of membership in this group, she participated in many of its national performances. In 1979 the group's performances were curtailed and until 1986 when Mojdeh moved to Canada and pursued her training and joined the Fringe Festival, she was not able to dance again. Later in 1988, because of physical injuries she received while practicing, she was forced to abandon ballet. After the revolution of 1978, Mojdeh joined a street theater group and despite discrimination against women, she performed on the streets. She also acted in several 16–millimeter films produced by the Center for Intellectual Development of Children and Adolescents. In 1985 she wrote and directed a play portraying life under the Islamic Republic. This play was performed in France by an Iranian theater group.

Mojdeh's strong urge for independence led her to seek employment after she graduated from high school. For a couple of years she worked in factories doing packaging and making leather purses. She was thrown out of both factories for "stirring up the workers." Then she was employed as a substitute teacher in a suburb of Tehran. After a year, she moved to northern Chalus, a city by the Caspian Sea, and taught in a boys' elementary school for four years. She recalls, "I loved working in a school where every child was a troublemaker; it's hard to believe that I was able to keep the promise I made to myself not to engage in physical punishment."

Mojdeh moved to France in 1985. She fell in love with a Muslim, whom, because of her family's religion, she could only marry outside of Iran. The marriage took place in France, days before Mojdeh's departure to Canada. She now studies sociology and film studies at University of British Columbia in Canada. Mojdeh has published short stories, plays and poems in Iran, and since her arrival in Canada she has made several short films and videos and directed a documentary film. She is also the author of several unpublished stories.

The Girl in the Rose Scarf

by Mojdeh Shahriari

The sky lazily paved the way for dawn. Along the desert the shadows resolutely held the line against the regiment of light which was approaching from a distance. The air, still weighted down with indolence, was motionless. A breeze, feeling like a warm vapor, blew occasionally, agitating the tears that rolled down Charghad Goli's protruding, red cheeks. The pale shadows of high, cobbed walls, crisscrossed to create strange impressions in the restless silence. Occasionally, there was a harrowing noise of trucks passing in the distance. Every now and then a man passed her. Then she imagined footsteps behind her, as if she were being followed. "But...why are these people out so early? What's their hurry? Are they running away from bad luck too? Or maybe they are security guards.... But security guards aren't fidgety, and they usually don't hum. Besides, what would a security guard be doing in an abandoned alley like this? They're paid to watch streets, streets that are full of interesting things, elegant stores and buildings, buildings built with solid bricks, stones, and metal; not with sun-dried bricks like these. God only knows what wonderful things are hidden away inside those buildings! Money, beautiful carpets... They hire security guards to protect other streets and buildings against burglars. But in this neighborhood of poverty-stricken Zoroastrians, who would need a security guard?"

Charghad Goli untied the knot of her scarf again, maybe for the fifth time, and wiped her tears with its corners. She put it back on, rearranged it, and tied it under her chin.

"Where can I go now? Who would take me in? God, how will my mother feel after she finds out I've run away? And father? God, forgive me! They'll die of grief."

Her heart sank.

"Why did I come here? The stores aren't even open yet. Besides, I'm not going home. Never. What if Mahmoud is here, too?... How strong he is! He can break a big bone with a single blow!"

She started to feel chilly. Her knees trembled. She stopped. She didn't want to go any further... She was ashamed of herself.

"To hell with that stupid vagabond!"

She thought about her older sister, Gohar. It was when Gohar got married and left home, that her troubles began.

"What's she doing now? Well, it's obvious! She is lying down next to her husband, prattling away. No... Not at this hour, anyway. They're probably sleeping like logs. What a shame! Isn't it awful that lovers fall asleep holding each other? Sleep is good for lonesome people. Well, this is another game life plays on you. When you don't have anyone, you can't sleep, you constantly toss and turn and think about how miserable you are; and then when you finally find someone, you are relieved, so you sleep well. Nature and its games! If nature was more thoughtful, it would bless lonesome people with sleep so that they might forget their misery; and it would keep happy people awake so that they might enjoy their happiness.

"Well, if I had been able to sleep last night... If I had been able to keep myself from thinking about crazy Jamshid and stupid Mahmoud, I would have never thought of running away and leaving my parents... And an aimless escape, at that.

That day their small house had been full of joy. Gohar was going to the "House of Fortune." Marriage was no big deal, and Gohar knew that she would be following her mother's steps and going through the same routine her mother went through. Nevertheless, Gohar was excited and treated the wedding as a unique, personal event, an event which would certainly transform her life, replacing past dependencies with new bonds... It is one of the contradictions of human beings, desperately straining towards the seductions of the new while retaining an unconscious loyalty to the old. And it is at the height of this contradiction that sorrow and happiness overlap; while one foot stays behind with the comforts and securities of the past, the other touches base with an unknown land of the future. The new always provokes attraction and fear.

"Gohar, you're not going to live with us anymore?"

And Gohar, with tears running down her cheeks, had only looked at her.

Her father, with his dark, emaciated face, sat in a corner and silently watched the crowd. His smile was glowing. His bent back was visible even when he sat. Years of work in the fields had bent him to one side. Father's body always bent towards the ground. His whole world gravitated toward the earth; he felt no need to look at the skies.

Her mother, assisted by female relatives, was swamped with the extra work she had to do on that day. She no longer had the frame of her youth and could not do all the household chores. As far back as she remembered, she had worked in the home and in the fields, always keeping the vague hope of a tranquil future fresh in her heart. On that day, she summoned all her energy to work. She looked after the guests and offered them refreshments; she went to the kitchen aimlessly. At one moment, she yelled at Charghad Goli for no reason, and at the next she praised her. She had mixed feelings about her daughter's wedding. On the one hand she felt relieved that she would have less work and worries after her daughter was gone, and on the other she felt uneasy because she was entrusting her daughter to an unknown fate. On the one hand she felt proud that she had brought up a chaste, efficient and energetic girl, and on the other hand she felt cheated because Gohar was leaving them just at the time she was old enough to contribute to her family's income by working in the field. Why should she offer her physical strength and youthful beauty to another family?

Charghad Goli was sixteen years old and wore a new rose scarf bought for her on this occasion of her sister's wedding. The scarf complemented her beauty and accentuated the glow in her big eyes. Those eyes were characterized by a sorrowful grace that suited her lean, frail figure. When the guests wished her luck she couldn't hide her excitement, an innocent smile erupting on her face.

She missed her older brother, who hadn't made it to the wedding. He had married years ago and moved to Tehran; since then, he seldom visited his family.

It was still dark when Charghad Goli rolled over in her bed and opened her eyes. She folded her mattress, wrapped it in a cover, leaned it against the wall, and went out into the yard. The warm, morning breeze was not pleasant. The same routine of the past day's chores was in store for her: she would wash her face, turn on the Samovar, and eat her breakfast—stale bread and hot tea—with her parents; her parents would then go to the field and she would remain in the house all by herself till dusk when they returned home, exhausted.

Her mother stirred in her bed, then woke up her husband. They both resented the daylight. For them darkness meant comfort, something to look forward to. But light—which always arrived too early and didn't give them enough time to rest before it stubbornly called them to the unmitigated, hard work—was ugly and painful. "They say polar bears hibernate six months of the year. How wonderful it must be! When they wake up they're refreshed and cheerful, not like us—always more tired than the previous day and aching to sleep a while longer." Her father would repeat this refrain before he got up.

Her family's income was constantly shrinking. They leased a field far from their shabby home. At first, her father and older brother worked on the field and her mother and sister worked at home. Their income was slightly higher then. But when her brother, and then Gohar, left, her mother was forced to go to the field to help her husband, leaving all the chores for Charghad Goli.

For some time now, many of the peasants, mostly young, talked about curious things. Rostam, Charghad Goli's cousin, was one of these people. He spent most of his free time playing with his portable radio, trying to get all the news: the direction the revolution was taking, the Reconstruction Effort, and in particular the seven-member councils. He often talked with Charghad Goli's father, promising him that the land they were working on would soon become theirs. The councils were taking the land from the landowners and turning them over to the peasants. He was sure that before long, it would be their turn.

Rostam's words seemed exaggerated but promising. After the Shah's escape from Tehran, their landowner disappeared. The rumor was that he, too, had escaped. But he soon reappeared.

For a while he went sneaking around, but it didn't take him long to build up his courage and turn up in public. Now, not only was he bold, but optimistic about the future.

The girl stayed at home. She would wash the tea glasses and saucers and then clean the house. Gloomily, she would go outside, and silently, stare at the old, decaying cypress tree, the only tree they had in the yard. At first, she thought she would soon get used to her sister's absence, but her melancholy got worse. She was isolated from the outside world. She stayed home and did the chores and sorely missed her sister's companionship.

That day she was thinking about her sister more than ever. She tried to hold back her tears. She wept in silence for a while, then shook herself and remembered that she was supposed to prepare stewed beef and beans for dinner. She felt slightly better. Al least for a few minutes, while she was at the market, she could see some people. She decided to wear her rose scarf. She had not used it since her sister's wedding because she wanted to save it for special occasions. But now she needed to feel its beauty and feel the pride of her shoulders beneath it. She carefully folded it into two equal triangles, took the ends in her hands, set the scarf on her thin, black, curly hair, and gently tied the ends together under her chin into a firm knot. Then she rushed to the mirror, looked at her head from all angles, and stared at her image with satisfaction for a few minutes. She was elated. She was thinking that as soon as she stepped outside, everyone would stare at her admiringly. She removed a twenty *toman* bill from inside the sacred book of Zoroaster and ran outside.

She saw some of the neighborhood women in the green-grocer's shop. Most of them were Zoroastrians. She greeted them as she passed them. Then she furtively turned around to look at them. They paid no attention to her. Perhaps they hadn't noticed her rose scarf at all. Or maybe they had noticed it but decided to ignore her out of envy. What if they were making fun of her now? But Charghad Goli didn't want to be pessimistic. She told herself, "I'm probably imagining it."

But behind her back, in the circle of the women, the whispering had already begun: "Did you see how the little devil has made herself up?"

"She looks as if she were on her way to a wedding party!"

"Maybe she is up to something, her own wedding, perhaps!"

And everyone broke into laughter.

But Charghad Goli was happy. She didn't feel depressed any more. She stopped to watch every little shop, store, and sidewalk stand. Even the fight between two little boys rolling over in the dirt, hurling insults at each other and tearing each other's shirts, was amusing to her. She wished she could spend all her time on the streets. She wished these damned houses did not exist at all. She hated their own small house and adored the streets, alleys, stores, people, even the stray dogs. Even the dry, annoying heat of the desert outskirts would not detract from this love of the outside world...

The shouts of a woman scolding her son interrupted her thoughts: "God damn you, Mahmoud! It's almost noon. Where've you been?"

"Mahmoud! Oh my God! I forgot all about the meat!" She hurried along the curve in the alley and made for the street. The closer she got to the butcher's shop, the more anxious she became. She could hear her heart pounding. Her cheeks were hot, and drops of sweat made their way down the curves of her face.

Mahmoud, the butcher's son, was standing on the side-walk, closing the shop. The girl froze momentarily, then walked toward him.

"Please don't close the shop yet. I need half a pound of meat for *abgusht*."

The boy threw a pointed, inquisitive glance at the distressed girl, and said very gently: "... But we're out of meat; you're late."

"But...."

She quickly turned her face away and started off. Mahmoud ran after her and touched Charghad Goli's shoulder.

She felt a flame rising inside her. She didn't know what to do. She wished to remain there forever, feeling Mahmoud's hand on her shoulder. Instead, she quickly moved away.

"Why did you get upset? Come get the meat!"

Charghad Goli didn't respond; she just kept walking.

Since that day, Charghad Goli left the house everyday and took to the streets, and whether she needed meat or not, she always passed the butcher's shop.

Her cousin came to see her one day, and out of the blue asked her not to leave the house anymore.

"People are talking about you. They say you're acting wild, that you make yourself up and walk all over the place."

Even Rostam, her cousin, started giving her advice. He had promised to come to her house and teach her how to read and write, but one day he stopped by to tell her that some ignorant people were talking a lot of nonsense behind her back.

The girl decided not to leave the house anymore unless she had a reason, but she couldn't abide with her own decision. The house was oppressive and an inner desire directed her to the outside world again. Mahmoud was very kind to her. She was falling in love unknowingly. Every time she went to see him she put on her rose scarf. Everyone knew her secret.

One evening when she was at home with her parents, her aunt came to visit. She was younger than her mother but had five children and the youngest one, who was Charghad Goli's age, was her friend. Her aunt's family always came to visit all together, but this time she came by herself. It was very unusual. When the girl brought them tea, she noticed that her parents looked sad. She asked, "What's wrong, Aunt? Has something happened?" Her aunt answered coldly, "No, it's nothing!" Well, something wasn't right! Her aunt had come alone and everyone was sitting there looking worried. Her mother said, "Go sprinkle some water in the yard! It's all covered with dust." The girl understood that she must leave them alone. She got up slowly and went to the yard. She took the hose, turned the faucet on, and stared at the old tree.

Charghad Goli's mother turned her gaunt face toward her husband and said, "What are we going to do now? How can we hold our heads high after this scandal? Instead of helping us, this foolish girl has ruined our reputation." Her husband said,

"But these could be all lies. People talk a lot. I don't think she is that sort of girl..."

Her aunt responded without hesitation, "There is something to what they say. I've seen her in front of the butcher's shop a couple of times myself. People don't just make up things. You didn't pay enough attention to her, didn't watch her closely. Pardon me for being nosy, but it isn't right. And her mother said, "But sister, how could we help it? We're in the field all day long and there's no one else. What are we supposed to do?" Then the three of them were silent. The mother was melting inside, shaking her head from time to time. The father had a bitter smile on his face, making him look even more miserable. The aunt, who looked more relaxed now, was also thinking. They all mulled over the problem. The girl was accused of serious misconduct. She was no longer the same innocent, chaste girl she used to be. The mother blamed the butcher's son, murmuring that he was a Moslem and shouldn't have messed with their daughter, damaging their reputation like this.

Finally the aunt broke her silence, "The only solution is to marry her off."

Her father said, "But how? We can't go soliciting for her!"

Her mother said, "Besides, with all these rumors going around, who's going to marry her? God, please help us!"

The aunt tried to console her sister and told them that they must start looking, that they would be sure to find someone to marry her.

Charghad Goli became restless outside. She cleaned the yard meticulously. Then she just stood there motionless. Finally she decided to go in. "We haven't had a visitor in so long, and now that we have one, they isolate me." She told her mother while keeping her head down, "I've finished." She didn't hear an answer. She sat down while everyone ignored her. By now she was scared. What had happened? Why didn't they speak to her? Her mother's dull eyes were full of tears and her father's bent back looked even more crooked.

She didn't know why, but she somehow knew that she was responsible for their grief. Her aunt was not acting like the kind of woman she usually was, and looked at her grudgingly. She couldn't bear their silence any longer so she said, "What's the matter, here?" But before she could find her voice, her aunt got up and left. Charghad Goli had no idea what could be wrong. Her aunt bade her good-bye, looking as parched and unfeeling as desert sand.

They did not speak to her. Speaking wouldn't do them any good now. They felt they didn't know their daughter anymore. For the past year or so, the sense of family unity had been lost. No one had much to say. When evening came, they all went their own way, absorbed in their own thoughts. The distance between the parents and their daughter now seemed as long as the walk from their home to the field. The girl became anxious and sensed a disaster approaching. She didn't know what it was or why it had to happen, but an intense anxiety had taken over her being and she awaited a catastrophe. She avoided everyone and kept her silence, but leaving the house was still the only thing that soothed her, and more than any other place, she found herself near the butcher's shop. She wouldn't even look up to see the butcher's son, but knowing that he was watching her made her heart jump. She did not delude herself. She knew she had no right to marry a Moslem man, yet she couldn't hold back her feet or stop the desperate beat of her heart. She continued wearing her rose scarf even though it was no longer new. Wearing it somehow made her eyes shinier.

That day her mother came home earlier than usual. She looked older, more fatigued, and more resigned. The girl became anxious. Her mother started cleaning the house silently. Then she told her daughter to wear something decent. The girl was startled. She gathered that a guest was expected but she couldn't understand why her mother acted so reserved or why she didn't tell her who the guest was. She could do nothing but wait. She put on a clean dress and shrank back into a corner. Her father came home. Having found more strength because of her husband's presence, her mother came to her and said, "Today you should act properly because your future depends on it. Try to be nice, but keep your head down... They're coming to ask for your hand. It's time you got married."

The red on the girl's cheeks extended to her heart. She couldn't describe her feelings, but she knew she was excited. She viewed this as a blessed opportunity; maybe her luck had struck. For a second she pictured the butcher's son in front of her and her heart sank deep down. It can't be... She pushed the thought back. Such a thing would be impossible. She couldn't think of anyone she knew among the Zoroastrians, though. She asked her mother, "Tell me who it is, mother. Please tell me before he comes!..." Overcoming a lump in her throat, her mother said, "It's not important, my daughter. You have to accept whatever your fate has in store for you. We're not the ones who decide these things." Charghad Goli needed to talk more but her mother rose and moved to the kitchen, leaving her stupefied daughter alone.

There was a knock at the door. The father approached the door with feeble, reluctant steps. The girl was standing in a corner in the kitchen while her mother arranged a beautiful white scarf on her daughter's head. As the sound of the guests entering the house reached Charghad Goli's mother, her hands froze on her daughter's shoulders, her eyes fixed on her daughter's. She was as still as a rock, as if the exhaustion of years of hard work had taken the last mite of her energy. The girl surrendered, realizing incredulously that it would be futile to resist. A remote hope replaced her fear, the hope of leaving her present state behind and putting an end to the neighbors' gossiping. She resigned herself to the old in the hopes of the new.

Suddenly she heard a familiar voice. She was so confused that she asked in an innocent, naive tone, "What? What's crazy Jamshid doing here?" Her mother's look was resigned and guilty: "My sweet daughter, everyone's fate..."

Charghad Goli cried for a few days. They had decided to marry her off to Jamshid and be done with it. It was a cruel decision. It would ruin her life. Jamshid was retarded. Now they wanted her to spend the rest of her life with him. She couldn't accept this cursed fate. And her parents wouldn't pay any attention to her objections. They were thinking only of their reputation, their honor, and how this man could help them win back what they had lost. Her father had shrunk even more and her mother's face was lined with new wrinkles. But they had made up their minds, and perhaps they had no other choice. The girl could only cry.

Now Charghad Goli had shrunk back in a corner, and was sewing; she looked pathetic. Her eyes had sunken deep in their sockets, and her face had lost its freshness. She heard a noise. Someone had come to visit. She kept on sewing, motionless, as the noise got louder and closer. It was her cousin Rostam who was making all this noise. He greeted her parents warmly, then he noticed Charghad Goli, a frown developing on his face. He came near her and kindly asked her how she was. The girl threw her shoulders up, coldly. Rostam sat down and said, "Things have worked out beautifully for me. I have some free time now. I've come to start those lessons with your daughter, that is, if you don't mind." The girl raised her head and while staring at his face vaguely she said, "Lessons? But it's not possible, now." The father said, "Dear Rostam! What good will lessons do her?" Rostam said, "Dear uncle! When are you going to realize what's going on around you? Nowadays, every day is brimming with new events. After the riots two years ago, people are waking up. In the village where Uncle Cyrus lives, people have thrown the big landowner out and divided the lands. I hear they are much better off. Now it's our turn to show them we can do it, too." The father said, "Rostam! Settle down, boy! I don't believe any of it. Besides, what does that have to do with my girl learning her letters?" Rostam retorted, "Then she can read the paper and tell you what's going on in the world!" The girl saddened by his idle enthusiasm, answered with a trembling voice, "No, I can't learn now, because I'm getting married." Her fury had found an outlet. She ran out to the yard so she could cry by her loyal companion, the old tree. She couldn't hear their conversation anymore but she sensed an argument developing. She knew that Rostam was arguing against the marriage. But her father's loud voice cut short any hope. His agitated, feeble voice bleated out angry and unkind words: "Get out, Rostam! Go away! Don't take sides with her!" Losing Rostam was going to be costly to them. He had been a loyal friend, someone who cheered them when they most needed it.

Rostam's departure was the end of a phase in their solitary lives.

At dawn the girl shook her lean body and got up. She got dressed quietly, packed a bundle, and went to the yard. She stood in front of the old cypress tree for a few minutes. Then she calmly looked at her parents. Tears formed in her eyes, making them glitter. She pulled her hair back and walked towards the door. All of a sudden a smile broke on her face. She quickly returned to the house and got her worn-out rose scarf. She arranged it on her head in front of the mirror, a proud lump forming in her throat. She approached the door again. She stopped to look at everything once more, then she opened the door and shut it behind her, knowing that she was leaving that house and her parents for good. The hot early morning breeze penetrated the scarf and lifted strands of her hair. Slowly something hardened in her eyes: a new resolve settled in, preparing for a long stay.

Mahdokht Dowlatabadi

(1933–)

Mahdokht Dowlatabadi was born in Tehran in 1933. She lived in Tehran most of her life, but recalls the year she spent in Isfahan with her grandmother (during World War II and the subsequent invasion by the allied forces) as the most enjoyable time of her life.

Mahdokht discovered her creative ability while still in elementary school where her classmates persistently praised her writing. She possessed a unique sense of expressing how girls her own age felt. Her continued interest in children led her to choose early childhood education as the field of her doctoral work, a project which she is now in the process of completing.

Mahdokht wrote and translated for children from an early age. Her stories, articles, and translations were published in a Persian periodical called *Peyk* to which she has devoted many years of her career. Some of her earlier stories are: "Sparrows and People","The Story of Pari" and "My Body."

In 1978 Mahdokht left Iran after a series of family and marital conflicts and moved to England. From this point on, she started writing for adults. The English translation of her first short story, "Being Nobody" was published in the British magazine *Honey*. "Scapegoat" was her second short story to be published abroad in *Par Monthly Journal* in 1987. "Escape From Madness," a short story she wrote in the U.S. in 1983, was also recently published by *Par Monthly Journal*, a Persian periodical published in the U.S. for which Mahdokht frequently writes. She is also on the editorial board of a Persian children's magazine (published in the U.S.) called *Touca*. After several years of living in the U.S., where her daughter and son have settled, Mahdokht recently returned to Iran to work and be near her mother.

Scapegoat

by Mahdokht Dowlatabadi

Mahmood was heading home, walking leisurely down the dark, quiet street. His head was lowered and his face sullen. As usual, before crossing the street, he checked both directions for cars. It was then, despite the darkness, that he saw a woman's figure resembling his mother's at the street corner. He was sure that his mother would never leave the house at that hour. Many years had passed since the time his mother used to wait for him at that corner, carefully wrapping herself up in her long veil so that no one would recognize her. He was a child then. It was his first year in school, and the school days had not yet been cut in half. He didn't live far from his school, but his father, God rest his soul, advised him, "If you want to become a man, don't return home for lunch!" Every morning, he would take his lunch along, wrapped in a cloth. During the first few months he anxiously awaited the minute he could go home. Every evening he would find his mother at the corner, waiting for him. Mahmood would run toward her the minute he saw her. They would walk inside the house together, and after washing his hands, he would sit down and wait for her to serve him sweetened tea with bread and cheese.

In the twenty years since, his father had died and his mother had grown very old. She seldom left the house after her husband's death. She lost the inclination to do anything after her daughters had married. With them also gone, she even gave up weaving carpets, as her eyes couldn't endure it anymore. She spent much of her time sitting with her prayer rug spread before her. These days, with all the killings and looters on the loose, her isolation grew as her inquisitiveness shrank.

Mahmood crossed the street. Frowning more deeply, he narrowed his eyes and rounded his lips, mumbling, "I'll be damned! It's her all right! Has she heard something? Is she standing there to check up on me?" The thought made his blood boil. He felt very hot.

With a bent back and a slow pace, the old woman walked toward him.

"It's you! What's wrong?" Mahmood asked.

His mother pulled his coat collar down, and standing on her toes lifted her body to reach his height.

"You have a guest. Nasrollah, Haji Ali's son," she whispered in Mahmood's ear.

Nasrollah's name turned Mahmood's thoughts back to his youth. They had gone to school together. He saw vividly the image of Nasrollah's house, surrounded by that huge garden at the end of their alley. Then he put that picture next to their own house, tiny as a matchbox, with a pool the size of a sieve and with a single walnut tree they had for vegetation. He remembered Nasrollah's dark skin, and his face with a soft mustache emerging on the upper lip. He even remembered the lower part of Nasrollah's trousers, always too short to cover his ankles. He thought about all the strikes he took part in in high school—Nasrollah always standing aside, his currying favor, never willing to lose his wits. Mahmood realized that he had been completely out of touch with Nasrollah for ages. He had seen him a few times since his family moved out, but not at all within the last year. Nasrollah had quit the streets, the main square, and even the bank. Mahmood's face assumed its sullen, frowning and curious expression again.

"Is this the Nasrollah who lived in the garden at the end of the alley? I didn't think he was around any more."

His mother started for the house, murmuring, "My son, it is him. I don't know what has brought the poor soul back this way. It was just getting dark when I heard the doorbell ring. I didn't open the door. I asked from behind the door who they wanted. Then I heard his voice saying, 'It's me, ma'am. I want to talk to Mahmood.' I told him that you were not home, but he insisted, 'Please let me in! I'll wait for him in the doorway.' When I opened the door I saw his pale face. He was white as a corpse. I took him inside and poured him a glass of tea. He didn't touch it. He kept wiping his face with a handkerchief. He didn't talk at all, but I think he is in trouble. I think something bad has happened. I didn't want to ask him anything, but I couldn't sit there and watch him twitch either, so I came outside and waited until you came."

Mahmood opened the door with his key and entered the house noisily. The only light in the house came from a lamp in the anteroom. Through the windowpane Mahmood saw

Nasrollah looking outside intently, with a hand placed over his brow, trying to concentrate. Mahmood took off his shoes before he went in. He sat next to Nasrollah and spoke excitedly.

"What a surprise! What's made you remember humble people like us?" He was scrutinizing his friend's face while he spontaneously uttered this cliche of a greeting. Nasrollah's small, black, intelligent eyes betrayed only fear. His colorless face was covered with sweat, and desperately trying to control his emotions, he bit his lower lip. Mahmood grabbed Nasrollah by the shoulders. "What's happened to you?"

Nasrollah lowered his head, as if expecting Mahmood to know everything already, like when they were in school. If a teacher was unfair to a student, Mahmood would speak up on his behalf. If the principal bore a grudge against a teacher, Mahmood would immediately sense it and mobilize the other teachers and students to support the teacher. If he sensed that the boys were picking a fight with some poor defenseless kid, he would appear in the nick of time to prevent it, cunningly distracting them and getting the troubled kid out. The students both in the lower and the higher levels respected him. Seyyed Sina's son was unknowingly the beating pulse of the entire school. How could he be sitting in front of him now, not knowing what was going on and why he was there? Could he really not know? Or was it because he wanted to hear the story from Nasrollah himself? Mahmood shook him again.

"Talk! What the hell is the matter with you? Where have you been? You're shaking!"

He took Nasrollah in his arms like a baby, trying to warm him with his own body heat, hoping to calm him so he could talk. Nasrollah was the same size as Mahmood, tall and slim; but he fit in his arms like a child. When Mahmood felt the wetness of Nasrollah's face on his neck, he pulled himself back and looked at Nasrollah's face, amazed.

"Are you crying?"

Nasrollah shook his head in denial, and whispered in a voice that could hardly be heard. "I am a sitting duck. They've made me a scapegoat!"

Mahmood's mother knocked at the door. "Do you want something to eat?"

Realizing that his mother was standing outside, Mahmood shouted, "Come in! Come in! Haven't you heard anything from the neighbors?"

The neighbors were the same people Mahmood didn't want his mother to mingle with. After his father, Seyyed Sina, died, and his sisters were married, an implicit contract was drawn between Mahmood and his mother: the latter would keep all her worries and the neighbor's gossip from her only son, her last child, and attend to her prayers in pursuit of securing a position in heaven; and Mahmood would remain in the same house in Najafabad and try to play the game according to her rules, busying himself with the task of securing their material needs. When he was offered a job in a bank in Isfahan, he brushed his greed aside and did not stir. Each of his married sisters had insisted on taking her mother along or having her come for visits, but their mother had rendered their persistence futile. She could not stand cars; rides upset her stomach.

After the revolution, Mahmood had become involved with a woman about his own age—a woman not so reputable, and for a few months now he had kept her in a small house in a garden in some remote area. The banks were open only for one or two hours a day. He would make a short stop there in the morning and then he would go directly to Pari and stay with her till late in the evening. It was not so much the sexual attraction that drew him there; he didn't wish to be alone with himself or his friends. At first he was cautious. He didn't want his sisters and his mother to find out. In a small town things are noticed, especially with everyone always watching.

Until the revolution, he had a very clear idea what he wanted. As a child fetching firewood from the forest for the kitchen stove; when accompanying his father, a dealer, to the bazaar; or years later, helping his sisters weave a row or two of carpet—he always found a contradiction between his observations and his elders' explanations. He committed himself to the establishment of good and justice. People, one or two generations older than his, feared their shadows. And these days, no one discussed the state of affairs . Those less fearful occasionally said a few words about the good days of the past regime, or talk about the books that were outlawed, or would insinuate their ideas by reciting this verse from Hafez, "Don't be grieved, as the dissipated Yousef will return to Canaan." His intuition rebutted the newspapers and radio. If he could afford it, he would become even more destructive than those who took part in the riots. He envied them. Before the revolution, he had shouted himself hoarse in anti-government demonstrations. Now he had doubts. He lost his desire to think. Braving now only the neighbors' gossip, he visited Pari every day and enjoyed ordering her around.

The doorbell made Mahmood jump. They looked searchingly at each other for a clue to the identity of who rang the bell.

Wiping the sweat of his face with a handkerchief pulled from his pocket, Nasrollah whimpered, "Mahmood, I'm a sitting duck. Please don't betray me!"

Mahmood, already preoccupied, was vexed dumb. Nasrollah must not know him, or he would never say such a thing. Of course, he wouldn't betray him! Who was he and what had he done, anyway, to be so scared? Pounding on the door had joined the incessant bell. Mahmood went to the door barefoot and opened it right away. He saw the glint of the gun barrel whose weight he felt on his chest a moment later. A group of young men, mostly armed, glared at him. One asked, "Whose house is this?"

Mahmood told him his name and his father's and explained that he and his mother lived alone. One of the revolutionary guards asked about Haji Ali's house and said that they were told it was in that alley.

Mahmood, terrified, paused, "Which Haji Ali? What are you looking for?" A short, young man in back shouted, "None of your business! Where are your identification papers?"

"Good Lord!" And as he was about to throw some offense at them, Mahmood heard his mother's calm voice asking, "Which Haji Ali, the one who lived at the end of the alley?" She continued undaunted, "They moved out a long time ago. Haji Ali is no longer here. He may live in the next alley."

"Bullshit! We've traced his son to this neighborhood. Haven't you seen him? Did you say only you and this old woman live here?"

Mahmood responded more confidently. "Of course!"

Suddenly the guards started pressing against the door separating them from the mother and son. The door gave in.

"What do you think you're doing? Who's given you the right to break into my house this late at night?"

"Shut up! We'll turn this house upside down, and we'll turn every house in this alley upside down, and we won't stop till we find Haji Ali's son. Where are your identification papers?"

They overpowered Mahmood and poured in. After a short interchange, three of the guards stayed and the rest left for other houses. Just as the three of them were about to enter the anteroom, they saw a pair of men's shoes.

"Didn't you just say there's no one but you here? Whose shoes are these, then?"

Mahmood could only think of the room Nasrollah was in. His eyes were fixed on the entrance.

"These belong to Mahmood," his mother intervened. "Look! He forgot to put them on when he came to open the door."

Mahmood went into the closet to get his papers; one of the men followed him. He felt like a mouse being shoved into a trap. When he saw that Nasrollah was hiding neither in the closet nor behind the doorway, he was sure that he had gone up the stairway to the roof. But no. They searched every possible place, even inside their bedding and his mother's chests. Relief was mixed with confusion in Mahmood and his mother. Nasrollah had sunk into the ground like a drop of water.

After going around the same circle several times, the short, young man said, "So far we've fixed Haji Hasan and his sons. God willing, we will eliminate these ungrateful bastards. We will protect this city's purity against all the Bahais and Jews. We'll find Haji Ali's relatives, even if we have to turn over rocks, and burn them alive. We'll burn their bastard corpses, too."

Then they passed around a box of Winstons, each taking and lighting a cigarette before rejoining their friends, the true believers of Islam, in the war against all others.

Now Mahmood checked their house. He looked in the doorways, behind the curtains, inside the closets, and everywhere else, calling Nasrollah's name. Sometimes he called him "Nassy," as when they were children, but he found no trace of Nasrollah. He put his jacket back on and told his mother that he was going to look for him. He neither waited for a response nor said good-by before leaving.

It was after he closed the door and stood in the dark alley that he felt utterly helpless. Where to start? Was Nasrollah still hiding in this neighborhood, in the alley in which he spent his childhood, or had he gone some place else, to take refuge with people who were more courageous than himself? Mahmood tried to put himself in Nasrollah's shoes. His mind was blank. He passed a few small alleys, and, as if looking for a small puppy, thrust his head into dark corners and occasionally called out "Nassy, Nassy!" Finally he came to Pari's neighborhuod. He had never gone there this late and although he trusted her loyalty he did not wish to test it. Ringing her doorbell this late would scare her. He did not want to scare her. Was he being followed? The mere sight of a man and a young boy passing by frightened him. He hid in the midst of a tree's branches by a brook, consoling himself with the thought of finding Nasrollah when the sun was up again. He could secretly bring Nasrollah to Pari's house until things calmed down. He was sure that the insanity would end, that someone would take charge and straighten out the mess. Now, anyone with a J-3 gun thought he was king. "Nassy" was too preoccupied for women, and this arrangement would work out better for Pari as well, since she wouldn't be alone to be deceived by the devil. He remembered that early on, when he had seen his mother waiting for him at the street corner, he had suspected that she had heard something about his affair with Pari and had come to confront him. He asked himself, "What's my problem? Why am I so afraid? Is it what people say about Pari or is it fear of my mother's disappointment? My mother seems to be interested only in seeing me settle down. Maybe it's because I still don't know what I want, I've made my mother a scapegoat. What's wrong with marrying Pari, anyway? I'll catch up with the old crowd and drop the indifference... Being apolitical is no different than siding with the oppressor."

Mahmood had always kept the seed of these thoughts alive in his mind, but the unforeseen events of the previous night fertilized them, and they became urgent. He wanted to wake up Pari and tell her all this. He was no longer afraid of ringing the bell or scaring her. He would go from one alley to another, with Pari on his side, and together, they would find Nasrollah's house and his friends. They would persuade his friends to stand up for Nasrollah. They would convince them that living in a society and benefiting from its privileges, naturally involves them in that society's problems.

He rang the bell. Normally the door would open as soon as he rang, as if Pari always waited for him behind the door. He didn't expect that at this hour of the night, but the protracted silence and stillness in response to his rings unnerved him. At last he climbed the door, and standing atop the wall, called Pari's name a few times. A jump and he landed in the yard. He went straight to her room. The door was locked and there was no one in. Now fear seized him. They had agreed: she went nowhere, or accepted any visitors without telling him first. He had left her house at eight the night before, and she had not mentioned a word about going out afterwards. Martial law was not in effect but people were afraid of being outside after dark.

The man whom she must be out with, who must visit her after I leave, might be even richer than I, and have a car. So naive! Betrayed.

He sat on the steps leading to her room and waited for her return. Being in this house with Pari gave him a sense of security. He was always in a good mood around her. But every night after leaving her, misery gave rise to suspicion. He would only continue this relationship until the end of the month. How could he have trusted her and given her this place so she could move out of that whorehouse? He must have lost his mind to get involved in a mess like this. What will he do if he sees her come in with a man? Beat her up, or just spit in her face and leave her for good? He was too tired to decide. Sleep overcame him.

Pari's voice calling his name woke him up. The sun had spread its rays over the whole yard, and Pari was still in her formal long veil.

"How did you get in? You left your key here. Why didn't you break the lock and go in? Are the banks closed today?"

Mahmood pushed sleep away and said with a gloomy voice, "Cut out this nonsense and tell me where you've been!" Pari, covering her face with her veil with one hand, extended her other to Mahmood and said, "Get up and let's go in and have a cup of tea. I'll tell you everything."

Mahmood wanted an explanation, not just stories. He ignored Pari's extended hand.

"I won't move from this spot until you answer my question. I should square my account with you first."

Pari took her veil off, went toward the pool and said, "All I need now , in the midst of this mess, is to have you getting on your high horse." She stuck her veil under her arm and poured some water on her face. Her eyes were obviously red and swollen from crying. Noticing, Mahmood was relieved of the miserable suspicion that Pari had been enjoying herself in the company of a man. In fact, he felt slightly alarmed about her condition and spoke in a more gentle tone.

"I've been miserable since last night. I came here to see if your silly mind can come up with an idea. At first I was reluctant to wake you up, and then after I pulled myself up the wall like a thief, I didn't find you inside. Where were you, for God's sake, that late at night, and with whom?"

"At my father's grave," Pari yelled peevishly. "Where was I? These days I get so anxious I can't sit still and stay home. I am not worried about myself, you know. I am worried about those children who are still in that house; I am worried about the storekeepers whose shops are being set on fire; I am worried for Haji Hasan, for his son; I am worried about this stinking odor of burnt human flesh and the burnt corpses that are still lying on the street , no one daring to get close to them. I went with a few other women to find Haji Hasan's relatives. So what if they are Bahais! That's not a sin. They're human beings, too. I heard that all of the Bahais, even older women and children have escaped to the mountains for fear of their lives. The rascals are after them on horses in the desert, and in the city they raid people's houses. If I can't help these people, I have no recourse but crying in sympathy for them. It's our own fault. If we weren't such cowards and didn't give free rides to anyone who came around..."

Mahmood bent over the pool to wash his face. All the while Pari was talking, he remained bent listening to her. When she finished, he straightened his back and extended his hand toward Pari.

"Let's go visit my mother. Last night we were visited by one of them. When the guards came after him and forced their way into our house, he disappeared. I came here to get your help in finding him. When a man is accompanied by a woman, he doesn't arouse suspicion. I haven't eaten anything since I had lunch with you yesterday, and I'll be damned if I eat till I've found Nassy."

Pari shook her head in approval and said, "How can one keep an appetite with this stinking smell in the air, this anxiety, and so much pain and suffering inflicted upon human beings? By the way, what did you say? It just registered: you asked me to go to your mother! Did I hear you right? Aren't you ashamed of being seen with me in public, of your mother knowing that you've been seeing me, a woman with all the wrong connections, a nobody?"

Mahmood looked down. He saw a few ants carrying food on the ground. He spoke after a long pause.

"It's not true. Everybody is somebody. You are superior to me. You were quicker than I was in going out to find out what you could do for them."

****

His mother was not surprised to see Pari with Mahmood. She poured them tea in fancy tea glasses. Once sure that she could trust Pari, she spoke.

"I stayed up late waiting for you, thinking about Nasrollah. I finally got sleepy and turned off the light. I had barely sat down when someone knocked on the anteroom window. It was Nasrollah. When we were at the door talking to the guards, he climbed the walnut tree. And when you called him he didn't answer you, fearing that a trap had been set. I insisted that he come in and sleep here, but he refused, saying that he had to leave Najafabad before it was too late. God bless all his God-fearing slaves."

Mahmood answered, "I wish God would do us a favor and make life easier for us. I think life would be better if there were less fear. Don't you think so, Pari?"

Pari nodded, but her imagination had wandered to Nasrollah's fate, wondering where he was, how scared he must be.

A. Rahmani

(1948–   )

A. Rahmani (a pseudonym) was born in 1948 in northern Iran. Later she moved with her family to Tehran and finished her high school and college education there. She studied architecture at Tehran University and was employed by the Ministry of Road Construction while still in college. After several years of employment there, she left her work and changed her major to sociology. Having obtained her bachelor of arts degree in 1982, she moved to England and entered Sussex University for graduate study and received a masters degree from this university in sociology.

A. Rahmani is presently living and working in England. She has been married for seventeen years and has a son who lives with her in London. She is co-founder of *Nimeyeh Digar* (The Other Half), a woman's periodical published in Persian in London, and has continued to work with this publication since its inception in 1983. A. Rahmani has published articles and translations in Iran. "A Short Hike," the story in translation here, was her first work published outside of Iran in *Nimeyeh Digar* in the Spring of 1984. This work was followed by another short story called "Avesta, I, and My Uncle" which was published in the same periodical.

A Short Hike

by A. Rahmani

The orange sun perfected the art of spreading its wings on the snow. The first snow had continued for several days non-stop. The city gradually turned white. In the white of the pavement, people looked like poisoned mice, moving from one line to another. There was something prevalent, heavy, and permanent in the air, something that made breathing, forgetting and escape difficult. It was as if each moment was ever-present, and it was. We lived the past three years experiencing this illusion. When we woke in the morning, its presence imposed itself upon our minds, transforming it into a cold, dark space, and it stayed. And we, the poisoned swarm, living the moments between childhood and old age simultaneously—unaware of the customary sense of Time—swung back and forth. At times, we childishly turned the event into an imaginary one, a journey into fantasy, into the depths of hell, or to the gathering of devils. Oftentimes, we were patient and resigned, as seasoned as old people...

Every one of us had devised a stratagem fitting his or her circumstances. Some planted trees and flowers, some jogged, some wrote, and others knitted, sewed, fed the dogs, the cats, the chickens, the pigeons. And still that heavy, poisonous air prevailed, continuously contaminating people's lungs, minds, and the atmosphere. To become political beings, however, was a necessity emanating from the circumstances. In a sense, we had all become political beings. We read newspapers, we listened to the news on all the other radio stations that broadcasted in Persian, we gave each other shelter, we hid each other's banned books, and thus we lived in this network of daily necessity.

I said that we were all political beings; whether optimists or pessimists, believers of this or that theory to change the prevalent poisonous atmosphere, or members of this or that organization, this was a prerequisite to our survival. Before, under the previous regime, you could do as little as withdrawing to your safe corner, closing off your eyes and ears, or choosing a solitary life in a secluded area, to survive. But now things were different: everything was closed out there, as if you were faced with an iron door; the university, the bookstores, the movie houses, the theaters, the bars, the streets... To survive under these circumstances, you could no longer stay on the sidelines. There was nothing there to hang on to. This was why, except for the few agents of corruption and darkness, all of us, despite our varying viewpoints, were political.

Last night, a couple, who were my friends, stayed over at my house. We extinguished the candles, as our neighbor was a member of the "Party of God"—the Hezbollah, and sat and talked into the wee hours. The sight of the first rays of the sun on the mountains tempted us, so we left the house, taking along my mother, too.

There was a line of cars from Mahmoodieh to Valenjak, and the flock of pedestrians climbing the slopes of the hills extended as far as the eye could see. Everyone seemed to be in the same mood: eager to see the expanses of snow and the open solitary of the rocks lying under its humble surface and the clear, kind sky—a sky unaffected either by the distant, sluggish heaven or the tangible, convenient hell. Lately staying home had become as unbearable as going out. Both had turned into traps, driving us to such insane acts as pounding our heads against the walls, hoping to end our miseries that way. A futile act.

We passed the gate opening to the slopes designated for public use, surprised to find it open. On a Friday? Permission to pass through the gate would be granted to those who abide by the Islamic code of conduct! The guards, armed or unarmed, were driving on the road leading to the chair-lift, imposing their unpleasant presence on people, and "fraternally" splashing the soft dirty snow all over them. There were many guards inside the ticket office with pointed guns, inspecting the size of our head-covers, and permitting those who passed the test to go on to enjoy the "fresh" air. The area around the office and the mini-bus station was covered by slogans: advice, warnings, declarations of "Enjoining the good and forbidding the evil," and finally threats; all crooked and nonsensical statements by this or that agent of punishment by hellfire. There were pictures, too; some showing men wearing turbans and some of the children who had unquestioningly offered their necks as projectiles for the canons of their government's establishment. "Waves of Martyrs," "Caravans of Martyrs," "Lineage of Martyrs,"... As if mothers of the Martyrs had tolerated nine months of pregnancy, the labor pains, and all the subsequent anxieties to be endowed with the honor of having their sons' pictures decorate ridiculous posters hanging from trees whose fruits perish as quickly and easily as this, before tasting the sun that is needed for their maturity. Then the government announcements came. Announcements of organizations rooted in the spiritual world but established in this earthly world! The "Forbidding" section was prohibiting the unveiled women from entering the area. The Ministry of Guidance was recounting the various kinds of adultery...adultery involving the eye, the throat, the nose...and so on.

There were people, too, either passing by or waiting in the bus line. Someone, possibly in his sixties, carrying a walking cane used by professional mountain climbers and wearing a carefully trimmed beard, had come with his dog. Later I heard a young woman ask him, "Are you an architect?" Was there supposed to be a connection between her question and the man's appearance? Then I saw a woman wearing a long veil halfway soaked in the mud, trying to climb the rocks. I could see a pair of military boots sticking out of her veil. I could also see her pants, her Islamic gown, and even her sweater; she reminded me of the inside layers of an onion. She was annoyed by the impurity of the architect's dog. Someone passed us hurriedly and bade us a "Take it easy!" in the manner of professional mountain climbers. He must have been one of those people who draw their daily dosage of satisfaction from greeting people who had fallen behind. Then I saw a few women, probably colleagues in some office, in their overcoats, high-heel shoes and fancy purses. They strolled ahead without any concern that they might be blocking other people's passage. The path was not wide enough to accommodate all the people. When there was no car, people used the road. Coming towards us was a group of school children accompanied by their coach, who was a member of the Revolutionary guard and to whom I would not entrust my child, if I had one, under any circumstances. They ran along the gravel side of the road and shouted, "God is great!, Death to anti-revolutionaries!" thus passing their leisure time.

We rented a chair–lift at the second station. When we got off, my mother and my friend's wife joined the people waiting for tea, and my friend and I moved on for a short walk. My friend's brother had left the country illegally a few days ago. He had yet to notify anyone of his whereabouts. He was one of the many people with no choice but to escape across dangerous borders. The revolutionary guards besieged his parent's house periodically and forced their way into the house. They arrested him once before his escape. He confused them by acting as if he were someone else and they let him go. A few days later, after realizing they had been tricked, they tried to confiscate his father's house. He stayed at our house for a few days, too. A few days after he left our house, they came after him again. My friend told me that once he had gone with his brother and friends to the mountains and stayed for a few days. He pointed to the area where they had set up their tents and prepared for the climb to the summit. The conversation absorbed both of us. I knew he was troubled and needed to talk.

After we were finished talking, we jumped down a steep rock, both feeling much lighter.

I saw the line of the school children coming down the opposite slope. I was watching them as they ran, rolled around, and played with each other. I thought to myself, "How could anyone confiscate their merriment and liveliness and institute such cruel concepts as sin, misery, elegy, and miracles in their place?" No matter how hard the preacher tried, acting like a clown in ridiculous children's shows on T.V., trying to turn the saints Muhammad and Ali into familiar heros who kill the Indians in massive numbers, he would never succeed in getting close to their minds. Not a chance! Even their epics turned out clumsy and sickening.

The wind had blown off my head-cover. It must have happened while my mind was wandering beyond the present surroundings. A voice, a male voice, shouted something from the end of the line. The children were closer now and I was carried away, enjoying every moment of the scene they created. The voice brought me down from the clouds: "Put your head-cover back on!"

It was a young boy's treble voice. It prompted me to laugh.

"Even a sky as wide as this, mountains as white as these, and the vast expanse of trees underneath your very feet, aren't enough to distract your attention from a meager, uncovered head?"

"One must note the Bad and the Good!"

"When you were learning the Bad and the Good, didn't they teach you to mind your own business?"

"I'm not acting beyond my scope. It's respect for the principle of 'Enjoining the good and forbidding the evil.'"

"Who said a bare head is the Evil? The wind has removed my head-cover. You don't have to look!"

"I'm not just defending my rights; it's for everyone's sake."

"Who asked you to speak on everyone's behalf? Other people can express their opinion themselves. Besides, who said everyone minds a bare head?"

The children were slowly gathering around us. The voice of my young assailant had grown weak and hesitant. He said, "Our coach has instructed us to speak up." I thought he probably didn't understand the significance of his action. I started to respond, "Your coach isn't everyone...," when a rough, nervous voice stopped me.

"What is it? What's the matter?"

He threw an angry gaze at the boy. A gaze that could frighten any young boy his age out of his wits.

"Didn't I tell you not to argue with people? What's the matter?"

I volunteered, "It's nothing. Just a minor disagreement between him and me."

I had intended to end the fuss, but I made him more agitated. How could there be something just between him and me, not involving them? He didn't even look at me. Instead, he repeatedly shook the boy's body violently, waiting for a response. The boy was flabbergasted. I imagined him thinking, "Now, what do I do? I don't believe my good intentions have created such a big mess!" And I imagined myself responding to him, "That serves you right!" when a voice coming from the group of children said: "Sir! He only told her to put her head-cover back on!"

131

I wondered if the word "sir" was intended for the man standing in front of me: a mercenary revolutionary guard who worked as a coach but acted as a pathetic preacher in his spare time; a man reduced to considerations of sins and inhibitions, who, unable to harness his own, is desperately determined to control others' so that he might have peace; or maybe a deprived soul whose contact with the earthly world was primarily through the television programs of the past regime, leading him to believe that the world was full of debauchery such as Jamilah's belly dance and vulgar songs.

The "sir," who was wearing a dark green jacket and a pair of army boots, who was skinny and pale, whose eyes looked ill and frightened, and who did not look at the person he was talking to, said: "I don't see what the argument could be, then. You must put your head-cover back on. What made you think you could argue against that?"

How arrogant! Who did he think he was to order people around like that? If he had a gun, I would at least understand where he was coming from. Has it really become this easy? I thought perhaps his students' "dutifulness" has boosted his courage. If I don't confront him now, his students would believe their coach was really an important person, that he was right all the time, that he was everyone's guardian as he claimed to be.

"Can't you see that I have it on...? Do I have a choice?"

He didn't like my response. He started lecturing about the time when *we* had *exploited* the *mountains* and *they* had made a revolution to *free* everything including the mountains; about how they had succeeded and how the mountains now belonged to everyone—including them—and how that entitled them to remove us from this territory and take us *there* if we violated their dress code. Where was this *there*? Everywhere we went, in the food lines, bus stops, streets, taxi rides, the workplace, and literally everywhere there was a fanatic Hezbollahi, we heard the mention of this *there*. It had turned into a catch word to frighten people.

Things were getting out of hand. I knew that the smallest risk I would be taking was to waste the rest of my day. But I had lost my patience with them. The way things were going, one could end up *there* any moment, anyway. I decided not to back off. Now that my mother and my friends were there to see them take me and to see why they had taken me, and now that I didn't have to worry about my family and friends not knowing where I was, yes, now I would risk asking, "On what legal grounds...?" But I decided it was useless. They could show me an identification card from a Komiteh, a mosque, or some other revolutionary organization. And even if they were not authorized, what could I do about the CIA-like Savakis and their spies and the ever-present body of Believers?

"You keep intimidating people! Black will take no other hue!"

The crowd had grown very big by now. I saw my friend's face among them. Her eyes pleaded with me to give in. But I was thinking, "How could an ordinary citizen, just because of his so-called association with the Hezbollah party, become both the law and the law enforcement agent at the same time: condemn another citizen, arrest her, and execute the punishment?" This was a bad joke history had played on those who believed in breaking the traditional boundaries of the present order of the division of labor!

A few revolutionary guards had shown up and circled around me, aiming their guns towards the crowd. They did not ask me anything. They didn't even look at me. The so-called coach told them the story of my insolence and asked them to take me *there*. The guard then looked at me. I imagined him saying to me, "You are a conspirator!"

My throat was dry out of anger. I saw a canteen in someone's hand. He looked queer, although there was nothing in particular wrong with his appearance. Had I noticed it earlier, I wouldn't have asked, but it was too late and I started: "Will you give me a glass of water?"

He looked startled. To make sure I was talking to him, he looked around. Then he became nervous and stepped back, pathetically calling, "Why me?" And then he was lost in the crowd.

Meanwhile two of the guards left. I imagined that they hadn't found the event as exciting as they expected. Or perhaps they were up to something else, since they hurriedly ran all the way down the slope. One of them stopped suddenly, as if he remembered something, and shouted, "When you're finished, come down to see..." I didn't hear the rest because of the wind, but the guard who stayed behind waved to him in agreement.

Then he made a gesture I interpreted as an attempt to compose himself. He was very young. He turned to face the crowd and yelled, "Gentlemen, please don't gather here! Come on, go mind your own business!" Then he addressed me, "You come with me!" We started to walk: the guard, I, and the so-called coach who didn't forget to remind his students of their duties. The children started shouting the slogan, "Death to unveiled women!" They had formed their lines behind us and started following us right away. They threw a few small rocks randomly at me, but as they managed to build up their courage, the number of rocks that bounced off my body increased, indicating a systematic and conscientious attempt at stoning me.

I was not intimidated. You must be a woman to understand how much of the efforts of this massive body of turpitude is directed toward the creation of devices to make women believe that they are contemptible. And if you, as the object of these attempts, fall into their trap, then you have accepted their values and will naturally fall apart. You have to interpret each rock and each shout of "Death to unveiled women!" as the sign of their desperate reaction to your resistance. As insignificant as it may seem to you, your struggle to hold up your chin and your endeavor to convince yourself that you exist, is an expression of our freedom—despite those vultures' attempt to reduce our existence to those of slaves whose only recognized right is to breathe. They want me to believe that I do not exist, or make me accept the distorted, unidentifiable images of their Islamic holy saints as my role models.

What is so special about *outside* after all? It's a purgatory, at best. And we, the people, are kept in suspense on a bridge as narrow as a strand of hair waiting to err and be shoved; and *there* was the hell awaiting us.

We walked down the hill to the station. The coach had calmed down considerably, and exchanged a few words with the guards. It was clear that they didn't work for the same Komiteh and didn't know each other. The children had fallen behind and added a little spice to their shouting activities, chanting, "Death to anti-revolutionaries!"

The guard was much younger than the coach. A young man of about sixteen, with a strong, healthy bone structure and a beard, fluffy but tight, that betrayed the boundless effort he invested in its growth. He was also more talkative than the coach. It was evident from the way he talked that he wasn't impressed by the coach. He talked about the heavy volume of responsibilities he was given by his district's Komiteh; about the problems created by both his enemies and friends on the weekends; about the two missing schoolboys they had to search for the previous week; and about himself and how, because of the recent state of alert, he hadn't slept in twenty-four hours. It was evident that he had little tolerance for leisure time activities. The coach was slowly getting the message: acting more Catholic than the Pope, in someone else's district? He looked confused. The guard was looking for a justifiable offense or a way to rid himself of the intruder. Whichever it may have been, it was apparent that he didn't have much in the way of authority to arrest anyone. In his own district's Komiteh, maybe... Things could have looked different there... The least he could do was to reprimand me. But here? Even the other guards had abandoned him. Where then was this cooperation between revolutionary organizations they so boasted about? Even I, the convicted party, had sensed this guard's restlessness, his uneasiness over being there and his anxiousness to get rid of these intruders.

On the way back I saw my mother and friends standing some distance from the restaurant and the tea house. My mother was holding two glasses of tea, one waiting for me. It was probably cold by now. I didn't feel like drinking tea anymore. I felt nauseous again. For the last two years nausea had seized me occasionally, both at home and in public. I thought to myself, "This is not as bad as the attacks of asthma, headache, and nettle-rash other people are suffering from..." The thought consoled me. I stopped under the pretext of tying my shoelace. Before I knew it, my mother, using her motherly wisdom, had struck up a conversation with them. In my ear hummed all the world's bees. I was exhausted; I wished to hand down the load I was carrying to my mother. I wished to stay beside her and be protected against all the worries, fears, and nightmares of the past few years. I didn't want to stay out there anymore. I had completely lost my desire to get fresh air. I was only thinking about my mother's hands. I wanted to touch them; to feel their consoling, real weight, to make sure that compared to my mother's real hands, all that had happened, the tumult, the shouts of "Death to unveiled women!", the rocks, the coach's sick look and the guard's gun, had been imaginary.

The guard seemed pleased to have finally found a conciliator. I heard him report that this woman (he meant me) had refused to put her head-cover back on, that the children had been about to beat me up, that he had gotten there in time to save me, and that he was now trying to get me out of there. I was too tired to argue with him. Besides, it wasn't wise. I was supposed to be lucky to have gotten away with that much already. If the coach and the guard had cooperated with each other... If the guard had known someone in that district's Komiteh... If a few people had spoken up on my behalf... Who knows? One could lose her life as easily as that. These days, the distance between life and death was not bridged by a first-degree or second-degree offense, a four-year or ten-year or a life-time sentence, but by a mere event... Such as a hike.

The conversation went on and the coach who realized his words were less effective than he had imagined, stood there silent, listening to my mother and the guard. My mother was benevolently advising them to stop the acts that discredit the revolution and Islam, acts that give the wrong people an excuse to take it upon themselves to become agents of the government, to frighten everybody by threatening to take them *there* and to spread among people exaggerated lies and stories. I was wondering how anyone could possibly exaggerate the existing savagery and barbarism... I should ask my mother later if she meant what she said. The guard went even as far as claiming that no one had intended to take me away and that I had insisted on it myself. And my mother succeeded in mediating between us, and things got cooler. They left and the children followed them.

We were in no mood to stay around to enjoy the mountains and our little exercise. Silently we sipped our tea and walked downhill toward the exit. My stomach was intensely upset, as if a hand was pulling the muscles violently. My ears were filled with noise. I could occasionally hear the people's voices in the tumult created by the noon-hour call to prayer and other humming noises: "What's this expiation we are condemned to pay... If only more women dared to... Such a pity... This is one of those cases of serving a prison sentence before you're proven guilty... Actually I'm against speaking up in protest; it makes them bolder..." I thought to myself, "This must be the wife of the man I requested a glass of water from. How many times we asked them not to... A heroine... War-time... Fight against Imperialism... Why don't I throw up? We should have confronted them from the start... A few days ago I saw the same thing on the street..."

I can not bear it any longer. We take a short-cut. We leave the road and the crowd behind. A stream of water is flowing in a gap between two rocks. Sometimes it disappears under the snow, but it soon surfaces again a few yards away. Cheerful, carefree, and mischievous, it is capable of amusing us all the way to the end of the valley. We lose it some distance below. We carefully look for it. The snow has covered the rocks. We walk cautiously lest we slip on the snow-covered rocks.

Mihan Bahrami

Mihan Bahrami was born into a traditional family in Tehran. The loss of her father at the age of two affected her intensely, drawing her into a world of emotional solitude. By the age of five she had found a loyal friend: painting, an activity she describes as the first cultural expression in which a human being is capable of engaging . She produced her first short story, "Garden of Sorrow," when she was fourteen. As a young girl she devoured works by Tolstoy, Shakespeare, Marquez, and Goethe. "Along the path of a solitary life, I found no world better than that of literature and no activity more exciting than writing."

Her first collection of short stories entitled *Animal* was published in 1985. It contains many of her earlier works, previously published in magazines and periodicals, intended for "an audience who enjoys observing the natural development of a mind along the path of maturity." "Animal" is an exception. It is one of her most recent short stories, "an experiment in working with our cultural molds, the relationship between human beings and objects and the feelings and acts of people."

Mihan graduated from Tehran University and then became a graduate student of psychology at the University of California at Los Angeles. "Studying at a school in the U.S. is an isolated event in my life." She left her studies incomplete and returned to Iran. "Commentary on a Ballet" is a short story she wrote during this time. "I have truly breathed that suffocating, dreadful air which is called nostalgia; that alarming symptom of a disease," she writes. "'Commentary on a Ballet' still flows in my veins. What has turned into a short story is the essence of painful moments I have experienced."

Mihan is presently living in Tehran. She is author of the much acclaimed novel, *Haj Barek-Allah*. As a successful artist, she has had many exhibitions of her paintings. She is also translator of several books in psychology. She is married and has a nineteen-year-old daughter.

Animal

by Mihan Bahrami

The peasant woman crouched next to her daughter's bed, wiping with her finger tips the tiny drops of sweat glistening around her daughter's lips and nostrils. The only noise that broke the silence in the room was the sound of their breathing. Both were silent and calm. The younger woman closed her eyes and breathed heavily, while her mother, sitting as silent as a rock, looked at her daughter's face, but seemed drowned in the memories of the recent past.

She imagined that the woman lying on the bed was her master's wife, Anis, lying unconscious inside the enormous harem, taking short, interrupted breaths. Someone had rested a Koran on her chest, and now a woman was holding to her nose pieces of cotton soaked in perfumed earth and rosewater. A stream of disconnected but clear words escaped through the sick woman's locked jaws.

In the other room a military official wearing a stiff peaked cap and a brass badge sat on a cushion and spoke softly to Haji Agha. An intolerable harshness governed his face. Haji Agha was frightened. He had pleaded with him desperately, but the officer had not budged. His determination scared everyone stiff. Terror crept into the other room like an ugly snake, forming a ring around Anis's heart. She fainted, and the other women squirmed nervously, beating on themselves desperately. Everyone in the room was praying; resorting to all the saints for help. Aunt Bibi, who was like a mother to Anis, cried incessantly.

Anis, who had been lying there like a corpse, suddenly jerked and groaned. Everyone rushed to her bedside. They called Haji Agha to tell him that his wife had regained consciousness. As soon as he walked in, Anis rose in her bed and seized him by the collar. She was trembling and a white froth foamed out of the corner of her mouth. She talked weakly and painfully, as if she had just survived a heart attack. "Haji... Haji! I'm appealing to you today and my soul will appeal to you on the day of resurrection. If you betray me, you'll be dishonored in the eyes of my ancestors..."

And with a tone of voice so destitute it could have melted the heart of a rock, she begged, "Hasan. Don't let them induct Hasan into the military. If they take our son, I'll kill myself. I'll hang myself."

And she flung herself on the floor and wept helplessly.

Haji looked about, eyeing everyone gathered around Anis. His look was beseeching everyone, even the peasant woman who was holding the brazier containing the burning incense. Her heart missed a beat and she looked down helplessly. Never having seen her master look so pitiful, she realized how serious the matter was. "What's this commotion all about?" she thought to herself.

She had no idea what military service meant. She visualized the gendarmes in her village. No one minded them. They were like any other person there, and if the villagers were generous to them they could even expect a favor in return.

Aunt Bibi who had never removed her veil in Haji Agha's presence, was now standing in front of him uncovered. She didn't even notice it. She turned to him and almost shouted, "Haji, have mercy on her ancestors! My child will be wasted."

And she beat on herself. Haji murmured, "Dear, what else do you expect me to do? Hasan is my child, too. I am at my wit's end. I don't know what to do. They say it's required by law. He says Hasan should report within three days to the service office and join the soldiers at the front..." And he pointed to the adjoining room.

Anis groaned. She clutched at a clump of her own hair and pulled it hard. Haji rushed to stop her and while he held her strong hands in his he said, "Dear, I beg of you for the love of your ancestors, don't act stupidly. Don't you know the organs of your body will judge you on the day of resurrection?"

Aunt Bibi said, "God help us! Why do we have to live in such awful times. Isn't there anything we can do at all?"

Haji shook his head despairingly and said, "Nothing."

And then in a gentler voice he said, "That is, it's too late, now."

Anis, having thrown her veil over her head, jumped up like a leopard, stood by the door, and said, "But I won't let them. No way I'll let them take my Hasan away from me. Look, my fellow Moslems, I've only got this one! I've suffered greatly. I've reared a good son. I'm so attached to him, as if we're still connected. How can I let them take him away and subject him to God knows what?"

Beating repeatedly on her chest, she started to groan and curse loudly. Someone coughed in the other room.

Then Anis ran to the other side of the room and took out a black metal safe she had hidden behind the heater. She opened the safe with trembling hands, took out a small box of inlaid wood, walked towards Haji who was standing by the door, and said, "Give it to them! This is everything we own. Give it all to them, but don't let them take Hasan away."

Haji shook his head, rejecting the box, and said, "Keep it, Khanom! If they accept a deed to someone's property, I'll give it to them. But if, God willing, cash is the answer to this problem, I'll come back for it."

And with that he left the room.

Anis threw herself on a cushion, crouched down, held both her knees in her arms and broke into tears. She wept desperately. The room was turned into a place of mourning once more.

Her daughter rolled over and groaned. The peasant woman took the water jug and wet her lips. She heard the noises coming from outside: voices of women talking and men issuing orders. It was a full house upstairs. The woman was not curious at all. Her heart froze with an unknown fear. She felt as if she were paralyzed in an open desert in the midst of a storm. Her teeth chattered; she held her feet tightly together. Fragments of memories swept her like a flood. She remembered her master returning to the harem with drooping shoulders and a bent back saying to his wife, "He won't accept it. He says he's only following orders."

Anis shouted, "O Great Prophet! Tell me who has the key to this problem! Is it God, heavens forbid? Whoever it is, he must have children, too. Dear ones, too. He should do something."

And then she paused, stared into her husband's face cunningly, and whispered, "Tell him he has a cripple for a mother. I'll break my arm. I'll cripple myself. I mean it. I swear on the prophet's tomb! I'll blind my eyes. Hasan will act crazy... I'll spread the rumor that he's gone crazy..."

Haji interrupted her, "Woman, we have already discussed this matter fully. There's no way. He says they'll make an investigation. The draft office has its own physicians. They'll examine him and we'll be caught. It's an offense. We have to take all this into consideration."

The woman's sanguine eyes, which until now gazed abstractly into space, suddenly burst into maddened fiery balls of rage. Like a coiling snake, she made her body as small as she could. And with a flat, hard voice she said, "I'll kill myself... I'll hang myself... I'll go to the rooftop and throw myself down to the yard right in front of their feet. I won't let them take my Hasan away from me."

Haji made a jerky movement out of restlessness and said, "Woman, you are always stubborn. You think the last word should always be yours. If you had listened to Aunt Bibi then, we wouldn't be in this mess now."

Anis shook her torso and said groaningly, "Why are you blaming it all on me? It's not fair. Didn't we do everything he asked for?"

Haji said, "We should've married him off many years ago when he first entered puberty. If he had a wife and children, they wouldn't draft him."

All of a sudden Anis stiffened as if she were being electrocuted. Her burning eyes fell on her husband's face and then on Aunt Bibi's. Like one that is possessed, she clapped her hands together and said, "I'll marry him off. Yes, I'll get to work immediately."

Haji and Aunt Bibi exchanged puzzled glances. "Has she gone crazy?"

The woman talked endlessly. She become happy one moment and worried the next, and she kept repeating, "I'll find a poor soul and make this a home for her. It doesn't matter who she is. There are plenty of girls. There are plenty of Believers. Their mothers will understand what I'm going through."

Then she pointed to the safe box and added, "I'll spend it all... I'll put his hand into someone's hand tonight... It must be what God wants. There's nothing wrong with it."

And after a pause she added, "No, tomorrow... Aunt Bibi and I will work as a team and find someone. It's not the end of the world. There are plenty of girls..."

Haji found a moment to interject, "But Khanom, who'll marry a daughter off in the space of a few hours?"

Aunt Bibi squinted her eyes and said, "He's right, Anis. We have to think about this carefully. It's not as easy as it sounds. We should've thought about it before. We can't ask the Sadria family. We can't ask for his uncle's daughter's hand either."

Anis broke her silence enthusiastically and said, "To hell with them! I won't bother with them. I'll find a common law wife for him. No pain at all. As they say, 'Find a head, a hat is no big deal!'"

And she started to laugh violently. Her tears were still fresh when she lowered her voice and said, "May those who can't see my happiness be struck down! And those who want to tear from me the fruit of my heart, may God truly blind them! I'll find a girl to marry him for the time being. This will solve Hasan's problem. And we'll arrange to have an earlier date written on the certificate."

Haji said, "But this is only the easy part of the job. You're not just playing an exciting game. They'll investigate. He has to have a woman living in his house. And then the woman may get pregnant, and what will we...?"

Anis replied without a moment of hesitation, "If she gets pregnant, we will make the marriage official. What difference does it make? Whoever we end up having is a servant of God. And under my supervision, she'll become a real lady."

And she laughed and thanked God, as if all her troubles were over.

Realizing that her master's wife was happy once more and didn't need her, the peasant woman collected her perfumed earth, rosewater, and basil seeds and left.

The next thing she remembered was sitting next to the pool with her daughter Sanam. Sanam's long braided hair reached all the way down to the ground. The house cook had been telling them the story of Anis's fainting, and although she had seen it all herself, she had to keep quiet and listen. In the middle of the story, Hasan, the adopted son of Anis and Haji, came running in. He was a mute. His real father had lived all his life at his master's house and had begotten Hasan, his only child, when he was old and resigned.

The woman was reluctant to leave Sanam alone with the cook, but he sarcastically said, "Zarbegom, hurry up! They've sent for you." The woman became anxious. Something she couldn't put her finger on bothered her. She hesitated before leaving. Hasan was trying to tell her something, making gestures with his head and hands, but Zarbegom's thoughts were traveling in a different world. She couldn't remember what she was thinking, but she was walking as if she were on thin air. When she reached the harem, Hasan had disappeared. Zarbegom sensed several people watching her. She hid in a corner and waited. Then she heard Aunt Bibi say, "Zarbegom, come in! What's the matter? Why are you hesitating?"

Her tone of voice was much different this time from her usual tone. What did they want from her?

Her daughter's groan brought Zarbegom back to reality. She noticed that the tumult upstairs had intensified. She rose from her seat and went to the door. Men were chanting religious slogans. Someone was shouting, "I swear you by Muhammad's green turban, chant louder! Don't get mute now, chant...! Don't hesitate, make it loud!"

Zarbegom opened the door hastily and dragged herself out to the vestibule. She saw a short, stocky workman who balanced a round, mirrored tray and a chandelier on his head, whirling around, entertaining the guests. Zarbegom forgot what she had come after and stood watching attentively. The man chanted a slogan while whirling about. A huge crowd had formed by the house entrance and up on the roof. Women, who were conscientiously holding their long veils with one hand and their children's arms with the other, had formed a thick wall. Haji's son-in-law moved towards the whirling man and deposited a coin in his palm. The workman stumbled a few times and feigned falling to make them laugh. The foot-boys rushed towards him and helped him with the tray. The colorful tassels hanging from the lamp shades were made of such fancy material, the likes of which Zarbegom had never seen. What a scene! She couldn't decide what to look at first. The variety of colors and lusters entranced her. Suddenly she saw the cook's reflection in the mirror. His cruel, cutting look pierced her heart. He spun the brazier containing the incense around the tray and said sarcastically, "May the eyes of the envious and the stingy be blinded! Cheers to the one who planted these incense seeds! Cheers to the one who reaped it! Cheers to the one who burned it for the sake of Saints Hasan and Husain! May the eyes of the impudent go blind! God willing, this will be a blessed unity..."

And Haji's son-in-law had thrown a coin in the brazier as well. They had decorated the area all around the pool and the passage leading to the entrance of the harem with mirrored trays. Zarbegom's look passed along the fully stuffed colorful satin and laced cashmere bundles, cushions made of brocade, trays made of copper, and china made by Haji Mamd-Hasan. It landed on an enormous dresser with a full-length oval mirror, the likes of which she had never seen. What a unique piece of furniture! Zarbegom stared at the reflection of her own ragged figure—her worn-out veil and her black twill pants—and she mumbled to herself, "They must be rich..."

Her gaze then passed along the line of trays containing toilet articles, chandeliers, candelabra, colorful delicate china ewers and basins with silver chains hanging from the ewer handles, and a mirrored tray containing three tiny cushions; two pink satin cushions decorated with pearl tassels on each side of a white one. Zarbegom knew what the white cushion was for.

A sharp pain stabbed her heart. It was a peculiar pain, something she had not experienced before: she was envious.

She was walking along the line of mirrored trays when her eyes met the cook again. He was helping the men unload the dowry but each time he got a chance, he looked at her with smiling eyes. Zarbegom looked down and carried her bitter pain to the basement. She paused at the entrance. She was afraid of seeing her own daughter. She thought to herself, "Good thing Sanam didn't see any of this." When she was calmer she went downstairs. Sanam stirred in her bed when she entered. She

145

fixed her inquisitive eyes on her mother. Then she calmly asked, "What time is it?"

Zarbegom didn't know, but said, "I think it's almost noon."

"What's all this noise? Is there a party upstairs?"

Zarbegom's body jerked. She didn't answer. She couldn't answer.

Her daughter asked again, "It's the guests, Mother, isn't it?"

No doubt her daughter had sensed what was going on, yet Zarbegom shook her head repeatedly, "No... They're about to slaughter a sheep..."

Sanam rearranged her head cover, turned her back to her mother and sighed. Zarbegom sat by the bed. She crumpled her veil in her lap and stared helplessly at her daughter's ripe belly. She said aimlessly, "Are you sure you're in your ninth month?"

Sanam turned her head toward her and responded with her head. She didn't feel like talking. They had calculated this together several times. They both looked down, staring at the threadbare flowers of the worn out quilt.

"Only ten month..."

This thought became etched in her mind. The cook had tolerated their presence in the kitchen for ten months. For ten months, the two women, Zarbegom and Sanam, whom he considered his inferiors, ate the food he prepared. Sanam was sometimes given allowances. Hasan liked her. From the moment the common law had been performed, he had become fond of her. When Sanam got pregnant he promised her an official marriage and a private room in the harem. This was what Anis had promised, too. The evil cook was dying of grief over his failure to jeopordize Sanam's happiness. He groaned and cursed and used every opportunity to make sardonic remarks: "Now you can start a new business up town. How far do you think your luck is going to take you? There's a proverb that says. 'Don't give up your hair because not all bald people are lucky!' God help her! I guess we'll see..."

But Zarbegom was confident. She lived for ten months with the hope that they'd finally become city people and that her daughter would live comfortably like a lady. They could finally hold their heads up in the presence of the cook. She longed to wear pleated dresses, beautiful veils and high–heel shoes. How many sleepless nights she tossed and turned in her bed, thinking about her daughter's dowry! She would sell the melon field they owned and spend the money for Sanam's dowry, as dictated by her husband's will. She would buy a fancy hand-made wool carpet, nice copper pots and brocade bed covers. The pillow cases would have tassels and the sheets would have laces around the edges. She would sew fancy ornaments with pearl flowers for the ewer handles. She would make calico curtains for her with small delicate prints. What a wonderful dowry it would be! She thought so much about each item of Sanam's dowry that she had a vivid picture of what her room would look like. The only thing left to do was to wait for the day they would perform the official marriage ceremony.

But now the dowry came to the house from somewhere other than her imagination, and it did not belong to Sanam. The two pink cushions were exactly what Zarbegom had in mind for Sanam.

A tremendous weight oppressed her, as if she had been buried under a landslide. She could hardly breathe. All her dreams had collapsed. She felt trapped, unable to do anything but react to the danger.

Several times a day she remembered when she had sat in the basement patching up old socks, and Sanam whose belly had grown big would slowly waddle down the stairs with tearful eyes. Zarbegom bitterly remembered how often she would get up and embrace her and tell her that crying wasn't good for her and that high blood pressure wasn't good for the baby. It was getting more and more difficult to believe that Sanam was the same young bride who wore the white lace scarf over her delicately braided hair, the red lipstick and the fancy diadem on the day of the ceremony. When she went upstairs that night she resembled a glittering peacock. What a night!

That night Zarbegom did not sleep out of anxiety and fear. Her daughter became the bride of Haji, the bride of the master's son. You never know... It must have been God's wish. They said they would first perform a common-law ceremony and then an official marriage. If she brings a son, then she will undoubtedly be the favorite one. They would transfer the title of the house over to her... And now Sanam had returned... with a full belly, saying, "Hasan says it's better if I stay with you for a few days. But I don't want to, Mother."

And she broke into tears. Zarbegom tried to get her to talk more, but she wouldn't. Then her mind started to work and she searched for the reason in the past: the women's group outings, the whispers that stopped when she walked in on them, and Hasan's mood changes. How often they tried to poison Sanam's mind and she hadn't suspected anything because she was just a child. God knows what plots were being hatched against her up there, behind those sash windows with their stained glass. In the richly adorned, calm atmosphere of their quarters, her daughter's fate was being determined by those women. What made Hasan, who was so crazy about Sanam and couldn't stand a moment's separation from her, send his pregnant wife (who was about to give birth any day now) to the basement? She remembered one day a week or two ago, when they had a family party for which they made enormous preparation. They did not allow Sanam to go. They sent her to the basement and gave Zarbegom the day off to go to the bath.

The more the peasant woman thought about the past the more she realized that they had been victimized and that their time was up. Worst of all the pain was becoming more frequent. Her daughter was now struggling like a wounded snake. Although she had anticipated this moment, now that it was upon her, she was as frightened as if a catastrophe were underway.

She interrupted the train of her thoughts momentarily and walked to the kitchen to get hot water. In the middle of the stairway a sound resembling a sick dog's howling stopped her.

"Oww- Ooo... Oww-Ooo..."

Zarbegom looked back. Hasan's jaws and the swollen, red-and-purple flesh above his large teeth caught her off guard. He resembled a clown making a wry face.

Zarbegom knew that Hasan wanted something from her. She made a gesture with her head to tell him she was busy and showed him, by holding her hands in front of her stomach, what she was doing.

Hasan nodded, repeated the howling sound and pointed to the quarters upstairs. Zarbegom paused, immobile. Her whole body felt lax and her heart beat so lazily it seemed about to stop.

She looked into Hasan's eyes. She always found his look comforting. His big olive eyes with their dark ring around the pupils reminded her of a lamb's eyes when looking at its shepherd. Zarbegom sensed that Hasan felt sorry for her. The sound of his breathing rattled by like a tired cow.

Zarbegom reached the top of the stairs. The cook's happy face added to her distress. He acted as if it were his wedding day. Zarbegom asked herself, "What've I done to him?"

But she really didn't know, and the cook didn't bother to ask himself that question. He needed to hate her. He hated her for the small privileges she had. At times, when no one else was around, he would ridicule her.

He always blamed her for things that went wrong if he could get away with it. But any favors? Zarbegom couldn't remember any favors he had done for her. None of the kitchen staff hated her as much as he did. But the cook's attitude encouraged them to talk behind her back and they felt entitled to it.

Their whispers would start as soon as Zarbegom started down the flight of stairs heading for her basement room, looking like a ghost clad in rubber boots and hitting the stairs slowly with her dry skinny feet.

The cook would stand by the oven holding a ladle in his hand and make fun of Zarbegom. He would make Nanah Ali's daughter, who was tall and slim, walk like Zarbegom and imitate her. Then he would start roaring with laughter—a laughter indicating more nervousness than gaiety. A numb feeling in his heart always reminded him that in spite of all his jokes he respected Zarbegom's character. He made no effort to hide his envy; rather, he sometimes made it the subject of his performances. He would say in his most exaggerated mocking tone, "Vicious peasant woman! She acts as if she were the daughter of Rockefeller! She has the nerve to carry herself like that. Who else would dare do flip-flops in front of a judge? But really, why doesn't anyone tell her who she really is? That she is the one who came from her village wearing a wooden clog on one foot and a sandle on the other? What is it she is so proud of? What for...?"

Nanah Ali's daughter would flatteringly interrupt him and say, "Drop her, Sir! You can't make a packsaddle for a donkey out of old cashmere, same way you wouldn't roast a puppy just because it's chubby. As long as there is no harm in her showing off, let her do it. Let her have fun with it, let her walk and act coquettishly! Her ass won't get any bigger, you better believe it."

The cook would then calm down. Nanah Ali's daughter knew that every time she talked like that the cook felt better. She didn't expect any favors from him nor were there any secret games between them. They were just killing time, standing there by the pot. The kitchen had its own unique atmosphere, with its smoked brick walls and wooden framed ceiling. Its air was always saturated with other aromas of rice, vegetables, meat, grilled onions, condiments, cardamon and saffron. Its space was full of endless and unrelated gossip the women spread around from early morning till after midnight when they finally washed all the dishes and swept the floors.

Zarbegom dreaded going to the kitchen. She seldom went near the cook. She was intimidated by the privilege the cook had earned because his birthday coincided with a holy holiday, and she also knew that everyone was watching her there. She heard their whispers and ignored them.

When Hasan called her on her way to the kitchen, she returned to the yard, but deep inside she wanted to go back to the basement. Her frenzied soul was being pulled toward the basement by a strong force, but she had to go to the harem. She could hear Aunt Bibi's harsh, coarse voice in the middle of the corridor. She was talking about her first childbirth experience. Her story was constantly interrupted by other women's comments. In the middle of the story Zarbegom heard Anis's voice, saying, "Pardon me for interrupting you. That's why I prefer her skin to be swarthy. Hasan himself, may God preserve him, has a skin as white as milk. If he drinks water you can follow its path down his throat. His body is worth a hundred gold coins. One would think he bathes in milk..."

Zarbegom saw Aunt Bibi's stunned eyes through the glass tube of the lamp. Then she heard her exaggerated tone, "May God preserve him." Anis who was enjoying the attention, continued, "I swear Auntie, women don't get enough of his body...!"

Aunt Bibi said, "It's all because you breast-fed him yourself. Your milk must have done him good. Besides, it depends on when a baby is conceived, too."

Anis narrowed her eyes and looked embarrassed. Aunt Bibi became more persistent and said, "Yes... I remember that my sister, God bless her, always used to say, 'Don't eat any vegetables on that night or your baby will turn out dark-skinned, don't let it coincide with the last days of your period or the sperm will be conceived in dark blood!'"

And then she added with exaggeration, "God bless my sister! She used to recite verses from the book of Joseph following my post-menstrual bath, and blow her breath over pieces of red apple. Afterwards, she'd give me and Akbar the apple to eat."

Zarbegom paused in the stairway. She visualized the two thick strands of black hair that had grown out of a mole on Aunt Bibi's face, and shuddered with disgust.

Then she heard Aunt Bibi's voice. She spoke rapidly but her tone was low. Her tiny, round body resembled a bundle of clothes sitting on a porch. Zarbegom was overwhelmed and speechless. Her knees felt loose. She wanted to hide herself. She wanted to go back to the basement, pack, and leave with Sanam. Suddenly a desire to leap filled her entire being. The entrance to the landing place of the spiral stairs, with its beautiful red wood edges was calling her. She felt a sudden urge to fly to a far-off land. But it was too late. Aunt Bibi's eyes were fixed on her. Zarbegom could immediately sense that something about her look was different. Her heart jumped a beat and she looked down. In spite of her confusion, she tried to grasp the motive behind that queer look. Aunt Bibi's eyes had always been expressive of her arrogance and strength, but now they showed only modesty. Zarbegom felt satisfied. She was free of a heavy burden she had long felt in her heart. Her sorrows began melting away. Maybe fear of God's wrath had made Aunt Bibi think twice. Maybe it was because of the works of the white witchcraft Zarbegom had resorted to, or perhaps Bibi's ancestors had appeared in her dreams to scold her. They must feel guilty for what they've done to Sanam and her. She flitted another glance at Aunt Bibi out of anticipation and fear. No, she wasn't wrong. Fear and despair had settled in Aunt Bibi's big yellow eyes. She heard Anis's voice, "Zarbegom, how is she?"

She was startled. All her fears and doubts were wiped out.. She felt a sharp pain in her heart. She wanted to ignore her badly. Her mouth was squeezed shut so tightly as if her lips were sewn together. Her teeth were biting the tip of her tongue. A moment passed in silence. Aunt Bibi made a gesture toward her niece and asked with a more confident voice, "How's your daughter Sanam, Zarbegom?"

The woman tried to look into their eyes again. She felt she needed to intensify her hatred of them. The faces of the women sitting on the colorful velvet cushions all around the room reminded her of portraits done in oil paintings. Zarbegom was nervous. She was disgusted and felt very lonely. Her knees were trembling and she felt she was going to faint. Aunt Bibi's voice and the words she had spoken echoed in her mind as if she had spoken in a cistern. Zarbegom tried to fight her own resistance, and talk, but what she had found out about these people intimidated her. She opened her mouth with a great deal of effort, and said, "She's fine. Her stomach hurts a little. I think the baby is still way up there."

And then she heard nothing but muffled voices coming to her from all directions. She felt exhausted after saying those words. She leaned against the door and with her trembling hand held her veil tightly. She heard Aunt Bibi say, "Zarbegom, if the pain gets worse, tell Batul to grease her hands with lamp oil and turn the baby around. Don't worry, it isn't due yet. She can't be in her ninth month yet..."

She heard Aunt Bibi's voice whispering to Anis, "Couldn't she wait? Maybe it's her monthly pains."

And a tumult erupted and gestures were exchanged amongst the women, but Zarbegom didn't see or hear any more. The next thing she heard was Aunt Bibi addressing her again, "When the men are back from their baths, go back to the basement and stay with your daughter. Don't let her figure out what's going on. I'll send the cook with the brazier containing the incense later."

Then there was silence. Zarbegom felt that they were whispering. Before she realized what she was doing, Zarbegom found herself in front of Aunt Bibi. Aunt Bibi put a coin in her palm. She was asking for forgiveness. Zarbegom was confused. She thought that if she didn't accept the coin and begged them to have mercy on them instead, things might change. She must do everything in her power to save their existence in that house. For Sanam who was her only hope, she would submit to any disgrace. For Sanam who is now suffering in the basement...

She jerked. She couldn't accept this harsh reality any longer. Her mind started wandering around her past. She remembered her husband's rough hands hanging the fake gold earrings on her ears, and the smell of his sweat reaching her nose through the shirt he was wearing.

She remembered his words, words that were seldom affectionate, "You abusive bitch! I hope to God you don't live long enough to see your gray hair..."

And he would slap her bottom with his wide coarse hands. But that was just a beginning. And all of a sudden her thoughts shifted and she remembered how she had torn her shirt front all the way to her waist when she had learned of her husband's death. She ran all the way from her house to the graveyard, barefoot. She stopped several times on the way, as if possessed by the devil. She remembered the men and the women whose faces were covered by dust surrounding her and holding her arm, one wiping the foam pouring out of her mouth, a few saying "Cry! Cry! Crying is good for you!" and the one who splashed rosewater on her face. And she just stared at the ground. She collected a handful of soil, smeared it in her own hair and took off again running toward the graveyard after her husband's corpse. She suddenly stopped by a water tank near the graveyard and stared at the crowd moving ahead of her bearing the coffin on their shoulders, and at the dust behind them blocking her view. She remembered how she had stared at the group of people gathered around a ditch, their nervous movements, their cries of "God is Great" and the silence: the silence and blackness of the pit's bottom, and the big coarse hands that pulled her husband's body out of there. She remembered the coldness of the blood that splashed on the wet bricks around the watertap and the soft hands throwing a black scarf over her head. She was a widow now. A widow with a small girl to take care of. She had no son or guardian who would care for them. She heard her husband's voice again, "Listen, woman! If I die you must take good care of her. She should be as precious to you as the pupils of your eyes."

When they had talked in the room with the baby babbling in her cradle, their voices echoed under the dome-shaped ceiling.

Once, their voices were so loud that Zarbegom thought everyone had heard them, "Marry her off to someone who has a modest, legitimate income. Someone who can afford the necessities of life."

She put her hand on her chest and let out a long sigh. She needed to release the pressure on her heart. She was so preoccupied that she didn't hear Aunt Bibi's voice saying, "Zarbegom, what's come over you?"

Zarbegom jumped and saw Aunt Bibi's puzzled eyes staring at her. The others were talking to one another. Words swirled and formed funny shapes in front of her eyes, like the fireworks she had seen at the Tupekhaneh square on certain holidays. But this time they landed on her heart. The deed of sale. They were talking about the deed of sale. They had given Haji's Chal garden to Mr. Sadria's daughter.

She looked at Aunt Bibi and felt dizzy again. She felt as if she were flung to a distant place. Aunt Bibi's eyes were glowing. There was no trace of anxiety left in them. Something like the cruelty of a ferocious beast characterized that poisonous glow.

The memory of her house made her heart ache. The room with brick walls, the fireplace, the mirror with the brass frame, the wooden doors, and the two antique lamps sitting on the mantle. A lump formed in her throat. How homesick she was for it all! What made her give up all that? It wasn't easy. She felt dark and empty inside. She had begged, "Don't destroy me! Her father commanded us in his will not to move away from here. Don't make me homeless. I want to be buried right here, in this village, next to him."

She had bared her face in front of the village chief. She cried, showing him her black scarf, "A widow's lamp doesn't produce any light, but I want my child to grow on my lap. I want to work in my field. I'm not going to the city. I want to die in this village. What'll happen to my melon field if I leave? My house will turn into a ruin."

The village chief was calm and thought only of what he was asked to do. Haj Seyyed, her master, owned property in the village. They were from a noble family and the chaplain said that their family tree went back twenty generations. They wanted to hire Zarbegom to do bookkeeping and light housework. What difference should it make to her? Zarbegom was crying like a child. With her, crying always came before helpless submission. They put her bundle in the trunk of a big brown car in front of the tea house. Zarbegom had never ridden in a car before. She had once seen a car parked on a road and started running away from it like mad. That day she started taking off her shoes, but a blow from her daughter stopped her. Zarbegom managed to control herself and sat in the back seat, watching her daughter Sanam closely: what a real lady she was, as if she'd been in a car a hundred times before. She neatly covered her hair with her veil, and her tiny white face resembled an angel's. Zarbegom's heart was beating desperately. She was calling on the saints, "O Eighth Imam! O protector of the homeless!"

Now she found herself resorting to the saints again. Aunt Bibi asked with astonishment, "What's wrong Zarbegom? You dropped your coin."

Zarbegom's bewildered gaze was fixed on her. She bent down and took the coin.

Aunt Bibi said, "Go stay with your daughter, Zarbegom. Don't stand here like this!"

Then she turned to Anis and said, "What's wrong with her? What if she's ill? At a time like this with her daughter going through labor and all?"

Anis said nonchalantly, "There's nothing the matter with her, you simpleton! Peasants are all like that. She just stares at you instead of being grateful. Didn't you see her take the money without saying anything at all?"

Aunt Bibi shook her head and said, "No, Zarbegom is not that type. I am afraid she might cause us trouble."

The tumult in the room had intensified. The women were all talking at the same time, but the conversations went on all the same. No question remained unanswered. Zarbegom stood in the stairway by the handrails. The words all seemed garbled to her. Aunt Bibi was saying, "Anis, don't let the Sadria family hear any of this under any circumstances!"

Anis said, "If we move fast, everything will be over in a wink. The moment their daughter has stepped into our house, we are in charge and they will become the helpless ones."

155

Aunt Bibi said, "I'm afraid of Sanam and Zarbegom— What if they put a curse upon us?"

Anis made an offensive gesture and said, "What are you talking about, dear? Haji will make sure they are not left homeless. He'll give them the cucumber field. What else do they want? They've married off a peasant girl in a temporary marriage and they expect to live off it for a life time?"

Aunt Bibi said, "What if it's a baby boy?"

Anis answered, "We've already agreed that if the baby is a boy, she can send him to our harem right away, even before the wounds are healed. We don't have enough boys. We'll do anything for a boy."

As the voices moved away from Zarbegom, words got lost as if in a vacuum. The stairs drew her up as if chains had tied them together. In front of the corridor entrance, the cool, strong autumn breeze hit her in the face. Hasan was standing outside staring at her. He softly called, "Oww-Ooo..." and pointed to the basement.

Zarbegom jumped and ran towards the basement. The wind blew the curtain aside through a broken glass. She could see part of her daughter's body through the opening. Sanam was motionless and uncovered. Alarmed, Zarbegom kneeled in front of the mattress and touched her daughter's arm with a trembling hand. Sanam's hair was soaked in sweat. The pillow on which she rested was also soaked wet. She gasped as if she were taking her last few breaths. Zarbegom called her name several times. The girl opened her eyes and looked at her weakly. Zarbegom uttered something.

Suddenly, Sanam's sharp pains started. She crumpled her lower lip and violently bit it with her upper teeth. Her mother forced her fingers between Sanam's teeth. A sharp pain shot up her arm, as she held her hand there. A sound resembling the scream of someone with whooping cough escaped through the girl's mouth. She grabbed at her belly violently, as a white foam formed around her mouth. The white of her eyes turned black. Sweat streamed down her forehead, neck and chest, soaking her shirt. Her heart beat under her mother's palm like a trapped pigeon. A thick yellow substance oozed out of her hot hard breasts.

Zarbegom bent over her and desperately called on the saints, "O Sacred Lady! O protector of the homeless!"

She had an urge to scream for help but they had insisted that no one but Batul (who wasn't there yet) was allowed to get near the basement. Where was she? She kept saying, "I wish we had left last month. I wish we had never come here in the first place. I wish I had broken my leg.... May the village chief burn in hell..."

She remembered how Anis repeatedly brought up th subject of her return to the village indirectly. She knew now that she had yielded to an illusion of hope.

The pain subsided. The girl's fast and unsteady breathing went back to normal as she slowly let her exhausted body sink on the pillow. Zarbegom looked around the room helplessly. Then she got up, folded a cover in four and put it on the mattress under her daughter. She thought, "What else can I do?" She remembered that she must get Batul to turn the baby around... what if the baby came before a midwife could get there? Her feet were nailed to the floor; she dared not leave her daughter alone.

The pain returned once more with a maddening intensity. Sanam clutched the floor, the bed, and anything she could get her hands on. Zarbegom was standing there helplessly. Her mind was blank. She couldn't remember her own experience of having given birth. She was wondering why no help was sent down when she saw Hasan through the glass. She called him several times, but Hasan only stood there smiling. Zarbegom raised her voice, screaming, but Hasan couldn't see anything from outside and obviously couldn't hear her. Zarbegom gave up. She lifted her daughter by the arm and tried to hold her tight, but she trembled so violently that she couldn't keep daughter's body still.

Sanam leaped forward and fell on her bed again. She grabbed the mattress as she pressed her thighs together. She uttered a loud scream through her clenched teeth. Then Zarbegom heard an explosion, something resembling the sound of a balloon bursting open. Zarbegom knew this sound. She embraced her daughter, and with a stuttering tongue screamed repeatedly, "O protector of the homeless! O Sacred Lady, help me!..."

The girl turned her head and bit her mother's shoulder. When Zarbegom finally succeeded in opening her stiff thighs, a stream of blood and water ran down Sanam's body and covered the mattress.

The baby's black head grew bigger and bigger and the girl's face changed colors from pale to red and then to a blue pallor. Her tongue was trapped between her clenched teeth and a mixture of blood and saliva foamed out of her mouth onto her shirt. Zarbegom couldn't let go of her. She had forgotten everything she knew. She kept roaring and asking for help. Her daughter's glance was beseeching. She was speechless; she looked like a helpless animal going through the agony of death. They both trembled violently, as if caught in a storm. A strong and wild feeling of revolt was boiling inside Zarbegom. Revolt against fear and caution planted a roar in her throat. She screamed madly, begging for help. She even called Haji's name. Then she stared hopefully at the basement door and listened. She screamed again.

There was a commotion in both the harem and the rest of the house. She could hear people chanting religious slogans. She could also smell the scent of burning incense coming through the crack of the window.

A bass voice said, "Bless Muhammad and his descendants!"

And Zarbegom saw the baby's hands groping the air as if looking for something. His narrow claws opened like a blooming flower and his ceaseless cry filled the room.

Zarbegom bent on her knees instantly and sat firm. She extended her arm and grabbed the baby, measured the umbilical cord by spanning and cut it with a long-handled knife that lay on top of a pile of apple skins on a plate. She pulled the stained covers away, tidied the messy bed, rolled her daughter over on the mattress, and covered her body with a quilt. Then she got up. She tore the curtain hanging by the front of the wardrobe in half. She cleaned the baby with one piece and wrapped its body with the other. The baby's red face resembled a fresh apple of a pretty color—a healthy boy whose resemblance to his father was immediately apparent. His eyes were closed and he was calm. His red lips were covered with small feverish blisters.

A premature feeling of happiness flowed in her heart. Things started to look different at once. The room seemed bright, as if a hundred candles were lit in it. The cool breeze carried the scent of the burning incense and resin to the basement. Zarbegom was constantly praying. Nothing stayed in her mind longer than a second. All of a sudden she felt light. The desire to fly, to run outside and talk, filled her heart. But she was afraid to look at the baby closely. A remote feeling of grief and anxiety made her uneasy. She was afraid of losing this baby. After her deceased husband, he was the dearest thing she had known in her life.

She covered the crack of the window with a piece of cloth. She laid the boy next to his mother and hid him out of sight. Then she went out to get food.

Her enthusiasm had made her extremely cautious. There was still a crowd in front of the vestibule. The groom had been bathed and accompanied by his intimates to the harem. The cooks were running around preparing for the party and the house cook was dancing and snapping his fingers in the kitchen to the rhythm of Nanah Ali's banging against the bottom of a pot. Zarbegom went down without stopping anywhere. She looked as if she didn't see anyone. Her happiness was a sweet secret that closed her eyes to sorrow and envy.

She took some hot water and food and returned to the vestibule immediately. They were skinning the sheep they had slaughtered at the groom's feet, preparing it for roasting by the pool. The sheep's decapitated head lay at Zarbegom's feet. Zarbegom stared for a moment at the animal's suffering mouth and the amputated veins through which fresh blood still streamed out. Its half-closed and misty eyes reminded her of Sanam's eyes, when she suffered and beseeched wordlessly.

She shuddered convulsively. She saw a strong resemblance between themselves and this animal's decapitated head and ugly swollen trunk. She started to walk fast. She wouldn't allow them to oppress her and her daughter any more. She couldn't afford to.

The night was passing quietly in the basement. Everything that stood outside of the old brick walls of this room had lost its relevance to her. No one had bothered to inquire about them. Her daughter was healthy and calm, and aside from a mild fever which appeared to be natural, she had no pain. The excitement over the newborn baby preoccupied them. They watched it all night, and when Sanam fell asleep and the outside noises subsided, Zarbegom saw Hasan's red jaw appear at the basement doorway. He was looking at them with a big smile. Zarbegom jumped up and went to the door, using gestures to tell him what she wanted him to do. Hasan was confused and only shook his head. Finally Zarbegom thought of something and returned to the room. She took her small wooden box from a niche, dug something out of it and put the box back in its place. Hasan watched her all the time without blinking. Then the woman walked towards him with confident steps. She repeated those gestures and placed the gold coin she had been given that morning in Hasan's palm. Hasan stared at the coin for a moment and then, while making noises with his throat to show his happiness and excitement, ran upstairs.

Zarbegom did not wait any longer. She prepared her small bundle, wrapped the baby in a warm cover, and sat waiting.

The first rays of the sun had already appeared when Hasan stuck his head in the basement door and repeated his call several times, "Oww-Ooo!... Oww-Ooo!..."

Zarbegom jumped up and asked him to be quiet. She woke her daughter, took her by the arm and started moving towards the stairs. Sanam couldn't stand up. She was sleepy and bewildered. Zarbegom lifted and carried her all the way to the vestibule. Sanam looked back and watched the entrance to the harem with astonishment. It was as if she had never seen the place before. Zarbegom opened her veil and placed the baby in its mother's arms. Then she helped her out the door.

Hasan accompanied them to the carriage and helped Zarbegom lift Sanam and the baby into their seats. He waited until Zarbegom got inside. Soon after the top was pulled down, they disappeared in the twilight of the day.

Fereshteh Kuhi

(1949–)

Fereshteh Kuhi was born in Tehran in 1949. She was the child of an engineer working for the Iranian Airforce, and a nurse, but she was raised and brought up without the benefit of her father's financial and emotional support. She went to England at the age of 18 to become a college student. She soon became a loyal member of the anti-Shah opposition movement, on behalf of which she gave up her studies and traveled for years in western Europe.

Fereshteh returned to Iran in the early 1970's and was accepted into the English literature program of Tehran University. She was also employed by the Iranian Ministry of Education, teaching Persian language, history and English for eight years in all-girls' high schools of the poverty-stricken southern Tehran counties. During these years she continued her secret political activities against the Shah's regime.

In 1978 she graduated from Tehran University and continued working as a teacher for a year. Circumstances, however, forced her to flee the country and become a refugee in Turkey where she awaited permission to return to England for a year. In England she struggled for another year before she entered Oxford University as a graduate student. After obtaining her master's degree, she continued to pursue her education in political science.

Fereshteh is presently living in England. She recently married an American and plans to move to New York upon completion of her dissertation. "Mrs. Ahmadi's Husband," the story in translation here, was published in the winter of 1985 in *Nimeye Digar* (The Other Half), a woman's periodical published in London.

Mrs. Ahmadi's Husband

by Fereshteh Kuhi

Of the two vice-principals of the school in which I taught, one of them was different in many respects from the rest of the government employees. She was short and stocky but very agile. She reminded me of the women of the Qajar period I had seen in paintings: a plump, round face, looking even rounder and chubbier because of the tight wimple which ringed her face. I don't recall having seen her greet anyone when she entered the teachers' lounge. Her large, black eyes, and the thin, connected eyebrows were also identical to those portrayed in the paintings. Her name was Mrs. Ahmadi. A sullen expression characterized her dead serious face. Even with her own kind, the fanatic Hezbollahis, she hardly ever joked around. Everyone took heed of her. I myself had mixed feelings. While I despised her views with a passion, when it came to dealing with the Hezbollahis, I definitely felt more comfortable with her.

Unlike the highly incompetent Hezbollahi principal of the school, who I thought must have been given that position solely because of her preaching skills, Mrs. Ahmadi took her job seriously. Compared to the others, she was less inclined to confuse fair and unfair, at least as far as the daily matters of the school were concerned. I never saw her gossip like the principal did, nor would she get excited and engage in ideological flirtations whenever a young revolutionary guard came to our school for inspection. She simply believed in her work and was determined to do her best at the duties to which she was assigned. It was because of her conscientiousness and competence that she was practically doing the principal's job. The school precinct office was also aware of this. If she missed a day, the atmosphere in the school would be altogether different: a pleasant kind of chaos would rule everywhere. The principal would confuse her right hand with her left and the children would do as they pleased. Scarves would slide down the girls' heads leaving their hair uncovered, the bells announcing break time would ring late, and the teachers' chats in the office and in the hallways would last longer. If documents were needed, no one could find them. In short, Mrs. Ahmadi was the beating pulse of the entire school.

Mrs. Ahmadi was twenty-five years old. She was also a student at the College of Higher Education, majoring in math. She had married a young revolutionary guard, younger than herself, and was now three months pregnant.

We heard that her husband left for the war front voluntarily at the beginning of the summer. I felt sorry for her. These days volunteers aren't so lucky. After a few weeks we all started worrying. She hadn't heard from him for some time. We learned this from the occasional whispers exchanged between her and the rest of the Hezbollahis at the school. There had been no letter, nor any messages through his friends or acquaintances who visited the war front frequently. They would come back to Tehran every once in a while and then return to the front with a new assignment. They would continue going back and forth until they got killed. Within the last few months many people from our own district had been killed in the war: young men who were between twenty and twenty five years old, many of whom had controlled the Education Administration Offices in the district. I knew some of them; I had seen them harass the teachers.

Everyone, including my friends and I, was concerned about Mrs. Ahmadi's missing husband, about whom we had heard so much. Everyone tried to conceal their worries from the others. No one said a word about the subject. An obscure feeling filled the air. A vague sort of uneasiness. It was as if everyone had a premonition of disaster; but based on an unspoken agreement, no one wanted to be the first to admit to it. In particular, not a single word was said around Mrs. Ahmadi. No one wanted to be the first to plant the seeds of worry.

Nevertheless, Mrs. Ahmadi had become the center of everyone's attention. Her movements were followed by quick furtive glances or under a thousand different pretexts. Sometimes the glances met each other. If it were a friend who had caught another friend's glance, she would slowly move her eyes around the room and stare at some irrelevant object on the floor or a more irrelevant slogan on the wall, or the principal's long, white veil hanging from the clothes rack. And if our glances were caught by one of them, one of the Hezbollahis, then we would hastily look away. Even if eyes were arrested, minds would continue wandering, wondering about the fate of Mrs. Ahmadi's husband.

Although Mrs. Ahmadi tried to be calm, one could see that she was anxious and nervous. She stopped smiling altogether. She came to school early and worked nonstop. Because of the heat and her constant movements, her chubby cheeks would turn red and protrude from her head covering. Tiny drops of sweat would settle on her nose and upper lip; often we'd hear her making scornful comments. As the days passed, she won everyone's sympathy. Even her enemies gave up their secret hostilities towards her husband. Maybe it was because she was pregnant.

One day, when I had a free hour between my classes and was sitting in the office alone facing the window, the phone rang. I answered. They wanted Sister Ahmadi. I found her exhausting herself with the children in the hallway and called her. She lifted the receiver and said, "Yes, this is Ahmadi," then she was silent. I couldn't hear a sound from her or from the person on the other end of the line. A few moments passed. Silence. I noticed that her hand was shaking. She suddenly dragged her body along the table and sat down on a chair. "What is it?" I asked. "I don't know. They put me on hold." Now the hand holding the receiver was also shaking. Her gaze remained glued to mine, while her whole attention was still with the phone. It was as if she were looking for something, and hoped to find it in my eyes. Some sense of sympathy perhaps, as if to say, "What if something has happened to him?" It was the first time we had looked directly into each other's eyes.

She managed to control herself and sat straight in her chair. After a few moments' pause, she broke the silence: "I'll send them to you right away." Her tone was so formal that one might have thought she was responding to someone who had called from the school precinct asking for the school's account of the past three months' expenses. She placed the receiver back on the phone with great effort. Loosely, her hand slid from the phone to the desk and then to her thighs. She looked like she was feeling sick. Her face turned pale and was covered by heavy sweat drops. I moved closer to her. Her whole body was shaking. Her wimple was strangling her but I didn't dare re-move it from her head. She closed her eyes, leaned her head against the wall behind her and sat limply on the chair. She knew something terrible had happened to her husband. This was the first and the last time I saw Mrs. Ahmadi so defeated. It may sound very cruel, but this was also the first and the last time I saw her act naturally. I fixed a drink of sweetened hot water for her. I kissed her cheek and said, "Don't worry. Soon you'll hear a word from him."

Two days after that phone call, Mrs. Ahmadi missed a day at school. We learned that her husband had been martyred in the battle zone. We all cried. The next day, the office walls were covered by her husband's picture and his obituary. He was very young. Only twenty–one years old. His face looked exactly like the other Hezbollahis. My friends and I decided that we must all attend his funeral, anyway. I didn't look forward to coming face to face with her under any circumstances. I didn't know what to say to her.

Mrs. Ahmadi returned to work a few days after this in-cident. She was garbed completely in black. Upon her arrival at the teachers' lounge, we all gave her our condolences. It went much smoother than I had expected. She cried. And we couldn't stop our tears from pouring out. Then everyone was quiet. Things were difficult because we were divided into different cate-gories: my group, the non-Hezbollahis, and hers, the Hezbol-lahis. We didn't know what to ask or say and they didn't want to say anything about the incident in our presence. Heads were bent down and looks were fixed on the furniture. Fortunately, this situation didn't last long because we had to leave the of-fice and go to our classes.

When I returned to the office at break time, I noticed that the atmosphere in the room had changed back to normal. Mrs. Ahmadi had already succeeded in controlling her emotions and was going about her daily activities as usual. She worked as energetically and seriously as before, as though nothing had happened. Obviously, her attitude made things easier for us and we didn't have to go out of our way to act any differently from our customary casual ways. Yet, the speed at which she had accepted her new situation confused me somewhat. After that day, every time I saw her I felt a lump in my throat. I kept telling myself that she must feel sad inside, and that perhaps she was trying to appear strong in the eyes of the enemy, so to speak. But her reaction to this event somehow went against my accepted values. I could not comprehend how, in a few hours' time, it had turned into an event belonging to the past, to history. The death of Mrs. Ahmadi's husband was like a passing fever that came, lasted a little while, and then disappeared altogether without leaving a single trace. I closely observed her behavior to decide whether I should attribute her impervious and serene expression to the strength of character, or to some sort of opportunistic cleverness.

The day before the funeral, some of us agreed to take our long, black veils to school and go directly from there in the hired cars of the funeral processions.

The next day, when I entered the teachers' lounge in the morning, I noticed a large poster on the notice board. It praised Imam Khomeini and the martyred soldier. It contained information about the location and the time of the funeral and the following words in darker and larger print:

.....Based on the martyr's own will, sisters and colleagues who do not believe in Imam Khomeini's leadership and the Islamic Republic, and those who do not perform their daily prayers, the very core of our religion, should refrain from participating in this ceremony. We are asking that these colleagues respect this request for the sake of reverence to our martyr and the tranquility of his soul.

I couldn't believe my eyes. I read it several times. I thought how ignoble of them to have put something like that on the wall. They knew that we had decided to attend the funeral. I was very angry. And I felt insulted because they had totally ignored my sense of sympathy. For a moment all of my blood rushed to my head, flushing my face. I scorned myself for ever having felt sympathy for Mrs. Ahmadi and her husband. There were at least two of us who didn't qualify to go and they knew this very well. They had put up that poster to isolate us. I lost all my sympathy for them and wished I had the courage to tear the poster into pieces. I went toward the window. I pressed my elbow on the window sill and my chin on the palm of my hands. I busied myself watching the kids getting ready to form their lines. I told myself, "To hell with them. Now that they are being so despicable, I won't go at all." I was ready to snap at the first person who got near me. Someone entered the lounge. Since no word of greeting was exchanged, I figured it must be the principal or the other vice-principal. I did not stir. I didn't feel like seeing any one of them. I stood by the window until it was time to go to class.

On the way to class, Nooshin and I got a chance to exchange a few words. She also felt the situation was intense. We agreed on talking to a few other teachers at lunch break. I entered my classroom. I was not in the mood to teach or even deal with my students. I had seldom felt that way during the eight years I had been teaching. It was often quite the opposite. I always forgot my problems as soon as I entered school. We talked to the other teachers at lunch time and decided that, under the circumstances, it was best to remain calm and go on with our plan to go to the funeral. Cancelling the plan would mean that we were what they portrayed us to be. Going to the funeral had been a voluntary decision prior to the posting of the notice. It had promised a certain degree of excitement; I was curious to see how Hezbollahis mourned for their dead. But now things had changed. Now a feeling of anxiety set in. I sensed their power over my head. We had to go. We left after school.

It took a couple of hours to get through the traffic jam of the Aramgah road and Shush Square before we got to their house in a well-hidden street in Khorasan Square. We parked the car at the end of the street. We entered a wide alley that led to a smaller one where Mrs. Ahmadi's house was located. The alley itself looked lively. It was one of those old alleys lined with plane trees whose abundant branches created cool shadows. A large brook ran by the houses, and there were a few small grocery stores and shoe shops. The shopkeepers were all standing outside looking at us with sympathy and appreciation, randomly greeting people. The alley was meticulously swept and cleaned.

A long line of curtained canopies was set up in the alley extending all the way from the beginning to Mrs. Ahmadi's house (actually her parents' house). The first six canopies were decorated with Khomeini's portrait. The rest alternated between those decorated with pictures of Mrs. Ahmadi's husband and those with Khomeini's. Artificial flowers and colorful lights surrounded the pictures. Pictures of various sizes showing Khomeini and Mrs. Ahmadi's husband were plastered on all the walls of the alley, leaving little empty space in between. Posters and banners bearing Arabic verses and the famous revolutionary slogan, "I wish I were a revolutionary guard," filled the rest of the space.

The alley was crowded with neighborhood boys and friends of the mourning family. Heads were bent down and faces looked sad. Most of them wore black shirts, and had beards that were darker than their shirts. We were almost there. An old man with gray hair and a beard was standing at the entrance of the house, crying quietly. He looked pathetic. We greeted him and he showed us the way to the second floor. There were six of us: three science teachers, the principal and the two vice-principals. We climbed the stairs.

The second floor of the house was comprised of two very small rooms and a narrow corridor. The hall floor was filled with shoes, and the rooms with people. Mrs. Ahmadi's mother came forward and greeted us. Mrs. Ahmadi also came to welcome us. We kissed each other's cheeks. The trouble was that I didn't know how to relate to the Hezbollahis. Imam Khomeini had encouraged people to convey congratulations, and, at the same time, condolences to the family of the martyred. I knew that I wasn't capable of playing such a hypocritical role. I decided to take the risk of saying a few words of consolation.

The two rooms were filled with women sitting on the floor, all clad in black veils. It was depressing. There was no place to sit. We stood in a corner and gradually forced our way to empty spots to sit down. It was extremely hot. It was almost impossible to breathe, especially because I was wearing an Islamic frock, with tight cuffs and collars, and a black scarf covered by the requisite veil. Drops of sweat ran profusely down my head, face and body. The odor of perspiration made the room unbearably stuffy. A water jug and a glass were being passed around. I drank some water and fanned my body with the corner of my veil. I wished that I could at least rid myself of the veil to be able to feel some of the air. I was literally steeping underneath all my garments. They brought tea and dates for the newcomers. A young girl was standing by the door splashing drops of rosewater on the women's heads.

Mrs. Ahmadi was wearing a beige Islamic style dress and had no headcover. She had shed the formal air she carried with her at the school. For the first time, I was able to see her neck. She had pulled her long black hair back. She looked much younger and prettier without that constraining head cover. I found her mother exceptionally disagreeable. She was crude. She had tied her veil around her waist and was constantly storming through the rooms and the corridor, giving orders and disturbing everyone's peace. I could easily imagine her as the busybody of the neighborhood mosque, one of those people who hang around crowded lines and wait for a miserable soul to complain about being fed up with crowded lines, so that she can open her mouth and say, "Hey, you! You unworthy, anti-revolutionary, Savaki, monarchist, or cheap communist! Who are you to discredit the Islamic Republic, the Revolution, ...and Imam Khomeini?" Yes, one of those people who, after creating a scandal, would make sure that the poor soul was arrested and taken to the headquarters of the Islamic guards— the Komiteh.

I looked around. Because the available sitting spaces were scarce, my friend and I had been separated. I felt insecure and alienated. Although the women sitting around me looked harmless, I was nervous and suspected that they were Moslem Sisters and would start performing their strange rituals of reading the religious verses out loud and chanting revolutionary slogans. I wished I hadn't come. I knew that Nooshin was feeling the same way.

An old woman started chanting mournful songs, the usual type of songs that make everyone cry. The majority of the women started to cry—or at least, it seemed that way. They had hidden their faces with their veils and shook their heads while sobbing. Mrs. Ahmadi, with her almost white gown, looked quite distinct in the crowd of black–veiled women. I didn't know whether she was pretending or not, but she sat calmly in a corner and accompanied a woman reciting verses from the Koran. I didn't see her cry.

169

The heat and the stifling air were depressing. Eventually a spot became vacant next to Nooshin in the other room. I made for it. The spot was so tight that I had to sit with my legs squeezed up against my chest. I sat motionless the whole time. All of us were now in the same room. People kept leaving and making room for others. Because of the constant movement we were being pushed closer and closer to the end corner away from the entrance, and before we knew it we were stuck there. We found ourselves facing the walls and the windows, with a tightly packed crowd behind us. It was very hot and there was no hope of getting closer to the door. Nooshin moved her head closer to mine and while her body heat assaulted my face, she whispered in my ear, "How are we going to escape now? These people don't seem to be in a hurry to leave."

Meanwhile, I noticed that the principal, Mrs. Ahmadi, the other two vice-principals, and three of the teachers had formed a small circle. The principal and one of the teachers took small notebooks out of their purses and opened them up. Someone handed a bullhorn to the principal. I wondered why she needed a bullhorn in so small a room. The vice-principal announced that there was a request that one of the Sisters recite a certain prayer and litany for us. I understood that the game was just starting and that one of our teachers was a professional narrator of the religious stories. She spread open her notebook and first chanted some pro-Khomeini and anti-enemy slogans which were repeated by some of the women in the room, leaving others with bewildered looks on their faces. Nooshin and I exchanged glances and touched each other's arms, both looking at the walls so no one could see us smirking. It was a ridiculous scene. Then the teacher suddenly started reciting homilies. Her voice was high pitched, coarse, and annoying. The principal was accompanying her. Then they got to a part that apparently required everyone's accompaniment. I noticed that one of the teachers was watching Nooshin and me. I had decided to move my lips to give the impression that I was joining in too, but I couldn't keep it up long, so I covered my face with my veil. I didn't want them to see me crack up. Nooshin did the same. The heat was suffocating me.

I was so preoccupied with our discomfort, that I didn't notice the direction events were taking. Now the song was at its climax. Suddenly the principal and her gang started beating on their chests and asked the rest of the Sisters to do the same. I was caught off guard. I had never been in a situation like that before. I looked at the window. I wished I could escape.

Nooshin whispered in my ear, "What should we do now? This circus is lasting way too long. I left my child with the neighbors and told them I'd be home by six. It's seven thirty now and we're still here." I said, "As you see, we can't help it now. How can we leave in the midst of this? Let's wait for the first suitable moment to go."

Although no one could see our faces, we still had to be careful because people could watch our movements from side angles. All the women were beating on their chests and their hand movements could be seen through their veils. I loosened my veil so no one could see that I was just beating against my veil. This way I could fan my face too. I had never beaten on my chest before. I could hardly keep myself from laughing. I touched Nooshin on the elbow. She opened her veil and I saw that she was giggling. She was also beating on her veil from inside. She said in my ear, " I wish we could go before everyone figures out what we're doing." I said, "Don't worry. They think we are crying."

The chest-beating ritual lasted for half an hour. Then a new prayer started and all of a sudden everyone got up on their feet to repeat the Arabic verses and songs after the principal. We were instructed to whirl to the right, then whirl to the left, then whirl toward the east and then sit down. All this time I watched the others carefully so I could imitate them and hoped that things didn't turn more ridiculous. Then they announced a break. The water jug and the glass started on their route again. Nooshin and I exchanged signals and got up immediately. It was eight-thirty. After excusing ourselves, we said good-bye and ran out the door. The air in the alley felt heavenly. We passed through the alley quickly and got in the car.

Once in the car, the irony of the situation became apparent. It suddenly occurred to me that I must have missed something. The funeral announcement had read, "To honor the memory of this martyred soldier..." Yet the martyr's name didn't come up at all during the whole evening. I thought to myself, "That explains the bewildered expression I noticed on some of the women's faces when the revolutionary slogans were being chanted."

Nasrin Ettehad

(1945–)

Nasrin Ettehad (a pseudonym) was born in 1945 in Tehran. In 1971 she left for Germany to continue her education, and by 1979 when she returned to Iran for a few years, she had obtained her bachelor, master, and doctoral degrees in political science. During these years she was an active member in the Confederation of Iranian Students working against the Shah's regime.

In January of 1979, Nasrin, like many other Iranians living abroad who wished to return to their country at the outset of the Iranian Revolution, returned to Iran. There, she co–founded the Ettehad Melli Zanan Organization, and by 1981 she was leading an underground life helping women whose lives were in danger to escape Iran. In 1982, Nasrin herself had to flee Iran via the bordering mountains of Kurdistan to Turkey and then to Germany. Once in Germany, she co–founded a center for Iranian refugees to help women refugees re–establish their lives outside of Iran. In April of 1989, she began working with another organization of women against the death penalty.

Nasrin has translated a number of works into Persian. Among these are *The Little Fish* by Leo Liony; *The Strike of Santa Nicoli's Children* by Gunter Feuster; and *How Humans Become Slaves* by Ernest Rowter. She has also written a number of short stories, two of which were recently published in *Cheshm Andaz*, a Persian periodical published in Europe. The story in translation here is the first of the two published in 1987 in the above-named periodical.

Nasrin presently works as a social worker in one of the refugee camps in Austria. She frequently travels as a guest speaker to other cities to speak about the condition of women refugees. She has been married once, to Bahman Nirumand who is a well-known Iranian political theoretician, and has a nineteen-year-old daughter from this marriage.

A Veil with Tiny Aster Flowers

by Nasrin Ettehad

I first saw her at a party. A middle-aged woman, looking neat, fashionable, and energetic. She had no reservations about mingling with men, showing no sign of uneasiness or inadequacy in their company. She was working with one of the political organizations, independently of her husband, as I gathered from her remarks.

A few months later I saw her again at a friend's house. I didn't recognize her. She was wearing a veil with tiny aster flowers, which she took off upon arriving. She acted fidgety, and her watchful, green eyes moved about anxiously. There was no one but my friend and me in the house.

I knew that her husband had left the country, his life being in danger. She may have insisted, too. And now she was left behind with three children, the oldest of whom had been wounded by a bullet in a demonstration or a direct confrontation with the police.

She said, "I'm looking for a place to stay. I'm living in a janitor's house now, doing his housework. He's acting as if I were his official servant. He expects me to cook for him every day, and if I leave the house he screams at me. My daughter screams at me, too. She says it was I who chose to live a life like this, not she."

I was in the same boat myself, having no place to stay. My friend could not put up both of us. She left as nervously as she had arrived. I thought, "If a revolutionary guard noticed her anxious eyes, she would be in trouble."

I heard a few weeks later that she had taken a bottle of sleeping pills, hired a taxi, and asked the driver to drive her around the city. She must not have been able to find a better deathbed. Or perhaps she had not wished her children to watch her die. Whether the story is true, I don't know. I only know that she no longer lives.

The story that follows is the reiterative account of the life of another woman wearing a veil with tiny aster flowers, another woman with anxious eyes. I have made no changes, except of proper names, in this story that she told me.

174

"I was five years old when we moved to Tehran from the village. I had three sisters and no brother. My father was out of work for a couple of years, mainly because no one wanted to hire an illiterate man.

"We lived in poverty-stricken southern Tehran. My mother worked and supported us, but she made very little money; so little that my parents couldn' t even afford to buy books and other school supplies for their children.

"When my older sister turned thirteen, my parents married her off. Being passionately in love with school, I managed to finish grammar school in spite of my family's financial difficulties. I was about thirteen, and just out of school, when I started looking for work. I used all my resources and asked everyone I knew to help me. Soon, I got a job as a teacher in a grade school. It was a private school and the salaries were low; nevertheless, my salary paid for most of my family' s expenses. I taught for two years, and when I was sixteen, I met my husband.

"Mostafa and I knew each other for two years, occasionally talking to each other, mostly about political issues. I had no particular ideological tendency, but I did wonder why, if there were a God, He made people suffer so much. No evening passed in our house without agitation and quarrels. I often talked to Mostafa about what troubled my mind. And I was very curious.

"Two years later I married Mostafa. My mother prohibited me from working as soon as I got engaged. She said, 'Now that you're engaged you should stay home.' But she was wrong, because the other teachers in our school continued teaching and were hired as regular teachers later on, receiving higher salaries.

"Mostafa was a worker. His wages were very low when we first got married. We couldn't afford to rent a room for ourselves, so we lived with his brother's family. His brother had eight children, and his house comprised one room and a kitchen. We didn't encounter any major problems, since we got along very well. We lived in their kitchen for about six months, until we could afford to rent a room of our own.

"It was 1972. We had just settled down when Mostafa was arrested. I was in my third month of pregnancy. For the first six months of his prison term, he wasn't allowed any visitors. We

175

went to the prison, and, like the families of the 'regular prisoners,' looked at them from a distance. Sometimes we went to the Redress of Grievances Office of the military and protested. The university students used to gather there and ask us questions and we explained our situation to them. One time they went on a hunger strike for thirteen days.

"While Mostafa served his prison sentence, I stayed at my brother-in-law's house. My parents were afraid of getting involved and didn't approve of Mostafa's political activities.

"My time had come. I knew a doctor who worked at the Russian Hospital. He had treated me before when I had a miscarriage. He took three hundred *tomans* from me and said, 'Come to the hospital when the pains start. We will admit you then and you can stay until the baby arrives.' But he disappeared from that hospital before I had my baby.

"I was admitted to the hospital and went through a difficult labor. They had to use forceps to deliver the baby. When I was ready to leave the hospital, they asked for seven thousand *tomans*. I didn't have anywhere near that amount. I told them they could keep my baby and me both, since I had no place to go. They decided to release me, knowing that they really would get stuck with me.

"The baby was six months old when Mostafa was released from prison. No one was willing to give him employment because he belonged to an 'Organization' referred to as 'Saka.' Eventually someone hired him, offering him minimal wages. Mostafa was a technician, but he was paid only six hundred *tomans* a month. It was not enough; at the rate the rent, food, and clothing expenses went, that amount could not bring any balance to our lives. It was a tough time, and on top of it all, a good chunk of the money had to go for bottle feeding the baby.

"We were forced to rent a single room again. We found a cheap room for two hundred *tomans* a month. The walls were half-way damp. Later, we found out that our room had been a bathroom, but we couldn' t afford to get something more decent; so we struggled through. The baby got sick with bronchitis, because of the dampness. He couldn't breathe. We didn't have a family physician so we took him to a public clinic where my husband's insurance paid the expenses. They admitted him to the clinic and opened his throat right away. Three or four holes, to give him artificial respiration. My baby died after three days. He was two years old. We moved out of our room right after his death. Mostafa had two full time jobs; both day and night shifts. He came home to rest between his two jobs for an hour or so. Those were irksome days. We were determined to save enough money and cut all unnecessary expenses, and we were able to put down thirty thousand *tomans* on a house. It was on the south side of Tehran; more accurately on the outskirts of the city limits.

"Mostafa continued working with the 'Organization' after the revolution. I also participated in some activities in relation to his duties. I took part in all the demonstrations against the Islamic Republic. Even when Mostafa was busy, or working at his job, I took the children along and joined the demonstrators. I had all four of them, then. Kaveh, my youngest son, was very little.

"In the year 1982, on a holiday, Mostafa was arrested, carrying a bag full of newspapers. He was detained in the Civil Court No—. The same day I took all my children along and went to the court. I caused such a ruckus they let him go. I didn't want him to stay there long enough for them to look into his past records. I was very good at figuring those things out. But after that incident they kept harassing him. He had a car and they had identified it. Every time something happened in our neighborhood, my husband would have to prove his noninvolvement to the authorities. Once the Mujahedeen's leaflet was distributed in our neighborhood and they had suspected Mostafa. They arrested him on his way home and detained him for twelve hours. They let him go after comparing his handwriting with the one on the leaflet. Once they went to his work place and dragged him into a car and interrogated him. They threatened him; they wanted names of a few people. He didn't give them any names. They sentenced him to death right there in the car. But later they let him go.

"We were constantly molested, both by government agents and by some of our neighbors who had painted the slogan on our building, 'Death to Communists.' They had told my children that we were anti-revolutionaries, non-Hezbollahis, i.e. the fanatic members of the Party of God.

177

"One day we went out with the children for a walk. We decided to visit Mostafa's brother afterwards. Someone came to his house looking for us, to tell us that it wasn't wise to return to our house that night. We asked, 'What for?' 'Someone has given them your names,' he answered. We didn't go. Mostafa decided to take the next day off. A week later I went back to see what was going on. The neighbors came to visit, asking me where I'd been.

"I said, 'My mother-in-law was ill and she has passed away. I came to get my black garments. We're going to the funeral.'

"We stayed at my brother-in-law's and other relatives' houses for three weeks. After three weeks a revolutionary guard came looking for us. My brother-in-law didn't want to tell us at first, but he changed his mind later and said, 'He came after you.' Mostafa said after the guard left, 'We've got to leave.' Kaveh was asleep. I picked him up, got the other children ready, and we left for my mother's house.

"My mother was upset; not because we wanted to stay with her, but because she felt we were living a miserable life. We stayed with her for two days. Then the word came that we had to leave because they had my mother's address, too. Mostafa went underground after he left my mother's house, and I moved on to stay with other relatives.

"The first two months were very tough on me. Everywhere I went, I encountered strange looks, as if they were telling me, 'You may stay for an hour, but not longer!' I could sense these things. They were afraid... Some of my relatives were harsh on my children; they beat them in front of me. It's difficult for a mother to watch her children get beaten. Under these circumstances, we couldn't stay anywhere. I came to prefer the streets over the relatives' houses.

"One morning I took the children and we walked all the way to my sister's house. Her house was very far, on the way to the city of Saveh. We arrived in the evening. My brother-in-law became uncomfortable when he saw us. He said, 'You may stay here overnight, but you have to leave early in the morning! I will be held responsible for this!' My brother-in-law was a fanatic Hezbollahi... I had only gone to his house out of desperation. My children were feeling uneasy. They shrank into a corner and stared at me. I told my brother-in-law, 'What've we done to deserve treatment like this...? Why is everyone treating us as if we were criminals?'

"We stayed there overnight and left the next morning crying. I was insulted... Since that day, we took to the streets every day, as a matter of course. The children were smeared with dirt and their heels were callused from excessive walking. My foot was also wounded and bled. Sometimes we sat on a bench in a park. I would buy something for the children and they ate there. As for myself, I had lost my appetite altogether. At night we went to stay with our distant relatives who knew nothing about our situation. Often, we left early in the morning with empty stomaches and walked all day without having eaten anything. Once I made an arrangement with my mother to see her on a street corner. My sister came, too. We went to a restaurant. I said spontaneously, 'I wish they would let us sleep here at night.' My mother cried helplessly and said, 'You' re that desperate?'

"What could I do? Everywhere I went I got the message that I wasn't welcome. I wished I could sit on a restaurant chair, like that day, with all my children around me. I wished that I were by myself, but what could I do with four children? Some people told me that the guards knew we had four children; that we could be easily spotted. They told me that I shouldn't be walking the streets with my children. But what was I supposed to do? How could I leave them with someone else? The poor kids were suffering tremendously. People advised me to be watchful, to avoid the areas where the guards hung out, to be quiet, to avoid passing the the guards' headquarters, the Komiteh. My children would get nervous when they heard these comments. Women are at a disadvantage in situations like these. A man could go to all kinds of places and sleep on the streets, but a woman! Especially one with four children!

"After two months we received a message from Mostafa saying that we could go home; that it was safe now. He had made sure that they didn't know I was involved in any activities. I was reluctant to go. Although staying on the streets had made me miserable, I preferred tolerating this hardship over returning to our house. I was afraid the guards would come take my children away. I had heard they sometimes took the children and the wives hostages.

"On the way to my house I had a strange feeling, as if I were about to go crazy. When we got to our street and got out of the car, I suddenly started crying. I was going home without my husband. The children had been crying continuously. At night they pleaded for their father. The youngest one was particularly fond of him. He suffered the most during this period. He would go stand in the alley and watch the neighbors come home. Then he would come home and say, 'Everyone else's father came home; but my father didn't come. Why?' I would say, 'If he came, the guards would arrest him and take him away.' Then he would calm down a bit.

"Our neighbors' reactions to us changed drastically. They would come and ask us if we needed anything. If one of my children got sick, they would take him to a doctor and offer to help us when we needed help. They had developed affection and respect for us. I had told them Mostafa's mother was dead, but they had found out what we had actually gone through. They knew that Mostafa had been forced to go underground.

"Our neighborhood was mostly occupied by families of workers. But by this time most of them had turned against the government. Among the neighbors living on our side of the alley there were two Hezbollahi families; out of forty-four.

"But the guards continued harassing us. At night, at about two in the morning, they would ring our doorbell. I was unable to sleep at night. I just stayed awake, as I was constantly worried that they'd show up any time. I knew that the person they had arrested didn't know me, since I did my work independently from Mostafa. But I was afraid of being taken hostage. Once, in the middle of the night, someone rang our doorbell mercilessly. Keyvan jumped from his sleep so suddenly I thought he would lose his mind. I didn't open the door. I asked who it was; no one answered. I went to the rooftop to look; I didn't see anyone. This happened frequently at night, and everywhere I went I was tailed. Every now and then I went to my brother-in-law's house to let them know we were all right, that they hadn't come for us. The school children molested my son, Kavoos. They had made an older boy, one who had fallen behind the rest of the children, sit next to Kavoos and constantly ask him where his father was. Kavoos would get mad and tell him that it was none of is business.

"Kaveh would shrink back to a corner all day and cry. At night he kept asking about his father, calling his name. He was three and a half years old then.

"The children saw their father twice during the six months Mostafa was in hiding. We tried to visit him four times, but twice we were followed, so we didn't go. Kaveh was shocked the first time he saw his father. He was laughing and crying simultaneously. He hadn't seen his father for a long time, and Mostafa had let his beard grow. Kaveh was naturally confused. He could recognize his father's voice but not his face. He thought they had arrested his father and that this man was his friend. (A few minutes before, when asked who he missed most in Iran, he had said, 'My father.' He was slightly mixed up.)

"Once, after we had visited Mostafa, my mother, who wanted to test whether Kaveh was tight-lipped, bought him a lot of chocolate, candy, and pastry and said, 'Did you see your father, Kaveh? If you tell the truth, I'll give you all of these!' Kaveh said, 'No.' My mother kept showing him the baits, making him frustrated. Finally he started crying and said, 'No! Leave me alone! I didn' t see him!'

"We had asked him not to tell anybody that he had seen his father, and we said that if he did, they would take his father away and kill him. This request had stuck in his mind for a long time. After our escape from Iran, one day when we were at a motel in the city of Van, Kaveh woke up and didn't see his father. He started crying and repeated, 'They've arrested my father, they've arrested my father!' I told him, 'Don' t worry! We're in Turkey now. Your father has gone out to buy something and will return soon!' But Kaveh kept on crying until his father came back. He was very fond of him and when it came to his father, he was very difficult to deal with. My hair turned gray during those six months. Mostafa was a good father and the children missed him. I thought if he wasn't kind to them they would even welcome his absence, like most children who have strict fathers. But Mostafa treated them kindly and he is still the best father they could dream of. I don't mean to give him too much credit. Sometimes I lost my temper with my children, but he didn't.

"Finally, we decided that we couldn't go on like that forever. The neighbors knew the truth, the children were restless and frustrated, and most importantly, Mostafa knew a lot of people and was afraid he might talk if arrested and tortured. In fact, it was not just to save our own lives that we decided to leave the country. We didn't want to risk any of Mostafa's friends' lives... Anyway, we made all the preparations; and our friends helped , too, to get us out.

"We were not able to sell any of our belongings. Our house was under surveillance twenty-four hours a day. We only brought the clothes we were in. We set off at the end of November of 1983.

"One of my sons went to school in the mornings. I had received directions to tell my son that he should not return home on that day, and instead should wait on the street corner. My oldest son went to school in the afternoons. I was to tell him to leave the house at the usual time and, instead of going to school, to join his younger brother. I was to take the two young ones along and leave after my oldest son. They asked me to come up with a story to tell anyone who happened to see me leave. I was instructed not to take anything with me. 'Only wear as much as you can, but don't carry any bags,' they said.

"We followed the instructions that afternoon. I held my sons' hands and left the house. A Hezbollahi woman in our neighborhood stopped me and asked, 'Where are you off to?' I answered, 'I'm going to the city to see a doctor.' Luckily Kaveh's eyes were slightly red and inflamed. That settled it. We kept backtracking and changing our route to make sure no one was following us. Then we entered a building with two entrances. I entered through one entrance, took my veil off, changed my appearance and exited from the other door. A car was waiting for us there. We got in and took off. Mostafa was in the car, too. We drove to the bus station, bought our tickets and went to city A. From there we went to city B in Van. We arrived in a village at night and were given a room next to a stable to sleep in. We were ordered not to leave the room, lest the villagers see us. The children had to 'go to the bathroom' in the same room. They moved us from there in the middle of the night. We walked for about three hours; then they brought horses for us. It was very cold and we were all trembling. We didn't have sufficient clothing. We continued these rides for six days. We rode in the daytime and slept at night in one of the villages on our way. The children rode on horses, too. Each sat next to a guide. Once Kaveh almost froze to death. We wrapped him in a blanket. The guide was trying to rearrange his seat and put him down for a minute on the snow. Suddenly Kaveh started to cry. His feet were numb. His father rubbed his feet until they regained their senses. We were worried that the children might get ill, for we had not been able to bring any medicine or extra clothing for them. Nothing.

"In Kurdistan, they provided us with Kurdish outfits. After we crossed the border, they brought a car and took us to the city of Van. On the way there, our car was inspected once.

"We stayed in Van for thirty-eight days. We took a small room with two beds in the Aslan Hotel. (The room wasn't even half the size of this one. I don't know if you have seen the rooms in that hotel.) They were very dirty. We were miserable. Lice had attacked all my children and we didn't have extra clothes to replace their dirty ones. Our financial situation was hopeless. As we hadn't been able to sell our furniture, our friends had put up the resources for us: one hundred fifty thousand *tomans* went for travel expenses and thirty thousand *tomans* we had with us. We had to make this money stretch for an unknown period of time. We went through an extremely tough time. All six of us slept on the two beds.

"Then we came to Istanbul. We had to make two beds do there, too, since the rooms were so expensive. Then our friends in Germany sent us plane tickets, and here we are!

"The children were really calm throughout the entire trip. They wanted to behave their best to impress their father. When we were in Iran, I sometimes told them, 'Your father is planning to go abroad but we have to stay in Iran.' The children would say, 'No, we want to be with our father.' I would then say, 'How am I supposed to take four children along? What if we were caught on the way and got arrested, what then, would you still like to go?' They would say, 'Yes, we want to be where our father is.' They did not complain at all; not a word. Our co-travelers were amazed. So was I, because the children had really drained me before the trip. This was why the trip had actually been a relief to me, to the extent that I tolerated the freezing weather and the other hardships without much difficulty. God knows what I went through—during these six months. Hearing it is an entirely different matter. Our lives consisted of little more than that. Sheer misery and vagrancy. It is safe to say that our troubles are mostly over now. But the ones who've stayed behind..."